No Substitute

for Murder

Carolyn J. Rose

No Substitute for Murder

Murder

Carolyn J. Rose

2011

No Substitute for Murder

Copyright © 2011 Carolyn J. Rose

www.deadlyduomysteries.com

ISBN: 978-0-9837359-2-2

Cover design by Dorion D. Rose, Broken Cork Photography

Digital editions produced by Booknook.biz

For Mike, who almost always finds truth more amusing

than fiction

A substitute teacher must have:
a) certain credentials and certifications
b) stamina
c) the ability to communicate well
d) nerves of steel
e) a pulse

CHAPTER ONE

The problem with getting your life back on track is that there's usually another catastrophe hurtling down the rails to knock you off again.

Case in point: in January my attorney fired the final volley in a running gun battle of a divorce that demolished my savings. Living single is lonely but also lower-priced. I figured I'd recoup. After all, I had a good job producing the Rick Rivers Radio Show, the number-one program in Reckless River, Washington.

Until March, when the downsizing axe separated me from my paychecks.

Being jobless isolated me even more than getting divorced, but I qualified for unemployment benefits and my mortgage payments were low. I figured I was bound to find another job soon.

But the housing market crashed taking the economy with it.

In August, panicked by gloom-and-doom financial forecasts, I sold my house for an offer I was lucky to get, and moved to a one-bedroom condo. Then, in an effort to hoist myself back onto the rails, I signed on for a stop-gap job one notch above crash-test dummy.

So, at dawn on the Thursday before Thanksgiving, I drove through rain and wind worthy of a TV special to cower in front of Wilhelmina Frost, the woman in charge of payroll, personnel issues, and checking in substitute teachers at Captain Meriwether High School.

Despite the fact that she stood only four feet ten inches tall, Wilhelmina Frost was a legend in the Reckless River School District. Caustic and opinionated, she was also tireless, damned good at her job, and fiercely loyal to those she liked. Administrators walked softly when passing her office and teachers regularly laid tribute on her cluttered desk: chocolates, coffee, cookies—even sizeable gift certificates to restaurants and department stores. Big Chill, as she was called behind her back, was never without high heels, stoplight-red lipstick, and rectangular black-rimmed glasses. Her short white hair, rinsed a faint shade of turquoise and teased high, reminded me of an exotic fruity drink spiked with blue liqueur.

She inspected me the way a drill instructor might size up a raw recruit, taking in my rubber-soled sensible shoes, black slacks, and gray sweater. With a nod, she shoved the substitute pay form across the desk. "Phil Benson says you did okay for him."

Last week I subbed for his band and guitar classes. I'm no musician, but I recognize cacophony when I hear it. That evening, eardrums still throbbing to the mangled opening riffs of "Smoke On The Water," I went online and ordered a pair of heavy-duty earplugs to carry in my briefcase.

"It was interesting," I said in what I hoped was a casual tone. Big Chill had two lists—subs she recommended and those she'd refer only to a serial killer

2

in search of victims. Teachers advised me to play it cool and act as if my schedule was packed because Big Chill could smell need at a hundred yards. And I reeked of it.

I bent and printed my name at the top of the form: *Barbara Reed*. Barbara flowed from the pen, but Reed came out in slow and jerky strokes. I was still getting used to my family name after years of being half of a couple—first Mrs. Albert Peters and then Mrs. Jake Stranahan.

Big Chill narrowed her eyes. "He told me the kids liked you."

I filled in the date—*November 19, 2009*—and wondered if she was laying a trap. The list of what it took to be popular with kids was pretty much the flipside of requirements for being popular with teachers. Kids tended to like subs who let them get away with goofing off, napping, chatting, texting their friends, taking long trips to the restroom, and copying others' work. Teachers liked subs who knew the subject, taught the lesson plans, helped kids master the assignment, and somehow maintained that elusive thing called classroom control. Having kids like you could be the kiss of death, so I feigned surprise and attempted to skip around Big Chill's tripwire. "He did?"

She nodded and flipped a hand, sending a whiff of gardenia perfume my way. "He said you even got them to straighten up the instrument room."

Thanks to bribery—miniature chocolate bars are units of exchange in the high school trade and barter system—I had. But I wasn't about to admit that, so I just filled in the name of the social studies teacher I was subbing for: *Susan Mitchell*.

"He'll be gone for a few days in January," Big Chill said. "I'll sign you up to fill in."

I didn't so much as suggest I'd check my schedule. If the road to the top of Wilhelmina Frost's good list was through hell, high water, or the band room, then that was the route I'd take. "I'll be happy to do it."

I signed at the bottom of the triplicate form, ignoring a tiny voice in my brain that asked, "Where's your pride? What happened to your self-esteem?" Well, my scant self-esteem went through the shredder known as Jake Stranahan, and until this recession ended, pride was something I couldn't afford.

Big Chill slapped the form into a plastic bin and held out two keys, one for the classroom and the other more vital—it opened the faculty restroom. I clipped them to the lanyard displaying my school district badge, a rectangle of white plastic with a picture dreadful enough for any passport.

"It's a good thing you're early," Big Chill said. "Susan e-mailed that she forgot to get the atlases from Henry Stoddard's room."

Henry Stoddard.

My heart seized up like an engine out of oil.

"Those books belong to the whole department and Susan reserved them." Big Chill made sucking-a-lemon lips. "But Henry can be kind of cranky, especially with subs."

Cranky? Cranky was just the tip of the iceberg—an iceberg the size of Greenland.

Two weeks ago Stoddard was skulking in the hall when I let myself out of the unisex faculty restroom near his classroom. He'd glowered, yanked the door wide, and shoved my shoulder as I stepped clear. "This restroom is for teachers," he snarled, "*real* teachers."

"I didn't realize that," I said in a quavering voice. "There isn't a sign."

"Don't need a sign. It's tradition. If I see you here again, I'll get your name scrubbed from the sub list for this district."

I'd slunk off without another word.

Stoddard was a festering boil on the backside of the school; no one was willing to lance it. According to legend, he had truckloads of major dirt on those at the top of the educational food chain.

Hoping to beat Stoddard to his room at the far reaches of the building, I dashed from Big Chill's office, snatched up the attendance sheets, and raced for the first staircase.

Named for Meriwether Lewis, co-leader of the 1804 expedition to explore the Louisiana Purchase and reach the Pacific, the school was a sprawling heap of brick and concrete, an edifice built in stages, and reconfigured by random acts of budgetary desperation as student enrollment swelled.

As I trotted along a hallway smelling of disinfectant and splotched with flattened blobs of green and pink chewing gum, I wondered how Meriwether Lewis, an introverted man given to depression, would cope if he was scooped from the past and set down among today's teens. I imagined him studying them with the same attention he'd given to prairie dogs and grouse and then penning a journal entry: *These strange creatures insert plugs in their ears and move to what they tell me is music but is like no music I have heard elsewhere. It reminds me of war chants and the groans of men sick from meat gone bad. They clasp bits of metal in their hands and communicate by pressing lettered and numbered buttons. They eat baked dough covered with cheese and sliced meat. Their answers to my questions are vague and I am convinced they have little awareness of the terrain ahead.*

Briefcase thumping my right leg, I smiled as I zoomed along the English wing and panted up a dog-legged flight of stairs. The building had its drawbacks, but it had charm, too. It was surrounded by sweeping lawns, dozens of trees and shrubs, and enough parking spaces so even lowly subs could find a close-in spot during the rainy season. (For those who haven't lived in this neck of the woods, that season stretches from late September until the fifth of July, depending on ocean currents, prevailing winds, sunspots, global warming, the metric tonnage of the Brazilian banana crop, squid reproduction rates, and whether or not you have a roofing emergency.) The wings of the building enclosed an enormous courtyard with a pond where freshmen, much to the annoyance of the fish, often floundered despite the efforts of the security staff to prevent a rite of passage known as Sharks versus Suckers.

And, the staff was amazing. In spite of cutbacks and crowded classrooms, they went the extra mile and more for their students.

With the exception of Henry Stoddard.

He was as generous and caring as a hungry grizzly and had the sense of humor of a scorpion. Henry hated teaching. And he made that abundantly clear. But he stuck with it, perhaps for the joy of making everyone around him miserable. Kids had been known to transfer to other schools to avoid his classes.

I dashed down a short side corridor, skidded to a stop in front of the door at the end, fumbled the key into the slot, and turned it, taking up the slack in the lanyard and nearly choking myself in the process. Opening the door wide, I side-stepped along the wall to my right, fingers groping for the light switches. I flipped all three, but nothing happened.

"What the heck?"

Only anemic light from the hallway washed my shadow across a jumble of tables and chairs. I swatted the switches down and up again, then remembered the sensors designed to turn off the lights if no motion was detected for several minutes. Glancing around, I spotted a

6

tiny red light on the ceiling at the front of the room. All I had to do was get over there and create some motion—without major injury.

For the record, health insurance is out of my price range, so I was on the cargo plan. If I get sick or hurt, I'll get in my car, go for a drive, and hope someone with a lot of insurance hits me.

I propped the door ajar with a chair, put my hands out in front at table height, and advanced by inches toward the pale glow of the white board. The air smelled like corn chips, mustard, and baloney—the key ingredients in the lunch Henry Stoddard brought each day.

I bumped a chair with my knee and stepped on something that crunched. Odd. Henry Stoddard didn't let his students leave unless the floor was spotless, and the janitorial staff swept through the classrooms the minute school was out.

I inched forward, the smell of that baloney sandwich stronger, gamier.

The lights popped on.

Blinking, I scanned the room and spotted the atlases in a heap on a low table by the windows. I dashed over, shuffled them into a single pile, and gathered them into my arms. They were thin with slick covers, more like magazines than books, but thirty-five of them plus the briefcase was quite a load, and I walked hunched over like a tramp searching for cigarette butts.

I was almost to the door when I heard that crunch underfoot again. Craning my neck, I stepped back and peered down at a pale pink bit of plastic, a bent wire, and three white chips.

A dental bridge?

The responsible part of my brain urged me to wrap it in a tissue, take it to Big Chill, and accept responsibility. The practical gray cells in the other brain hemisphere told

7

me this was not my fault but that of the person who left the teeth behind.

That's when I felt that tingly creepy feeling you get when you're being watched.

Turning, I spotted Henry Stoddard sitting in a chair tucked between two cabinets. He wore his usual white shirt, his usual gray sweater vest, and his usual purple-veined scowl.

My heart constricted to a cold lump the size of a walnut.

"Sorry," I squeaked. "I, uh, didn't mean to step on your teeth. But, um, maybe you shouldn't have left them on the floor."

Henry Stoddard elevated the art of silent intimidation to new heights.

"Miss Frost told me it was okay to get the atlases because Mrs. Mitchell reserved them. I'm filling in for her."

Heart pounding, I clutched the atlases tighter. "I'll bring every one of them back just as soon as we're done."

Henry Stoddard's scowl didn't change by so much as a millimeter.

The muscles in my arms burned and my back ached. "I'll organize them exactly the way they were."

Henry Stoddard glared on, and a tiny flame of fury flickered at the base of my brain. I had no time to waste being bullied. Scuttling to the door, I kicked aside the chair I'd used to prop it open. "Shall I leave the lights on?"

He didn't answer.

Fine. I didn't have a free hand anyway.

As the door closed, I glanced over my shoulder. Henry Stoddard still hadn't moved. And, eyesight honed by rage, I saw why. His outdated tie—navy blue with thin red stripes—wasn't tucked into the V of his sweater vest. It was yanked to the side of his head and knotted beneath his ear.

The atlases tumbled from my arms and I swallowed a scream.

Quiz Answer:
a – definite requirements
b, c, d, e – helpful attributes

Which slogan best encapsulates a sub's job
philosophy?
a) living the dream
b) still standing at the end of the day
c) kindness, caring, and consistency
d) I'm outta here when the final bell rings
e) just another day in paradise

CHAPTER TWO

For a long moment I teetered against the half-open
door, hands pressed against my roiling stomach, atlases
spread at my feet in a slick swirl of red, yellow, and blue. I
tried to breathe, swallowed air instead, felt swelling pain
behind my heart.

"Do something," the voice in my mind whispered.

Obediently, I dug in my briefcase for my cell phone
and then remembered it was in the car, tucked inside the
purse locked in the trunk.

"Go back. Help him," that nagging voice demanded.

I turned and took one trudging step before Henry
Stoddard's scowl brought me up short. Never one to be
completely positive about anything, I felt ninety percent
confident that he'd been dead for hours. But what if I was
wrong? How long before a brain deprived of oxygen
passed the point of no return? Was the window of
opportunity still open a crack?

I used my briefcase to prop the door ajar and, with
gritted teeth and dragging feet, stumbled to Henry

Stoddard's side and placed trembling fingers beneath his jaw. No pulse. His skin was as cool and unyielding as that of a display mannequin. I touched his hand. His fingers were stiff, locked around his arm.

Along with fear and revulsion, I felt a vast relief. If rigor mortis had set in, I wasn't obligated to pump his chest and press my lips against his.

As my mind focused on *that* image, I shuddered, released a shrill and manic laugh and backed away from Stoddard's mortal remains, assuring myself that he would be every bit as embarrassed and humiliated by the resuscitation experience. He'd never married and, as far as anyone knew, never been involved with a woman— "involved" meaning any and all activities up to and including wild weasel sex. Shoving my shoulder a few weeks ago might have been the sum total of Henry Stoddard's female physical contact in years.

I laughed again, then tried to convince myself laughter wasn't a sign I was psychotic, but just an uncontrollable visceral reaction.

I headed for the classroom phone, then halted. It wasn't *entirely* impossible that Henry Stoddard strangled himself, but as a faithful viewer of all crime-scene TV programs, I suspected murder was more likely. In either case, I'd already left enough fingerprints, epithelial cells, and fibers in here, so the best thing to do was to call from Susan Mitchell's room.

Reaching the door, I felt a swirl of cold air on my ankles and heard the shuffle of feet and a mutter of voices. The buses had arrived. In a moment a sullen brood of students in hooded sweatshirts would straggle past. One might wander over and spot Henry Stoddard. Teen years were traumatic enough without seeing a man throttled by a component of his wardrobe.

11

I flailed at the light switches, settling a shroud of darkness over Henry Stoddard, then kicked my briefcase and the atlases clear of the door, and locked it tight.

"Yo, Miss Reed, you need some help?"

I yanked the key from the lock and spun to see a gangly boy with a black guitar case slung over his shoulder separate himself from the trudging herd migrating toward the cafeteria and slouch up the short corridor. A junior, he scored a candy bar off of me last week by helping a couple of freshmen with the chords to "Purple Haze."

"No," I told him. "I'm good."

"No problem." He dropped to his knees, raked atlases into a pile, then whisked them together like a deck of playing cards. "You trying to put these in Mr. Stoddard's room before he gets here?" he asked in a conspiratorial whisper.

"No. I just got them out of there." I glanced over my shoulder to make sure he couldn't see more than a few feet into the room and realized that by removing the books I'd disturbed the crime scene. For a second I thought about putting them back, then wondered how Susan's classes would get their mapping project done if I did. Damned either way.

"Would you mind carrying those to Mrs. Mitchell's room?" I hefted my briefcase. "I'll give you a candy bar."

"Sweet." He hoisted the heap. "Want this marker pen, too?" He held out a bright yellow felt-tipped highlighting pen. "It was on the floor with the books."

"Sure." I popped the marker into my briefcase. Waste not, want not. About seven minutes into my "career" as a sub I detected the existence of pen-and-pencil-swallowing black holes. Markers, rulers, and note pads were also sucked into the vortex. Most remained lost forever but occasionally some broke loose and fell beneath desks and in corners. An avid recycler, I scavenged those and put them back into circulation.

Hustling to Susan Mitchell's classroom—just around the corner on the main corridor and a few doors down—I felt another swirl of cold air and heard a series of squeals and high-pitched giggles. More kids arriving. Gotta hurry. I opened the door, snapped on the lights, flung my briefcase onto the nearest table, and dug out a couple of mini chocolate bars. "Put them down anywhere, uh . . ."

"Josh." His voice was wistful and the corners of his mouth turned down. "I thought you'd remember."

"Sorry." In the interest of moving things along, I didn't add the number of kids I saw each day—about a hundred and fifty—and how I tried but just couldn't learn all their names.

He dumped the atlases, snatched the candy, and then slouched against the wall, peeling the wrapper. "You going to sub for Mr. Benson again soon?"

I glanced at the phone. "Maybe in January."

"January." He munched chocolate. "That's, like, after Christmas."

"Right. Listen, I've got to get organized."

He nodded. Didn't move.

"I've got a lot to do to get ready for first period."

He peeled the second candy bar. "Being a sub can be tough, huh?"

You have no idea.

"Sometimes," I equivocated.

Like right this very instant.

"Today's going to be difficult, so I need a little time to think." I opened the door and held it for him.

He popped the second chunk of chocolate in his mouth. "I'll put the chairs down for you."

Before I could object, he leaned his guitar against a table and went to work at a pace guaranteed not to endear him to a future employer who paid by the hour. A quick peek at the clock showed I had twenty-one minutes before the bell. A peek back at Josh showed he was on his third chair. I peeled two ones from the emergency stash inside the feminine products container wedged at the bottom of my briefcase and poked them into his paw. "The first period kids will get the rest of the chairs, Josh. Go buy a cinnamon roll."

"Wow! Thanks, Miss Reed." He clutched the bills, slid an arm through the strap of his guitar case, and shambled off.

I locked the door, leaped for the phone, and dialed Big Chill's number. Situations like this hadn't come up during substitute training, but I figured telling her first was my best bet. She answered after two rings. "Captain M High."

"It's me, Barbara Reed. Henry Stoddard's—"

"I'm so sick of that man I could just spit," Big Chill raged. "I'll send Jessica up. I don't know who he thinks he—"

She hung up. I dialed again, got voice mail, and guessed she was on the horn to Assistant Principal Jessica Flint. I cringed. While easy-going sixtyish Jerome Morrow led by example and inspired with encouragement, Jessica Flint, half his age and new to the job as his assistant, nipped at the heels of the staff in an attempt to drive them to compliance.

Imagine a herding dog with streaked hair and lipstick.

Seizing my briefcase as a shield, I darted to Henry Stoddard's door, glancing back to the main corridor just as a sea of students parted for Jessica, a walkie-talkie clamped to her ear. She wore a knee-length dark green dress with huge gold buttons and a wide belt with an enormous gold buckle. A ring of keys clipped to the belt jangled like a wind chime in a hurricane and her three-inch heels struck the floor so hard and fast I expected to

14

see sparks. But while her body language from the neck down was all "my way or the highway," her facial expression looked more like "show me the off-ramp."

She stopped with a final clash of keys, clipped the walkie-talkie to the other side of her belt, and peered at the dark room with anxious eyes. Then anxiety gave way to feral aggression. "Henry's not in yet. What's your problem?"

I swallowed, feeling incompetent, defensive, and as if I'd acquired my clothing in a trade involving spare change and a bottle of fortified wine.

She snatched at her keys. "If you can't manage the simplest tasks then this school doesn't need—"

"Henry Stoddard's dead," I whispered.

She dropped the keys. "What?"

Several shaggy heads turned in our direction. She seared me with a glare, then peered over her shoulder at a tide of teens lapping toward us up the stubby corridor. "Cafeteria closes in ten minutes," she announced.

The tide receded and she retrieved the keys. "That's impossible. I just talked to him last—"

Something that looked a whole lot like relief flickered across her face, hotly pursued by panic. She swallowed a sharp breath and in another second was all jagged belligerence again. "How do you know he's dead?"

"He's cold and stiff. He has no pulse."

She discarded that with a snort of disgust and a head toss that released a cloud of industrial-strength perfume. "I better check."

I held my ground, squeezing my briefcase against my chest. "You shouldn't go in there. You'll contaminate the crime scene."

She moved closer. Another inch and I'd be wearing her makeup. From this vantage point, her pores looked like lunar craters and the mole beneath her left eye seemed too dark and irregular to be healthy. But this wasn't the time to warn her about the dangers of skin cancer.

"Crime scene?"

"Someone strangled him."

"Strangled?" She backed off half a foot, her jaw dropped, and her hand gripped her throat. Her gaze darted left and right and she licked her lips. "Who would strangle Hen. . .?"

Her words faded out and I imagined she was calling up a mental list of the entire staff, students, and alumni. The keys jangled again and I noted her hands were trembling. "Ridiculous," she said in a caustic tone. "You must be having a PMS hallucination."

Were there such things? And the larger question, could hallucinations make PMS worth putting up with? "I'm not."

"I'll be the judge of that." She set her hip against mine and exerted pressure, her heels scraping for traction.

My rubber-soled shoes held. "We've got to call the police. Or Mr. Morrow."

"That's my responsibility. Step aside," she panted, her breath fogging my glasses, her perfume assaulting my sinuses. "Let me in there."

"You'll contamin—" A sneeze burst from my lungs. With all the real problems I'd accumulated this year, why piss off Jessica Flint? Especially when I'd already messed with the crime scene by removing the atlases?

"Okay." I jumped aside so fast she lost her balance and clawed at the door handle. More smears for some fingerprint expert to sort out.

"Go to your classroom." She unlocked the door. "But don't think I'm finished with you. My office. Immediately after school."

I nodded, but walked away with baby steps, peering over my shoulder, wondering about the emotions that had flickered across her face.

Jessica turned on the lights and gasped. The door clicked shut and she bent to lock it, then straightened and shot me a Medusa-like glower.

So much for subbing in this school again.

With slumped shoulders, I turned toward Susan Mitchell's room, but caught a riffle of motion from the corner of my eye—Jessica letting down the blind on the door.

I halted, replaying her dread, relief, panic, and resolve, then crept back to Stoddard's door. Peering through a tiny gap in the blind, I watched Jessica Flint inspect the tie knotted around Stoddard's neck and then stoop and thrust her fingers into his pockets.

Either she had an unusual method of checking for vital signs or he'd gone to meet his maker in possession of something that she wanted.

Quiz Answer:
c – definitely the standard to strive for
b, *d* – what I often think
a, *e* – what I seldom think

You can tell a sub from a "real" teacher by
a) the size of the paycheck
b) the stack of grading to be done
c) which one goes to staff meetings
d) comparing their wardrobes
e) which one leaves immediately after the final bell

CHAPTER THREE

I knew Jessica had stopped searching and spread the news when, a few minutes before the first bell rang, the security staff closed off the spur hallway with a row of upturned tables. Counselors intercepted Henry Stoddard's students and herded them to the library while history teachers with rooms on the edges of the side corridor posted signs saying classes would be held in other locations.

Henry's room had a door to the outside. That gave cops and administrators a degree of control over what kids saw, but there was no way to keep the lid on tight. Allowing for absences—legitimate and otherwise—there were probably 1500 students at school that morning. That translated to 3,000 spying eyes, 3,000 listening ears, 3,000 whispering lips, and 3,000 thumbs texting updates on cell phones, texts like "OMG, dude, I think the Suck Master kicked." School policy called for students to keep phones in their pockets, purses, or backpacks during class, but most kids viewed that policy the same way they did other rules laid down by adults.

As a consequence, despite an official announcement citing only "an unfortunate incident that necessitated closing a portion of the school," stories and speculation about Stoddard swept through the building like a swarm of tornadoes, leaving a litter of myth and legend in their wake. During second period I heard students informing each other that he'd puked himself to death after eating a rancid baloney sandwich, tumbled down a flight of stairs while blinded by the light from an overhead projector, and gotten so mad he'd blown out an artery. I was on the lookout for kids who seemed troubled and should be sent to the counseling center, but didn't notice anyone brought low by the reality of Henry's mortality.

The only student I was at all concerned about was the one who put forth the abducted-by-aliens story. A waif-like girl dressed all in black with long bangs falling over her eyes, she mourned that the misguided aliens, mistakenly believing Henry Stoddard represented the epitome of educational excellence, would replace all the teachers on the planet with his clones.

Suppressing a shudder, I got the kids started on their mapping projects and hoped they wouldn't ask me if I knew what really happened. My defense, I decided, was to cling to that official announcement.

But before the problem arose, a teacher I'd seen only from a distance appeared in the doorway. He carried a green pen and a sheaf of papers covered with circles, squares, and triangles. "They want you in the office. I'll cover this period."

My mouth went dry, but I managed a few terse words about expectations for the assignment, gathered up my briefcase, and left on numb feet, aware that thumbs were already poised over keypads, my name about to be woven into the fabric of fiction.

19

Big Chill intercepted me outside her office, eyes glittering. "Why didn't you tell me Henry Stoddard was dead?"

Self-preservation made me discard the obvious and honest response and go for, "Sorry. I guess I was so shook up that I couldn't get the words out."

Perhaps the quaver in my voice sold it. "I had to hear it from Jerry," she said in a tone that implied receiving news from the principal instead of handing it off to him amounted to a failure on the scale of losing a world war.

"Sorry," I muttered again.

She waved that aside. "Was he really strangled with his own tie?"

"The navy blue one with the red stripes." I offered what I hoped was a detail she might not have.

Her lips curled in a satisfied smile. "He was wearing that one yesterday. Probably owned it since Mount Saint Helens blew its stack." She leaned close, gripping my arm. "Jessica's got her bloomers in a bunch about you, but if she tries to give you grief I'll see she's overruled so fast she gets whiplash."

I suspected her stance was less about me than about Jessica who probably had called Jerome Morrow directly to report Stoddard's murder, cutting Big Chill out of the loop and firing the opening shot in the latest skirmish of an on-going turf war. I had no doubt that Big Chill would triumph.

"Thanks," I mumbled, feeling like a chunk of thrashed-over real estate in the heart of No Man's Land.

Big Chill flipped fingers tipped with nails painted the same vivid red as her lips and spun on one heel. "Conference room."

Now that I'd been humbled, she was all business. "Police want to talk with you."

Cold sweat slicked my palms, but after the showdown with Jessica Flint, being grilled by Detective Charles Atwell—on high heat after I admitted to taking the atlases, which he called for an officer to collect immediately—was like an all-expenses-paid day at a spa with unlimited champagne. Unfortunately, champagne gives me a headache. So did Detective Atwell's repeated and rephrased questions. It didn't help that I was dithering about whether to rat out Jessica Flint and wondering how much wrath I'd incur if I did.

Atwell led me through everything that happened from the minute I arrived at school, jumped back to cover my brief past history with Henry Stoddard, returned to this morning's discovery and then, after an hour, retraced his steps once more. "Tell me again about the confrontation you had with Henry Stoddard earlier this month." He leaned back in a plastic chair, gnawing on the top of his pen.

I added that quirk to my mental list of what I didn't want in a man. Not that I was looking for a man. I was through with them. And not that I'd consider Atwell. For starters, with his wiry dark hair, jutting brow and nose, small eyes, and thin lips, he appeared about as warm and caring as a vulture.

"I wouldn't call it a confrontation." I picked at the skin around my left thumbnail that I'd worried raw even as I told myself I had nothing to worry about. Even before Big Chill clued me in about the tie, I guessed that, cold and stiff as Stoddard had been, he was killed yesterday evening. If Jessica Flint did the deed, she would have searched his pockets long before he assumed room temperature.

Atwell tapped the pen against the cell phone he'd placed in the center of the table next to a tape recorder. "You said he shoved you."

21

"It was more of a push. A little one. Just kind of to get me to hurry." I flushed with annoyance—at Atwell for what I saw as an attempt to blow the incident out of proportion, at myself for using the word "shove" in the first place, and finally for defending a man I'd loathed in the interest of self-preservation. My crappy-year-problems list was long enough without adding defendant to divorced, downsized, and demeaned. "He was in a hurry to use the restroom. We have only five minutes between classes."

Atwell rolled his eyes and cracked his knuckles as if to say that real men didn't have issues with bladder control. I added eye rolling and knuckle popping to my mental list of what I didn't want in a man. "And you didn't report the incident. Why was that?"

Because it would be his word against mine. Because I was afraid he'd blackball me. Subbing money wasn't great, but it had lured me into the habits of eating regular meals and paying bills almost on time. I shrugged and settled for, "I didn't think it was important."

"Not important? The man shoved you."

"Pushed," I corrected, noting that my thumb was oozing.

"And that's appropriate behavior?"

I glanced at the box of tissue at the end of the table, decided not to give him the satisfaction of knowing he'd drawn first blood, and wiped the smear on my slacks where it wouldn't show. "No, but everyone knows—knew—that Henry Stoddard was . . ."

Atwell shot forward like a striking snake, his elbows thudding against the tired faux wood of the oval table. "Was what?"

Psychotic. Malicious. Intimidating. Blackmailing.

Atwell was bound to get an earful about Stoddard—unless everyone remembered what I had just managed to forget, that bad-mouthing the deceased made you look like a suspect. "He was sometimes a little cranky," I mumbled, using Big Chill's euphemism.

"Cranky?" Atwell let the word hang between us like damp laundry, then made a squiggle in the notebook placed at right angles to the phone. "What do you mean by that?"

Cross, crabby, crotchety, grouchy, grumpy, snappish.

I ran through a list of synonyms. Stop digging, I thought, before the hole caves in. I spread my hands. "Just, you know, cranky. Teaching is a stressful profession."

Atwell gave me a measured head shake as if to say I had no idea what real stress was. I gave him back the same. What did he know?

He shook off my dismissal and rocked in his chair. "And in this politically correct and litigious age no one with any authority ever sat Mr. Stoddard down and had a talk about working and playing well with others?"

According to teachers' room gossip, the policy was that if you left Stoddard alone, you might avoid conflict and remain ignorant of any life- and/or job-altering dirt he'd accumulated on you. But, lest my own grime become part of the police record, I decided to let Atwell find someone else to pry the lid off that particular can of worms. I took refuge in my lowly position. "I don't know. I'm just a sub." Not only at the bottom of the totem pole but embedded deep in the earth beneath it. "You'd have to ask Mr. Morrow or Miss Flint."

Atwell winced and gave his knuckles such a ferocious crack I was certain he'd already explored this avenue and found it piled high with sandbags. "Henry Stoddard wasn't a large man. He probably didn't weigh much more than you."

23

Now there was an esteem builder for a woman who'd been weight conscious since childhood. I'm not fat, I told myself. I weigh less than the dead guy.

I slid my wounded thumb into my pocket, recalling how Stoddard's fingers had been wrapped tight around his arm, an arm smaller than my own. Was it possible that at 129 pounds—first thing in the morning, stripped naked, and with my eyebrows freshly plucked—I *didn't* weigh less than the dead guy?

Atwell's phone hummed and jittered in a circle. He snatched it up, flipped it open, and clamped it to one meaty ear. "Atwell." His eyes pinned me to my chair. "Uh-huh," he muttered. "Uh-huh. Huh." He snapped the phone closed, sipped at his coffee, grunted, and spat it back into the cup. "Cold."

I opened my mouth to volunteer to bring him a fresh cup, decided that was a manifestation of Stockholm Syndrome, and clamped my lips. I might be his hostage, but no way would I wait on him. Especially not with hands shaking worse with each minute beyond the 10:53 start of my designated lunch period.

I thought fondly of the sandwich I'd stashed at the back of the tiny refrigerator in the teachers' room. PB&J. 100% natural peanut butter, tart orange marmalade, and artisan bread. The jelly side would be just a little soggy about now, the crust still chewy. My stomach rumbled like distant thunder.

Atwell frowned and went back to gnawing the pen with front teeth a beaver would envy. "Where were you yesterday evening?"

With a little jolt of surprise, I realized he hadn't asked that question before and noted that he'd said evening, not afternoon. Had the phone call given him an approximate time of death? For the first time since I found Henry

Stoddard's body, I drew breath to the bottom of my lungs. "I was at school. College. Over in Portland."

"College, huh?" He picked up his coffee again, snarled at the cup, and set it down so hard liquid slopped onto the table. I hoped he wasn't considering a career on the professional poker circuit. He had far too many tells. "Until when?"

"The class got out around 9:30. It was my turn to drive the carpool and by the time I dropped the others off it was probably close to 10:30."

He rubbed his chin and made a note. "10:30," he murmured, his frown fading.

I figured that meant the timeline for my alibi didn't rule me out. "And then I walked my dog," I added, trying not to sound too hopeful.

The frown returned, creating a crease between his eyes deep enough to slot in a nickel. "Did anyone see you?"

"Just the guy who stakes out the space under the canopy that keeps the rain off the trash containers behind my condo complex." I didn't mention that, depending on his alcohol intake, that vagrant may also have spotted matching pairs of a whole range of exotic or extinct species.

Atwell made a note. "Do you know his name?"

I shook my head. My neighbors called him a lot of names: Sam the Scam Artist, Panhandling Pete, and even Fortified Freddy. I referred to him simply as Trash Guy.

"Where did you take the dog?"

"Not far. Just around my condo complex. And I picked up after him." I held up my hand as if I had a plastic sack over it, showing that I was a responsible dog owner who would never leave a pile of poo behind, not even on a dark and stormy night, not even if I was rushing to get to school to strangle Henry Stoddard.

25

Atwell gave the knuckles another workout and eyed the lanyard around my neck. His skinny lips tweaked into a smile. "You have a key to the victim's classroom?"

My gut cramped and words surged from my lips like lemmings leaping from a precipice. "Yes. It fits most of the classrooms. I picked it up when I came in this morning. From Miss Frost." I turned my badge so he could see that hideous photo and wondered briefly if a police mug shot would catch me at an angle that didn't show as much of the soft flesh beneath my chin.

"Subs turn their keys in when they leave the building," I told him. "We don't get permanent keys unless we take on long-term assignments and I can't do that until I get my certificate."

He considered that, rubbing his chin, fingers whisking against his stubble. "Did you work here yesterday?"

I let the lanyard drop. "No. I was at Reckless River Heights Middle School." And don't get me started on that. If there was a hell, and if it bore even the slightest resemblance to the drama-infused hormonal chaos of middle school, the staunchest atheist might get religion. Just my opinion.

He pinched the knob of his chin. "Do subs ever 'forget' to turn in their keys?"

"I never have." I dodged the insinuation that with murdering Henry Stoddard in mind I kept a set. "Miss Frost keeps the keys. You should ask her."

He tucked his head as if dodging a blow and I guessed he already had a close encounter with Big Chill and failed to score points for his side. If he planned to interrogate her the way he was going at me, I figured it would take about five minutes for griller to become grillee.

He peered at my lanyard. "What's the other key for?"

"It opens the restrooms." My bladder twitched and I tried not to squirm, telling myself the full feeling was due to nerves.

"Not the outside doors?"

"No. You need a key card for those." I flipped my badge so he could see it had no information strip or bar code. "I come in through the front door in the morning. It's the only one that's open until the buses arrive."

"What time is it unlocked?"

"I have no idea. You'll have to ask Miss Frost."

He ducked his head again and I realized I could use her name the way a vampire hunter wields a cross.

"What would you do if the front door was locked and you had to get in?" He leaned toward me, resting his chin on his thumbs. "If you forgot something important, your purse for example?"

I didn't need a GPS device to see where this was going. Would I jimmy a door or clamber through a window? "I leave my purse in the trunk of my car; I don't have a desk to lock it in."

"Suppose you left something else." He gazed at the briefcase I'd allowed him to rifle through earlier, blinked as if developing a snapshot of its contents, and then grimaced. "Maybe a book. Or some medication."

Talk about a reach. The only book in my bag was a paperback collection of short stories and the medication was a single ibuprofen tablet wrapped in a tissue and stashed at the bottom of the pencil case. "I guess I'd have to hope that one of the custodians heard me knocking and recognized me."

"Suppose the custodians were working where they couldn't hear you?"

I squeezed my sore thumb inside my fist. No one could accuse Atwell of being a quitter. "I'd come back in the morning," I said, keeping it simple, not mentioning evening athletic practices or teachers working late to get papers graded. Last night there could have been several doing just that, clearing the decks for the five-day holiday weekend ahead. Stoddard might have been one of them. He might even have opened the outside door to his killer.

Atwell grunted, made a note on his pad, and stood, running his thumbs beneath his belt and tugging it atop a narrow shelf of gut. "We'll need your prints. Then you can go. Don't talk about this interview."

He drew a business card from his pocket and tossed it across the table. "Call me if you think of anything and be advised that I'll want to talk with you again." He didn't say "don't leave town" like they do in the movies and I was so glad to be out of his presence that I didn't mention that oversight.

I also didn't bring up his other omission—he hadn't asked me if I knew anyone who would want to kill Henry Stoddard.

Quiz Answer:
All of these are possible answers depending on the day, the school, the assignment, and what didn't need to be ironed.

The daily rate for a substitute
a) isn't bad for part-time work
b) should include hazard pay
c) varies from district to district
d) may increase after a set number of days
e) is terrific if you have another source of income

CHAPTER FOUR

For the rest of the day, I was on automatic pilot, handing out maps and the few atlases I was able to scrounge and suggesting that kids work in teams. A few minutes after the bell rang I turned in my keys to Big Chill—making sure there was another sub as a witness—and told her I'd be in the building for a while because I had to meet with Jessica.

"She's in the staff meeting," Big Chill told me.

"You'd better wait for her," the little voice in my mind nagged.

"Could be at least an hour," Big Chill said as if she'd heard.

I ran a mental replay of Jessica's threat. She'd definitely used the words "immediately after school."

"She'll be angry," the little voice warned.

As if I didn't realize that. Would it be too much to ask for a conscience that gave me just a *little* credit?

Shoulders slumped, I thought of Cheese Puff, waiting for his walk, of the bubble bath I'd planned to take, the soft bed I longed to flop on. "Miss Flint wanted to see me right after school. But I have an appointment." Not exactly a lie. The appointment was with a dog. "What should I do?"

"Go." Big Chill flashed me a complicit smile.

"You won't get away with it," the little voice snarked. "You'll pay for this."

So what else was new?

I scurried to my car and on the way home made a furtive stop at the liquor store. Furtive, because when I started subbing, I realized there could be students lurking anywhere and everywhere, ready to text the 411 on my habits. And furtive because it was a small world, and if Detective Atwell spotted me, he might suspect I was attempting to drown a guilty conscience.

Having managed my clandestine operation without being spotted, I drove home with a bottle of rum, dreaming of something fruity, frothy, and packing one hell of a wallop. I parked under the canopy allotted to those with no-view condos, skipped across the parking lot, and skidded to a halt. There, on my miniscule front porch, her substantial butt parked in my swing and her magenta Mohawk aglow in a rogue ray of sunlight, was my sister Jeannine.

I swallowed a groan and tweaked my lips into a tight smile. The people who make up all those smarmy sayings about family never met Jeannine— Indigo Zephyr, or Iz as she's known to her fans. She's a big deal in some circles. And if you know what's good for you, you won't forget that for even half a second. My relationship with her was, to say the least, complicated. I owed her for salvaging what she could of my childhood after a family tragedy. She was aware of that debt and the guilt compounding like interest and that awareness gave her an emotional club she wielded with what I perceived as too much zeal.

"Well look who's finally here." Scowling at my paper sack, she lumbered to her feet. The swing creaked in relief. "I hope that isn't spirits in the bag."

She wasn't referring to ghosts.

Clutching the bag to my chest I decided that a lie would be pointless—Iz would check—so my best defense was to send her off on a tangent, and dodge as much conflict as possible until she left for the lecture I'd forgotten about until this magic moment. She e-mailed me a notice last month, something about reinterpreting the message of popular children's books from the perspective of blah blah blah.

Don't get me wrong, I have no problem with reinterpretation or perspective. I also have no problem with my sister's sexual, political, or religious preferences. What frosts me is my sister's belief that her views are supreme and what *really* frosts me is her condescending attitude toward anyone who doesn't worship at her feet. To my amazement, the league of foot-side worshipers was growing exponentially, making her even more pompous and despotic.

Iz smoothed a flowing green satin blouse over a spare tire the size of, well, an actual spare tire. "I said, 'I hope that isn't spirits.'"

"Didn't Nietzche say 'hope is the worst of all evils'?" I asked, ducking my head to hide a smirk. Iz hated people quoting anyone but her.

"I don't know and I don't care." She emitted a gale-force sigh. "There hasn't been a man born yet who had anything worth saying about anything."

I smothered a smile. If Iz got going on the foibles and failures of the male sex, she'd have no time to tee off on me. As I climbed the steps, I scrounged my brain cells for fuel to throw on the fire. "But didn't Shakespeare say—"

31

"Another male." She leveled a finger at my nose. "Don't depart from the subject. The point is that I'm justifiably concerned about your health. The point is that only a weak woman takes refuge in liquor, Babs."

I gritted my teeth. She knew I hated that nickname. But she'd brought up names, so to heck with dodging conflict. I manufactured a syrupy tone. "Then I suppose I'm faint, feeble, and fragile, *Jeannine.*"

Her close-set eyes narrowed. "You know very well I no longer use the name our parents chose."

Knowing she would never see the correlation, I turned my back, unlocked the door, and greeted the one creature who accepted and loved me exactly as I was—Cheese Puff. Ten pounds of wild orange hair, shoe-button eyes, and wagging tail. He circled me as I trudged to the kitchen, performing an intricate series of dips and twirls worthy of a top score on one of those reality dance shows. I set the booze on the counter next to the refrigerator and got a doggie treat from a bright blue canister—a splash of color against the beige wall. If I ever got an infusion of cash, I'd paint over the quick-sale neutral tones.

Cheese Puff sat up and begged, then leaped high to intercept the nugget I tossed. "Good boy."

"I don't know why you have that dog." Iz commandeered a chair, bellied up to my two-person dining nook table, and pawed through the bowl of chocolates I keep to practice self-control and demonstrate that food has no power over me—or at least slightly less power than gravity.

"With all the homeless female mutts out there you end up with a male," Iz groused. "The size of a flea. What could he possibly do if a rapist broke in?"

Cheese Puff bared tiny teeth as if to tell her he'd handle the situation by biting said rapist in one particular appendage.

32

I tossed him another nugget. "He's got ears like a bat. He'd warn me in time to lock myself in the bathroom and call the police. And you know I didn't set out to get a male dog—or any dog at all."

Back in the spring I spotted him cowering under a shrub along a riverfront trail, so thin his ribs stood out like ridges on a washboard, and so dirty his coat was the color of coffee. When I bent for a closer look, he peered up, eyes wide with fear, then blinked and launched himself into my arms. At home, he gobbled down what I had on hand right before the unemployment check arrived—stale bran crackers and lemon yogurt three days past its expiration date. I gave him a bath, cut the tangles from his coat, and blew him dry. At bedtime, he burrowed deep beneath the sheets and slept beside my feet. The next morning we shared a granola bar before I launched a half-hearted search for his owner. To my delight and relief, no one claimed him.

Iz unwrapped a pair of miniature candy bars and stuffed one into each cheek. Her way of demonstrating power over food was to decimate its ranks. "You knew I was coming," she fumed in a sticky voice. "Why didn't you buy milk chocolate?"

I longed to respond, "You need chocolate like the national debt needs a few more digits." But taking a more subtle approach allowed me to award myself points, so what I said as I cast a longing look toward my sack of liquid relaxation was, "I read a study that found dark chocolate is better for you."

"Probably a study done by a man." She smacked the table with a weighty palm. "But the point is that you don't eat it. You just play stupid torture games with yourself because you're obsessed with trying to attract another husband."

"Direct hit," the little voice in my mind said smugly.

I grabbed a glass from the cabinet, decided it wouldn't hold nearly enough rum, put it back, and stretched for a pint beer mug on the top shelf. I talked a good game about being through with men and marriage and making it alone, but I was lonely and a little scared. Atwell's face loomed in my mind, his lips set in a predatory grin. Make that a *lot* scared.

"You should have learned a lesson from the disaster with Jake." Iz devoured another candy bar. "But you always put yourself first."

I sloshed rum into the glass. Yeah, I was selfish to the core. That's why, after closing on the condo, I'd selfishly "loaned" money to Iz to have the tattoo of a heart and her previous lover's name removed from her left breast. *Sindie Lu.* In flowing script. And no, I'm not making that up. The odds of her repaying me were right up there with the chances of the Loch Ness Monster propelling itself up a Reckless River fish ladder to spawn.

"And this place is a perfect example." She swept an arm to take in the cramped kitchen, the living/dining space, tiny washroom/laundry area, and steep staircase leading to my bedroom and the master bath. "A dump I can hardly turn around in, a bed littered with allergy-inducing dog hair, and a futon mattress as thin as a tortilla. Fortunately the lecture organizers booked me a hotel suite, but I'm starting to think you don't want me to visit."

Bingo. I poured lemonade over the rum.

"Selfish and passive-aggressive." Iz fingered another chocolate.

I added a huge dollop of grenadine, stirred, and tasted. Not bad. I opened the freezer and snatched a handful of ice cubes. "Whatever."

34

Iz smacked the table once more. "Damn it, Barbara, the point here is I don't want you to end up like Bryce—dying before you realize your potential."

Bryce. I felt a crushing wave of sadness and regret. He died when I was ten, died saving six women from a burning college dormitory. I remembered him as the gangly boy who inhabited the room next to mine until he went off to school. It was a room crammed with books, sports equipment, and heaps of clothing, some headed to the laundry room, some bound for the closet, most never arriving at those destinations. I felt such freedom in that room, such a lack of boundaries. But I never relaxed the squared-away standards of my own room. Freedom, I realized early on, was a scary thing.

Which is why I don't kick Iz out of my life. When my parents fell apart after Bryce died, she took up the slack, making my breakfast, braiding my hair, getting me off to school, and helping with my homework. Being thrust into the role of surrogate mother when she was fifteen probably explains why Iz tried to manage my life and save me from heartache. And the parental attention she was deprived of might account for her look-at-me behavior.

"Maybe I'm realizing my potential at this very moment." My voice trembled on the final words. What if that was true? What if this was the high-water mark of my life? I shivered, took a long swallow of my drink and felt it deliver a punch to my gut that straightened my spine. I glanced around for Cheese Puff, didn't see him, and guessed he'd gauged the tone of the conversation, slunk upstairs, and sought refuge among my pillows. "Why is it such a big deal to you? Do you think my lack of success is catching?"

"Of course not." Iz laughed with all the sincerity of a salesman working on commission.

"Does it embarrass you?"

Iz went to great lengths to avoid mention of her family tree. Nowhere in her biographical blurbs was there a hint that she'd been born in Omaha, Nebraska, to parents who now resided in a gated senior community in Missouri, insulated by endless rounds of golf, tennis, bridge, and square dancing that salved—but didn't heal—the wound of Bryce's death.

Once each year, in early spring when the dogwoods were in bloom, I made a pilgrimage to their ranch-style home packed with trophies and photos commemorating friends and activities. High school graduation pictures of each of their children stood on a small shelf in their breakfast nook. When I presented them with a silver-framed photo taken as Albert and I cut our wedding cake, my mother thanked me, handed the frame back, and said she'd put the photo in the family album.

"I must be fair to the others," she said. "After all, Bryce will never have the chance to marry, and as for Jeannine . . ."

That was as far as she ever went on that topic. Moments after my arrival she would ask if Jeannine was well. I would report, omitting salacious and controversial details—i.e., anything that smacked of the truth—and subsequent conversations would center on "safe" topics like gardening, cooking, and the weather. During my last visit I'd omitted my divorce and in phone calls since explained my new address by calling the move "a sensible decision considering I never had much interest in yard work."

I gulped rum and felt both bold and curious. "Does it annoy you that I can't help advance your career?"

Iz flushed the color of marinara sauce and shot me a scowl. "In case you haven't noticed, my career is doing just fine." She unwrapped yet another chocolate and bit so hard I heard her teeth snap. "If you settle for what you get,

36

Babs, and you don't develop your talents, then your life will continue to be just one accident after another."

And there it was. The word that had colored my life since Iz first used it as a weapon on my fifth birthday. "Mom and Dad had Bryce and me on purpose, but you were an accident." Not yet old enough to understand the concept of sex, let alone safe sex, I recognized from her tone that it was far better to be on purpose than to be an accident. I'd run crying to my room and refused to come out for the rest of the day, not even when Bryce caught a garter snake and chased Janie Fuller around the yard.

Now I raised my glass in a silent toast to Iz for managing to resurrect that day with a single word, to stab me with such subtlety that the knife was deep in my heart before I felt the pain. Only those you love—or feel you should love—have that power.

"I just want you to realize your potential," Iz repeated. "As a woman and an individual."

That was Iz-speak for "Don't even think of getting married again."

"And as an artist," Iz added.

I took a long swallow. "I'm not an artist."

"We're all artists." She splayed her fingers across her ample breasts. This I knew from previous conversations was the prelude to justifying every project, passion, or peccadillo. "We all have talent."

Leaving unsaid that she had more than most and definitely more than I had. The only talent I'd displayed in the do-it-yourself project known as my life was dreaming up topics and tracking down guests for the Rick Rivers Radio Show. "Couldn't do it without you, honey," he told me a thousand times. But since I was laid off he seemed to be doing just fine. Maybe my real talent was for not leaving a ripple in my wake, not being missed after I left the building. Or missed with a sense of relief the way Henry Stoddard would be.

"I'm not an artist," I repeated, drinking more rum to make myself and my thoughts numb. Rum. Numb. Hmm, maybe I was a poet.

Iz sighed and unwrapped another chocolate bar. "If you're not going to make an effort to realize your own potential, at the very least you should help others realize theirs."

I gripped my glass. That was another bit of Iz-speak. Translation: she was short on funds again and I owed her for filling in for our parents. "I'm broke." Broke, and with a school loan hanging over me like an executioner's axe. Sipping, I searched for a rhyme, decided on, "And that's no joke."

She frowned. "It's just two thousand, that's all."

That's all? "I'll go in the red." I drained the glass and slammed it on the counter. "And my dog won't get fed."

"You have assets." She flipped a hand. "You have this condo."

"I won't add to my loan, so leave me alone." Darn, that was the same word, just spelled differently. What do you call that? Something ending in nym?

Iz glowered. "You don't need to be so PMSy."

I guess that's what some people call it when you finally speak your mind.

She stood with all the grace of a sack of spuds and brushed the front of her satin shirt. "I can take a hint."

"You never have before." I sloshed more rum over the ice. This speaking-your-mind stuff felt pretty darn good.

Iz glared. I swallowed rum to fortify myself against one of her legendary tirades, but she turned and tromped away. "I can't believe you're my sister," she yelled before she slammed the door.

Sister. Rhymes with blister. Or pissed her, as in pissed her off. Not quite. Gotta work on that one. I whistled for Cheese Puff, snapped on his leash, and, wobbling like a top about to plop, took him for a stroll around the complex.

And that explains why, when Big Chill called at 5:15 AM and asked me to cover Henry Stoddard's classes, I was in the bathroom kneeling before the porcelain shrine and vowing I'd change my ways if the room would only stop spinning.

Quiz Answer:
All of these answers work for me.

Teachers and administrators prefer subs who
a) show up
b) follow the lesson plans
c) don't whine too much
d) have good classroom management skills
e) care about the students

CHAPTER FIVE

"You'll be in a different classroom every period," Big Chill told me as I signed the sub form. "Naturally he didn't fill out his lesson plan book—Henry Stoddard was above all that—but Susan's putting something together. Check in with her."

In an effort to disguise what I suspected was the lingering reek of rum, I tongued a peppermint from cheek to cheek and kept my answer short. "Great." With quivering fingers I accepted the keys and clipped them to my lanyard.

Big Chill opened her desk drawer and took out a foil-wrapped packet of aspirin and three sticks of gum. Without a word she leaned over the desk and dropped them into my briefcase. I thought of half a dozen explanations for my condition—migraine, family crisis, sick dog, sudden appearance of ex-husband, car wreck, capture by pirates—then simply nodded. Big Chill had heard it all.

"Mr. Morrow wants to know if you could do a long-term assignment, Barbara."

I herded the mint back to the other cheek. If Morrow, who'd never spoken with me or seen me at a distance of less than twenty feet, was thinking of sliding me into Stoddard's spot, it meant two things: Jessica hadn't blackballed me and Big Chill had put in a good word. Letting her down didn't bode well for my future, but I had no choice. "Not until the end of spring term. I have a few more courses to take to be fully certified."

That class work, difficult and exacting as it might be, seemed a mere formality after the school district background check. You may not know this, but if you do a lot of bare-handed housework, use sandpaper without gloves, or play the harp, the whorls and ridges on your fingertips, unlike the wrinkles around your eyes and lips, smooth out. By the time you're my age—let's just say I'm pushing forty and it's pushing back—getting a clear image can be difficult.

While they inked and rolled my fingertips, I contemplated the ramifications of being unable to leave behind more than smudges. It seemed the ideal qualification for employment as a cat burglar or international jewel thief—provided I had coordination plus the audacity and flexible morality of a high-living investment banker asking for a bailout.

Now, after two months in the crucible of the educational system, facing down thirty teenagers every hour, my nerves have the tensile strength of carbon nanotube fiber. (For the record, I have no idea exactly what that is or what it's used for, but it's pretty darn strong. You could look it up.) As for malleable morality, well, that seemed to have developed yesterday when I kept quiet about Jessica's desperate determination to get into Henry Stoddard's room and the way she ransacked his pockets. I wondered if the cops would find her prints, then wondered if I left any behind for them to decipher.

"Not until the end of the spring term," Big Chill said with the same dismay I use for phrases like "bounced check" and "flat tire."

"Or a little later," I amended.

Big Chill sighed. My approval rating slipped with an audible clunk.

"But I'll fill in as long as I'm allowed," I offered. "I'll do a good job. History's practically my second major. I read history all the time." Okay, make that historical fiction, but there must be a *little* truth in those books.

She sighed again and I chomped the mint to stop myself from babbling about how my previous job had included gathering background information for Rick Rivers.

"I'll cancel my other subbing jobs," I volunteered. And with glee. The only thing I had set up for the rest of the month was a two-day stint in biology at another high school—a job I feared would involve dissecting some pale, pickled creature or, worse yet, one that was still wiggling. Teaching Stoddard's classes would be a cakewalk compared to that. Plus I could probably rely on students who loathed and feared him to cooperate with anyone exhibiting the least degree of humanity.

Big Chill tapped her pen on her calendar and turned to her keyboard. "I'll put you in until Christmas vacation while we look for someone."

Considering myself dismissed, I zoomed into the mailroom and rifled Stoddard's cubbyhole for attendance sheets, then popped a piece of gum between my jaws and hustled up to Susan's room.

"I'm glad you were available today." Her tired smile went with chapped lips, a nose raw with tissue burn, bloodshot blue eyes, and brown hair so limp and lusterless it made mine look like I'd just stepped out of a salon. "I'm so sorry about what happened to you yesterday. What a shock it must have been for you . . . finding him dead."

I almost assured her that finding him dead was better than dealing with him alive, but bit my tongue. My days in the radio business left me with a dark sense of humor—a protective shield against the seamier side of life—not always appropriate in other situations. "It wasn't the best day I ever had."

For the record, that was when I put my hand in my jacket pocket and found a twenty-dollar bill I'd forgotten about, got a reduction on my car insurance for getting older, and helped the demo lady at the supermarket clean up a nasty nacho spill and been rewarded with a strawberry cheesecake. Can you tell my life needs an upgrade?

"You've got a good attitude." Susan dug a tissue from her pocket and blew her nose. "I hope we see more of you around here."

"I'd like that."

She nodded and tapped a yellow pad. "Well, I'm sorry, but I have no idea where Henry was and I can't get into his classroom to search for lesson plans. When I found out what happened I dragged myself out of bed and polled two of his classes. 'Somewhere in the Dark Ages' was all I could get out of them." She slapped the textbook shut. "So start with the plague—that's always popular because they get to use words like pustule and talk about rotting flesh and carts loaded with dead bodies."

Now, you might flinch at that, but after ten weeks with teens, I only nodded.

"I've got a video here." She opened a file cabinet. "And plenty of worksheets. My TA got distracted and ran off an extra 200."

I gathered them up. The plague it was.

Rain was pelting down when, after five showings of the plague video and six aspirin, I pulled into my condo complex and nosed my car into my allotted space under the long metal canopy a hundred and twenty steps from a tall glass of orange juice, a hot shower, and a long night's sleep. Too many of those steps would be miserable. The laws of economics multiplied by the privileges of the wealthy determined that. Had I been willing to go another hundred and fifty thousand in debt, I would own a riverfront unit and a parking space a few steps from my door.

The moments devoted to running with shoulders hunched while icy rain spattered the back of my neck— because only visitors to the Northwest use umbrellas or raise their hoods on days when rain hasn't reached torrential standards—are when I really miss my house and its attached garage. But that was then and this was . . . well, this was pretty darn sucky.

I made it to the shelter of the rich folks' carport and spun in a circle, shaking water from my hair. A flash of yellow caught my eye and I noted a new resident by the trash bins. The previous Trash Guy was thin and stooped and made do with a bit of faded green canvas. Trash Guy II was sturdier and wore a yellow slicker and hat that looked like they came straight out of a New England harbor. I wondered if he was a more recent victim of the recession, one who hadn't yet pawned, traded, or worn out gear salvaged from the wreck of his life.

There but for fortune. I was down, but I wasn't out. Yet.

"Well look who's here."

That was the same greeting I'd gotten from Iz yesterday. But this wasn't the voice of my sister; this was the smoky, sexy voice of someone I wanted to see even less—my ex-husband.

Temporary insanity. That's how I'd plea if they hauled me to the Supreme Court of Stupidity on charges of committing marriage with Jake. Temporary insanity due to the loneliness of life without Albert—adoring Albert, the sweetest man who ever rubbed my feet and took my car in for an oil change. Forget flowers and candy. Albert knew what this woman *really* wanted.

That's not to say he was without faults. When he was bird watching—intent, say, on a towhee scratching in the garden—he was oblivious to anything else—smoke pouring out of the toaster, carpool honking in the driveway, me telling him to put on shoes that matched. He left the lid loose on the mayonnaise, snored like a walrus, and never got the hang of sorting the recycling.

Albert never got the hang of making money, either. So when, a few years after we moved to the Northwest from Nebraska, he leaned over a guardrail to get a closer look at a nesting puffin and fell to his death, he left me with a vast collection of audio tapes filled with chirps and trills, twenty-seven years to pay on our mortgage, and $12,283.63 in savings. I expected to spend a good chunk of that on funeral expenses, but the Coast Guard never recovered his body, so I had a nest egg and home equity.

Those, unfortunately, were the primary attributes Jake had been looking for in a mate.

"Jake," I said, in a tone I hoped was as chilly as the rain. "What are you doing here?"

He gave me what I recognized as his blue-ribbon smile, the one that showed off twenty-four of his whitened, straightened, and flossed-daily teeth. "I live here. Moved in a few days ago."

My gut clenched and the sound of rain pounding on the canopy above swelled like an obligatory drum solo from some wild-haired, no-talent, 70s rock group. I steadied myself with a palm pressed against the sparkling window of a big-ass sedan belonging to Myra Bancroft, a cold-hearted trophy wife who lived in the view condo that butted up against mine. "Moved in? Here?"

Since reclaiming my freedom and my name I'd avoided his usual habitat—fern bars and upscale fitness centers—and hadn't run into Jake. I'd hoped to keep it that way for, oh, the next ninety years.

"Yep." He feathered his baby-fine brown hair. Even in the dim light I noticed he'd added highlights. And he'd buffed up significantly; a tight red T-shirt beneath his open rain jacket defined ridges of muscle. He nodded toward the up-river side of the complex. "The big unit on the end."

Damn him. He had a view of the river *and* the frosty slopes of Mount Hood. How the hell could he afford that? His income as a real estate agent was, to put a positive spin on it, irregular, and under the terms of the divorce decree, he owed me half of whatever profit he made on a development deal leveraged with the contents of my savings account.

Given the state of the economy, I doubted that deal had gone through, but vowed to check with my mole in his office, one of several co-workers he dallied with while we were married. When, in a last-ditch effort to keep my roof over his head, he dumped her, she switched her allegiance to me. If Jake was trying to cheat, she'd rat him out him in the time it took to dial my number, and he'd have to answer to my divorce attorney—a woman who could give Big Chill a run for her money.

"How nice for you," I uttered with enough venom to take down a charging bull elephant.

"Yeah, it's great—three bedrooms, jetted tubs, big-screen TV." He gave me a venom-proof smug smile. "And my friend is giving me a deal on the rent."

I translated that to mean that his friend was a woman and still so enraptured she hadn't realized all she was getting was smarmy charm and athletic sex. Not that I have anything against sex—athletic or otherwise—but I have the selfish desire to be part of the bedroom equation. The deal with Jake is that if there's a mirror on the ceiling, you can bet a year's pay he's admiring himself. He never asked "Was it good for me?" but I always felt he wanted to.

"So you live on this side." He nodded toward my twenty-square-foot yard and the porch with its two-person—or one Iz—swing.

I wanted to say, "I live within my means," but only nodded. No point in letting myself in for the lecture on spending money to make money.

"Just down the way from me," he said.

Was he about to suggest that he might drop by some night? I shook my head hard enough to revitalize my lingering headache. "Down the way from you and your *friend*." I jangled my keychain. "Well, I've got to run. Enjoy your view."

"You're not going to invite me in?" He cocked his head and flashed his intimate smile, revealing a glimpse of his upper teeth. "For a drink . . . or something."

After last night, I needed a drink like a Chihuahau needs a hairnet and as for the "or something," the only way I'd ever do that with Jake again would be if he was the last man on earth and there were no batteries to be found.

"I've given up alcohol." Not exactly a lie since I didn't mention how long I'd given it up for. I consulted my queasy stomach. Definitely another day.

His eyes widened. "Really?"

I understood his surprise. During the final days of our marriage, I relied a lot on courage from a bottle to stay the course once I finally set one.

You see, ours had been one of those Titanic-iceberg relationships. Jake—in the role of the Titanic—steamed along, confident that I wouldn't get in his way or send him to the bottom. And for too long I was an iceberg with all the power and potential of those melting chips in the bottom of a paper cone after you slurp down the last drop of pumped-on syrup. I drifted on a current of infatuation, suspicions squelched by waves of his charm.

To say I stuck with him because I had no self-esteem is on a par with saying Death Valley can get kind of hot. But as Jake fell more in love with himself and took less care to hide his true nature, my emotional temperature fell, first by a few degrees, then with the velocity of a bowling ball dropped from a skyscraper. The day I discovered that one of his associates—a woman he claimed had stopped in for a meeting about a new listing— left lipstick smears on my pillow and appropriated a twenty-dollar tube of face cream, I set myself on a collision course with my two-timing Titanic.

"How about a cup of coffee?" Jake suggested.

I blew that off with a flip of my hand. "Too late in the day."

"Tea, then." He stepped closer and trailed a finger along the back of my hand. "It's been a long time."

I jerked away, irritated that he had the gall to touch me, furious at the tingling and tightening that touch set off. "Not long enough."

One of Jake's few positive qualities—and perhaps his biggest flaw—is that he doesn't think the word "no" applies to him. "Feels like too long to me," he said with a twist to his lips I recognized as his "bad boy grin," the one he practiced before he went out to persuade middle-aged women to buy more house than they could afford.

Did he honestly believe he could sucker me with something that looked so much like a sneer? "After those years with you, Jake, I came to the conclusion that Iz has the right idea about men."

Jake gaped. His hands dropped to his crotch as if I'd aimed a kick with steel-toed boots. "You mean you're—?"

"Yup. Convinced I can live without them."

While Jake was occupied with thoughts of his equipment becoming obsolete, I slid past and trotted to my door. As I thrust the key into the lock, I glanced over my shoulder. Jake was still gawking, but Trash Guy II had left his post and stood beneath the canopy next to my car, staring in my direction. I let myself in, scooped up Cheese Puff, and peered through the blinds.

"If that bum messes with my car," I muttered. "I'll call security."

Posted signs warned that "the premises were patrolled regularly by an independent security firm." But, considering that Trash Guy I had claimed his territory without dispute since September, I had some questions about the definition of "regularly" and "security."

Cheese Puff coughed.

"Okay. I'll call the police."

I shivered, seeing Detective Atwell studying me like a plague virus under a microscope. Innocent as I might be of the murder of Henry Stoddard, there was no point in calling attention to myself.

"But only if he's trying to break in, not if he's just, you know, leaning on my car," I amended. "I don't want to make trouble for a guy who has to sleep in a slicker under a trash bin."

Cheese Puff licked my chin in what I took for approval and together we watched Jake stutter-step off with a pigeon-toed gait, family jewels tight between his legs. Trash Guy II ambled along in his wake.

"Maybe he's planning to mug Jake," I whispered.

They'd never met, but Cheese Puff knew all about Jake. His lips curled into what, for a dog, passes as a smile.

I rubbed my nose against his. "Couldn't happen to a nicer guy."

Quiz Answer:
all choices are possible
e, *d*, and *b* are the biggies
a – that's a no-brainer
c – even whiners don't care much for other whiners

Many students believe that on days they're not at school subs
a) hang in closets upside down like bats
b) read dull books published before 1800
c) sit by the phone waiting to be called to the next job
d) practice being mean and crabby
e) temporarily cease to exist

CHAPTER SIX

Being the indecisive person I am, just before I fell asleep, I wasted a few seconds feeling guilty about hoping Jake would get mugged. Then I persuaded myself that a few bruises might build character of a less self-involved kind.

After that, because guilt was free and I could never resist a bargain, I felt sorry for Trash Guy II who would get very little for his effort. If Jake was running true to form, there would be no bills in his wallet and only parking meter change in his pockets. He always claimed there was no reason to carry cash when there was plastic and it was almost a year before I discovered the enormous unpaid balances on his credit cards. My shock fanned a spark of self-preservation and I searched out and copied statements going back to well before our wedding, then took steps to make certain that debt was his alone.

So on Saturday morning when Cheese Puff and I took advantage of a break in the rain, I was both relieved and disappointed to spot Jake, unscathed, with a tall, broad-shouldered redhead. She had the kind of grip on his arm I

51

reserve for bags of freshly roasted jumbo cashews and, when a pair of nubile joggers passed and Jake's head swiveled, she spun him against her, kissing him in a way that seemed more possessive than passionate.

"He's on a tighter leash than you are," I told Cheese Puff.

As if he understood, my tiny dog stepped high, and bounced into a front-leg-curling trot like a show pony.

"Slow down. I don't want another close encounter."

Cheese Puff obligingly stopped to sniff and Jake and the redhead got into—what else?—a low-slung sports car. She took the wheel and revved the engine. I guessed love wasn't blind enough to let him drive. Jake's head-swiveling attempts to check out all things female made for highway progress best described as erratic.

The car burst from their parking spot with a squeal of tires and roared down the short drive. We picked up our pace—a power walk for me and a slow run for Cheese Puff—and cut around the end of the condo complex to the riverfront trail. As we passed a common space where residents sometimes set up a volleyball net, I got the mental pricklies, glanced around, and spotted a man hunkered on a wooden bench in a small garden area sheltered by a curve in the brick wall marking the property line. He wore jeans and a navy windbreaker and, even though the bill of his black baseball cap was pulled low, I noted that his gaze was fixed on the departing sports car.

Probably just admiring it. Or her.

For a few seconds I wondered what it would be like to be tall and lean and have a wealth of coiling hair the color of sunset. Then Cheese Puff spotted a cat, dashed to the limit of the retractable leash, and did a canine mime routine of scaling an invisible wall. That had me chuckling until the rain returned and we scuttled for home.

That evening, after catching a television news recap of Stoddard's murder and suffering a bout of anxiety about how Detective Atwell might be twisting fact and supposition, I mixed myself a drink and headed upstairs, grateful for one small favor—the media either didn't have my name or had decided not to interview me.

No matter what aspersions Iz cast, my bedroom was graced with tall windows screened by maples still sporting a few orange and red leaves. It was spacious enough for an easy chair, and desk/computer workstation, and a queen bed. I fluffed up the pillows and plopped down with Cheese Puff sprawled across my stomach. Closing my eyes, I imagined a life without stressing out about making ends meet.

The clack and clatter of coat hangers interrupted my daydream. Those hangers were in the smaller bedroom of the riverfront apartment that backed against mine and I'd heard that sound often enough to know what it meant— Nelson Bancroft was on the hunt for Myra's unsanctioned purchases.

Nelson wore dark blue suits, carried a slim briefcase, drove a luxury car with leather upholstery, and came home on the dot of 5:42 each evening looking like he'd been dragged behind a combine at harvest time. Myra was an aerobicized twig with jutting collar bones, sucked-in cheeks, and platinum hair scraped into a bun. A few weeks after I moved in she tried to get the association to bar "filthy animals, especially little dogs that yap endlessly." She lost by a landslide vote—the penalty for discounting Cheese Puff's fan base.

Cheese Puff—who, for the record, barked instead of yapping—had quite a following among retirees in the complex. One of them—Mrs. Ballantine, next-door neighbor to the Bancrofts—formed the Cheese Puff Care and Comfort Committee. While I was at school, members came by to walk and brush him and deliver bits of roasted chicken breast or homemade dog biscuits. The Committee had led the charge to vote down Myra's proposal.

Something thumped against the wall and I wiggled closer. Trying not to eavesdrop was like trying not to breathe. And I felt no guilt. Nelson and Myra knew how thin this wall was.

"What's this?" Nelson bellowed.

"It's a blouse," Myra said. "It was marked down."

"$140 is marked down?"

"Yes." Her tone implied he was too stupid to live. "That's forty percent off."

"It's extortion. Take it back. We can't afford it."

"If you'd tell me what you make instead of playing Mr. Corporate Control Freak, then I could budget," she whined.

"Budget? You? The woman who thinks if we still have checks we still have money?"

"Fine. If you're going to belittle me, then I'll never buy another thing."

"Ha! You'll be at the mall before noon tomorrow. You're just like your mother."

Cheese Puff's ears shot up. "You're right," I told him, "they're not wasting time tonight. "Bathroom habits are coming right up.

"My mother is a saint," Myra screeched. "And you're a pig. No, even a pig could probably learn not to piss on the floor."

"Here it comes," I said. "Sex."

"And a pig could probably manage to last more than forty-two seconds," Myra howled.

"If this particular pig was allowed to have sex more than three times a year then perhaps he could."

"I've had sex zero times this year." I scratched Cheese Puff's ears. "Not that I haven't had opportunities. Finding a partner is a snap. Heck, I'll bet the guy out by the trash bin would be willing."

Cheese Puff drew back his lips to display tiny teeth.

"No, not the old guy with the yellow eyeballs. I forget you've got a distance-vision problem. We'll do a close-up walk-by tomorrow so you can scope out the new guy." And maybe I'd give him a few bucks because though he hadn't mugged Jake last night, he might do it sometime.

"You're always so critical," Myra wailed. "Nothing I do is good enough."

"Here we go again with that! Myra, I'm not asking for the moon. Just don't buy anything unless you really need it."

"Well, I need that blouse for the bank Christmas party."

"I told you last week there won't be a Christmas party. Money's tight. We have to send a message of fiscal responsibility."

"Note," I told Cheese Puff, "that sending a message isn't the same thing as actually *demonstrating* fiscal responsibility."

"If money's so tight, then I'll get a job," Myra threatened. "At a grocery store or a greasy little restaurant. Is that what you want? Do you want me to come home with broken nails, stinking of onion rings? Do you want your clients to see me wearing an ugly sack of a uniform?"

She burst into sobs and I felt the vibration of running feet. A moment later I heard distant knocking and pleading and guessed she'd locked herself in a bathroom.

The evening's entertainment was over.

Quiz Answer:

Find out for yourself by polling students in your neighborhood.

The most practical lunch for a sub to bring
a) doesn't need to be refrigerated or heated
b) can be eaten in ten minutes or less
c) is so weird, healthy, or disgusting no one will steal it
d) contains nothing breakable or crushable
e) all of the above

CHAPTER SEVEN

"So where did he hide it and who's got it now?"

All eyes in the teachers' team room swiveled to Aston Marsden, a man so caught up in history that he relived it each weekend through reenactments and encampments. He started with Civil War battle recreations, but soon branched out. For the past two years he'd been given to teaching dressed as a fur trader, Union Army sergeant, or doughboy, much to the delight of students and dismay of administrators who reminded him that even plastic replica swords and side arms were forbidden.

Recent rumor had it that Marsden, who was so tan he resembled a bronzed statue of himself, was learning phrases of ancient languages and practicing with shield, lance, and bow, hoping to be included in reenactments of the Battle of Thermopylae, the Punic Wars, and even Hannibal crossing the Alps. Unconfirmed student gossip held that he'd asked a local zoo to loan him a few elephants for a run-through but been turned down flat.

"Hide what?" Brenda Waring eyed Aston over a pot of something that resembled fat dark linguini in a sticky beige sauce with green flecks. Brenda was constantly experimenting with new recipes and bringing them in for taste testing. She taught Health and Nutrition, but I'd heard some teachers wonder which subject she knew less about. "What is it someone's got?"

"Henry's dirt collection." Aston gnawed off a chunk of jerky. "The secrets he held over us." He tongued the jerky into his left cheek, took a bite of a scrawny apple, and surveyed the group gathered around the rickety table. "Some of us. Not me. He had nothing on me."

"Or me." Brenda dug a spoon into the pot, filled a plastic bowl with a trembling hand, and offered it to the table at large. "Who wants to try this?"

Susan Mitchell elbowed my arm and shook her head a millimeter. I got the message and, even without knowing what was in that bowl, gazed with new appreciation at my sandwich: Jarlsberg cheese, tomato, avocado, and mayonnaise on rye. Susan smiled and stabbed her fork into a salad of greens, walnuts, dried cranberries, and feta cheese.

"I would but I can't," Aston told Brenda. "I'm eating in character this week. Fur trappers' encampment coming up." He shot Gertrude Suttle a grin. "Won't start using the lingo until Wednesday, but I haven't washed my hair or showered since Sunday. BO contributes to historical accuracy."

Doug Whitman, a first-year English teacher, moved his chair another inch from Marsden's and reached for the bowl Brenda offered. "What is it?"

"Eel Alfredo. With garlic, cilantro, and cinnamon."

Doug's arm snapped back like a bungee cord. "What a coincidence. I had that last night."

"Really?" Brenda narrowed her eyes. "Where?"

Doug's lips moved for a few seconds before words emerged with a squeak of panic. "Um, at Chez . . . Chez PU. It's over in Portland."

Susan poked me again and I stifled a smile.

"Chez Pew?" Brenda cocked her head. "Is that in a remodeled church?"

"Possibly," Doug said without missing a beat. "It was so dark inside, I couldn't tell."

"Atmosphere," Brenda sighed. "I love a place with atmosphere. I'll have to try it soon. How was the eel?"

Doug thumped his breastbone. "The sauce had way too much garlic. It's been repeating on me all morning." He shoved aside the ham sandwich he'd just unwrapped. "And the eel was tough."

"What a shame," Gertrude said. "Perhaps the chef cooked it too long. You should have sent it back. He'd want to know."

A counselor, Gertrude felt everyone should want to correct their errors.

"Send it back and the waiter pisses in your coffee," Aston stated. "Never send anything back. If it's bad, just bolt the bill. That's what I do." He eyed a wormy spot in his gnarly apple, then shrugged, said, "Protein," and bit into it.

Doug shuddered, stowed his sandwich in a padded purple plastic sack, and popped open a generic cola. "Well, whatever Stoddard had, wouldn't the person who killed him have it now? I mean, wouldn't that have been the whole reason for killing him? To stop his blackmail and get rid of the evidence?" He flipped his hand and his voice slid up the scale. "I mean, I'm just guessing. I don't know whether Henry was blackmailing anyone. It certainly wasn't me. All I know is what people say."

In the uncomfortable silence that followed, Brenda studied the bowl of eel the way a tea-leaf reader might scrutinize sediment in a cup, then set the bowl aside and opened a sleeve of crackers and a jar of pimiento cheese. "Well, whoever took it will destroy it." Her voice was as brittle as old glass and I wondered why she was under Henry's thumb.

"When pigs fly," Aston muttered.

Gertrude waved a stick of tofu-salad-filled celery. "What do you mean by that?"

"If you find yourself in possession of a cash cow, you milk it." He popped the apple core into his mouth and chewed without closing his lips.

Gertrude frowned. "Speak English, Aston."

Aston wiped his mouth on his sleeve. "I mean that the sword Henry was holding over your heads is still around." He speared each of us with a laser gaze. "And someday soon you'll find out who's wielding it."

I nibbled my sandwich, grateful that Henry Stoddard had nothing on me. I recalled Jessica's determination to get into his room. Was she searching for what he used to blackmail her, or for something she could use against others?

I set the sandwich down, wondering why I hadn't thought of it that way before and fingering the page from Jessica Flint's personalized memo pad I'd tucked into the pocket of my slacks. Josh, still with his guitar over his shoulder, brought it up to me during second period. A scrawl in the center of the page read, "I haven't forgotten! Be in my office immediately after school."

"I wonder where he kept it," Susan mused.

I studied her from the edges of my eyes and noted she was the only one who seemed merely curious, not nervous. There wasn't a harder-working more respected teacher in the district. If there was dirt on her, it had to be of the fictional variety.

"Maybe it was all up here." Brenda tapped the side of her head with the edge of a cracker.

"In the movies there's more to blackmail than he said/she said," Gertrude offered. "Blackmailers have pictures or documents."

"Pictures." Doug blanched and glanced in the direction of Henry's classroom. "Where do you suppose he kept them."

"Maybe in a safe deposit box at a bank," Gertrude offered.

"Nah," Aston said. "He was too cheap for that."

"He might have loaded them into his computer," I said. "Then saved them to a flash drive."

Aston laughed. "Henry using a flash drive? That's like saying dinosaurs used toilet paper."

"What a disgusting image." Brenda made the universal sign for "gag me."

"But Aston's right. Henry was a technophobe," Susan fumed. "He could barely create a simple word document, let alone a grading rubric. And he refused to learn. So of course the rest of us had to do more work."

"Well, I saw the police carry out his computer on Friday," Doug said. "So if he knew more about technology than he let on, they'll find it. Experts will go through his files."

"But if Henry was smart, he would have used another computer," Aston said. "The building is full of them. And how will the cops know they're looking at blackmail material?"

Susan pointed her fork at him. "Why wouldn't they?"

Aston gave her a pitying smile. "It's all about context, Susan. A picture of two people holding hands on the beach is innocent unless you know they're married to others." He glanced around the table. "When you were questioned by the police, did any of you mention that Henry dealt in dirt?"

After a second's hesitation, we all shook our heads. I thought back to my grill session with Detective Atwell and recalled my decision to let someone else open the can of worms labeled "blackmail" because what I knew was only rumor and bringing it up could make Atwell assume I was trying to direct suspicion away from myself. Apparently the others reached the same conclusion.

"Thought so." Aston aimed a finger at Doug. "Silence is golden. Especially if you have no seniority and huge car payments."

Doug ducked his head and I recalled seeing him in a glossy black SUV with all the trimmings.

"And you can bet the administrators kept their lips zipped," Aston said.

"Well, the police are looking for something," Susan said. "They took Henry's room apart."

"And went through his house," Gertrude added.

Heads swiveled in her direction and a flush crept up her cheeks. "I happened to drive by there. It's almost on my way home."

Susan laughed. "On your way if you go *out* of your way."

"Just a little," Gertrude admitted. "Half a mile."

"And I'll bet you didn't just drive by at the posted speed," Susan said.

Gertrude raised her hands. "Okay, I parked for a bit. I was curious."

"And . . . ?"

"Henry was quite a hoarder. Newspapers. Books. Boxes and boxes and boxes of papers."

Brenda crunched a cracker. "Going through that could take weeks."

"And if they don't know what they're looking for, they might not know it when they find it." Doug had the hopeful voice of a child making a Christmas list.

Aston gnawed off another chunk of jerky and grinned, displaying meat shreds between his teeth. "But if they find anything suspicious, they'll start calling us in, one by one, picking us off the way wolves—"

"Enough." Brenda dumped the bowl of eel Alfredo into the pot and carried the whole mess to the sink. "Let's talk about something else. Anything else."

Silence stretched and sagged like a pair of old undies and then Gertrude aimed a carrot stick at me. "How are things going in Henry's classes?"

"Good. Susan gave me lesson plans on the plague and she's helping me catch up on the grading."

"And how are the kids handling it?"

"With vast relief, I suspect," Aston snorted. "In a contest between Henry and the plague, those pustules win every time."

"How long will you be filling in?" Doug asked when the laughter died.

I fingered the note again. Would Jessica try an end run around Jerome Morrow and Big Chill and cancel my job? "I don't know."

"At least until Christmas break," Susan said.

She sounded so confident and cheerful I didn't have the heart to tell her she could be wrong.

Quiz Answer
e – no question about it

The smell in a high school locker room
a) is probably the same as when your parents were in school
b) has a life of its own
c) makes you appreciate everyday air pollution
d) could gag a maggot
e) is more powerful than any deodorizer

CHAPTER EIGHT

When I arrived at Jessica's office around the corner from the gym, the door was locked but the light was on. Her files were packed with sensitive documents, so I assumed locking up, even if she stepped out for only a few minutes, was standard procedure. I set my briefcase on the floor and perched on one of a string of cracked, wobbly plastic chairs reserved for students awaiting their fates.

Voices and the thumping of balls on wood echoed from the basketball court and the faint sharp scents of sweat and disinfectant swirled around me like wisps of fog in an old movie set on the English moors. The odors made me queasy at the same time as they resurrected the primal fears of my teenage years—being the last one picked for softball, breaking a leg trying to clear the pommel horse, and being judged and found wanting by girls whose bodies had matured in a more harmonious way.

Other girls' breasts swelled slowly. Mine erupted like young volcanoes over Christmas vacation. They had hourglass figures; I had a water glass figure. Straight up and down. Years of twisting exercises were all in vain.

The shrill of a whistle brought me back to here and now and I checked my watch. 2:27. Jessica must have been hijacked by a disciplinary problem—a fight or a skateboarder making a mockery of rules about railings and curbs. I unfolded the note and confirmed that it said "immediately after school."

Being as charitable as I was chicken, I settled back in the chair—keeping my weight on the side away from a razor-edged fissure. What was the worst that Jessica could do? Cancel my job? Bar me from subbing in the district? Have my certification yanked? Manufacture something to point Detective Atwell at me for Henry Stoddard's murder?

An icicle of fear spiked into my heart.

Would he believe her? Would he consider her more credible?

I rubbed my hands together, trying to ward off a spreading chill. How could I fight back? Should I wait until I had to, or go to Atwell now and tell him I saw her searching Henry Stoddard's room?

I rubbed harder, feeling no warmth. What if there was a simple explanation for that? What if she was, say, hunting for his keycard to make sure the building remained secure?

"Shoot," I muttered, and glanced at my watch. 2:41. Definitely not "immediately after school." Unzipping my briefcase, I scavenged a pad of yellow sticky notes from the folder crammed with information about fire drills and lockdown procedures. "Waited until 2:45," I wrote, intending to stay long enough to make that valid. "Had a doctor's appointment," I fictionalized. "Please call me."

Adding my phone number and initials, I stuck the note to the center of the glass panel in her door, shrugged into my rain jacket, hefted my briefcase, and departed. All the way to my car, the acrid scent of dried sweat from the locker room stalked me like a panther.

A stop at the market and gas station took up what I estimated would be the length of a doctor's appointment. My show and tell for this whopper was the diminishing bump on my wrist that Mrs. Ballantine last week declared a ganglion cyst.

"Nothing to worry about," she announced after prodding it with her fingertips. "If it doesn't go away in a few days, get yourself a brace at the pharmacy. If that doesn't work, you'll have to have it drained. Or I could thump it with my Bible."

I thought she was joking until she assured me that was the accepted remedy back in frontier days. "Bible bumps. That's what they called them. Give it a good whack and it should rupture and drain."

"Should" being the operative word.

Just thinking about it made my wrist ache so I could hardly turn the wheel when I pulled into the condo parking lot. Through the gathering gloom, I spotted a gleaming black sedan in my space.

"Damn it!"

Visitors were supposed to park at the end of the lot, but often appropriated empty spots. The first time my space was appropriated, I stomped to the manager's office, a partitioned-off area of the living room in a unit just slightly larger than my own. From reading the condo association paperwork, I'd gleaned that in exchange for managing the upkeep of the grounds and exterior, Bernina Burke lived there rent-free, got utilities and cable without charge, and collected regular paychecks and a yearly bonus.

"Someone's in my spot."

"Probably a visitor." Bernina Burke shrugged, the action swaying wings of pale skin dangling from the undersides of her arms.

I made a mental note to check the extent and swayability of my own underarm dingle dangle. "Well, what can I do about it?"

"Not much unless you know who it is." She glanced at the clock—for the record it read 10:25—and added, "Gotta meet someone clear across town for barbecue. If you find out I'll remind the resident of the visitor policy."

"Am I supposed to stake out the parking lot?"

She shrugged again, setting off another oscillation of spare flesh. "If you want."

Realizing I might need her goodwill for larger issues in the future, I reined in my temper. "Is there some kind of standard notice I could put under the windshield wiper?"

She rolled her cushy chair back from her cluttered desk and canted her head. "Nothing I know of," she said after half a minute.

"What about the security staff? Maybe they can do something."

She blinked like a mole exposed to June sunlight. "Security?"

"You know, the firm that patrols the grounds."

"Oh, those guys." She glanced at the clock. 10:27. "It could take hours to get hold of them."

Hours? That little factoid made me feel safe and secure.

"And the car will probably be gone long before they get here."

"Where am I supposed to park in the meantime?"

She'd hoisted a red leather purse the size of a bowling bag and trundled past me. "There's plenty of room in the visitors' lot." Jangling a ring of keys she opened the door wide. "If you think we need a form to stick under wipers, take it up with the association board."

If she'd been any more caring and helpful she could work for the IRS. This time, I'd handle things myself. I'd jam my car behind the offender and wait.

Intent on kissing the back bumper, I eased up behind the sedan and—spotted someone behind the wheel.

I braked, turned off the engine, and jumped out, fists clenched. This policy-flaunting parking-spot appropriator would get a piece of my mind.

The sedan door opened. Jessica Flint stepped out.

I skidded to a halt and clamped my hands behind my back. She planted hers on hips flaring from a waist that would have caused Scarlett O'Hara to tighten her corset strings another inch in a fit of jealousy. "Well look who's here."

No points for originality. I'd heard that from everyone who intercepted me in this very parking lot since Thursday.

"And how was your doctor's visit?" She tapped the toe of a shiny black open-toed shoe. "Will you live?"

"Yes, thank you." I wished I had my brace, but it was in my bedroom. Still, even without props, the best defense is a good offense. "I waited thirty-five minutes outside your office."

"I'm aware of that." She tightened the belt of her red raincoat. "I found your note. At 2:46."

A minute after I left. Coincidence? Or a fabrication like my doctor's appointment? I considered opening a discussion of the phrase "immediately after school," but decided the next move was hers.

She made it by stepping into my personal space. "What did you take from Henry's room?"

I blinked and inched a retreat. "The atlases."

She shook her head. "And what else?"

67

I held my ground. "Nothing."

She shook her head again. "No files? No computer disks? No keys?"

Her tone implied that all of the above had been present. The discussion in the teachers' room came back in a rush. Jessica thought I discovered Henry's dirt collection, recognized the potential value, and made off with it.

I swallowed so my voice wouldn't squeak, and squared my shoulders. "I didn't take a thing except the atlases." I leaned close enough to detect that her mascara needed declumping. "What's missing?"

Even in the dim light I saw something slither deep in her eyes. "That's what we're trying to find out."

We? Was that the imperial "we" or was Jessica working with someone on this retrieval project? The police? Mr. Morrow? Someone else? I cocked my head and made a show of being puzzled. "That doesn't make sense. You know something's missing but you don't know what it is?"

"It's none of your business what I know or don't know," she snapped. "If you've got something that belonged to Henry Stoddard, you'd better give it to me or . . ."

That dark fear slithered again and I knew she couldn't follow through on a threat because if I had Henry's dirt I might use it in retaliation. And if I didn't, I might go to Principal Morrow or even to the police, and tell them she was persecuting me.

We had a standoff.

"I'll have my eye on you," she muttered. "Don't think that I won't. If you step out of line so much as an inch, I'll—"

"Hey there, Barbie." That smoky voice cut through the evening gloom.

Oh crap. Not Jake again.

I turned to see him swaggering our way, a newspaper rolled under one arm. He posed a few yards off and riffled his hair. "Who's your gorgeous friend?"

Ugh. If there was one thing worse than being called Barbie it was Jake's misguided assumption that Jessica Flint was my friend and that I'd introduce them. On the other hand, I thought as Jessica licked her lips and looked him over, that introduction might distract them both from me.

"Jessica," I said, "meet Jake Stranahan." I didn't mention that Jake and I had briefly been a couple in the eyes of the law. "Jake, this is Jessica Flint."

"Pleased to meet you." Jake ran his tongue across his teeth and held out his hand.

Jessica drew a carmine fingernail across his palm, stepped close, and captured his hand in both of hers. Predator, not prey. "Nice to meet you, too."

Neither seemed to notice when I got into my car. As I drove to the visitors' lot I glanced in the rearview mirror and saw them doing what amounted to a mating dance. A flash of blue caught my eye and I braked and peered over my shoulder.

A man wrapped in a tarp crouched beside the trash bins. Even from this distance it was clear he wasn't Trash Guy I or Trash Guy II.

It was also clear that he was watching Jake and Jessica. Maybe they'd both get mugged.

Quiz Answer:
What do you think?

A sub's favorite food is
a) free
b) plentiful
c) quick and easy
d) prepared by someone else
e) accompanied by an adult beverage

CHAPTER NINE

What I needed was love or, at the very least, a few licks on the chin from a creature that depended on my opposable thumbs to open the biscuit jar. But no orange torpedo shot down the stairs to greet me.

I felt the kind of letdown I knew in second grade when I saw my bestest friend ever pair up with someone else for the walk to the cafeteria. "Cheese Puff?"

I heard nothing except the wheeze of the refrigerator.

"Cheese Puff? Where are you?"

I scanned the small bulletin board by the door where Committee members left notes if they had him out past my usual return-home time.

Not a single mark on the pad pinned to the cork for that purpose.

Heart hammering, brain conjuring up horrific images involving Myra Bancroft, I hurtled toward the stairs, stopping short at the answering machine and its blinking red light.

"Your darling is with me, dear," Mrs. Ballantine's wispy voice assured me. "I took a little spill and had to put my feet up. Let yourself in when you get home."

"Took a little spill" weren't words I wanted to hear from my sixty-or-possibly-seventy-something neighbor. I dumped my briefcase and purse on a chair, rushed out, crossed my miniscule yard, and hurdled the low hedge that screened her walk, landing with all the grace of a roller-skating reindeer.

I flung open her door and kicked off my shoes to protect polished wood floors buffed to a shine by her weekly cleaning service.

"I'm here," I called out.

Cheese Puff barked, but didn't rush to salve my emotional wounds.

"He doesn't want to leave my side, dear," Mrs. B called from the depths of a puffy chair covered in dark blue velvet. The focused light from a reading lamp made her flyaway hair resemble a corona of white flame and jeweled reading glasses magnified her sapphire eyes. She had both feet up on a footstool, one shoe and sock off, and a bag of frozen peas on the naked ankle. Cheese Puff was wedged into the chair beside her, looking more subdued than on the day we met. On the table beside her chair, next to a photograph of Marco wearing a tuxedo and raising a glass of champagne, lay a dog biscuit.

I gawked. Cheese Puff never left a biscuit uneaten.

Rushing to the chair, I felt his nose. Cool, but not cold. Damp but not wet. "Is he okay?"

"He's fine. He had quite a fright." Mrs. B stroked his back. "And so, I confess, did I. We've been sipping a martini and reading *The Godfather* to calm ourselves down."

I smiled. Given the snippets I'd gleaned about her background, it was probably a lot like leafing through her husband's family album. Bending, I lifted the bag of peas from her red, puffy ankle. Mrs. B had been a Las Vegas showgirl and, despite the tracings of veins and a few age

71

spots, still had lean and shapely legs that she showed off in walking shorts and sandals during the heat of summer. "Did you call your doctor?"

"Don't be silly. It's just a little sprain and I got it chilling as soon as I could. Inside and out."

Meaning the martini.

"How did you fall?" I put the frozen peas back and aimed a finger at Cheese Puff. "He didn't bolt after a cat, did he?"

As if denying the accusation, Cheese Puff drew his lips back.

"Oh no, dear. He never does that with me. I think he knows I'm breakable." Mrs. B patted Cheese Puff's head and he swelled out his narrow chest. "It was that woman's fault."

"What woman?" My fists clenched. "Myra?" I'd send that credit-card wielding harpie shopping for comprehensive medical coverage.

"No." Mrs. B pointed away from Myra's condo. "The woman who moved in down at the end a few weeks ago." She used the flat of her hand to mark a place in the air above her head. "The tall one with the muscles and red hair."

Tall redhead? That sounded like Jake's "friend."

I unfurled my fists. No point in being quick to pick a fight with an Amazon. "What did she do?"

"Nothing intentional." Mrs. B pinched the bridge of her nose. "She probably didn't even see me. She was wrapped up in her own problems."

And being involved with Jake, as I knew from personal experience, meant that those problems were multiplying.

"We were walking up to the river trail and as we turned the corner I heard her screaming at someone

72

named Jake—That name has come back in style, hasn't it?"

She peered up at me. "You were married to a man named Jake, weren't you, dear? Anyway, she was telling him if she saw him on the same block with 'that woman' again she'd castrate him and throw him out."

I nodded in answer to the questions stuffed into the middle of that sentence, but didn't admit this was the very same Jake. Why sign on for that humiliation?

"Then she slammed the door and ran past us," Mrs. B continued. "The little guy jumped behind me and I did a ball change step exactly the way I used to, but I lost my footing and went down. I almost landed on top of him."

Cheese Puff whimpered as if reliving the experience. I knelt and stroked his head.

"Then the leash handle slipped from my hand and smacked his tiny leg."

Cheese Puff held up a front paw for my inspection.

"There's nothing broken," Mrs. B said. "But it scared us both."

Cheese Puff lowered the paw.

"And that woman didn't break her stride—forget about helping me up. She jumped in her car and blasted off like she'd been shot out of a cannon."

"I didn't break anything, but it will swell up like a melon and I'll limp for a few days." Wincing, she flexed her ankle. "Don't you worry though, the Committee will see to it that this little prince gets his walks. Jim will get him every morning and bring him here after a nice trot, then Verna and Sybil will alternate afternoon walks. And we're still going out for Thanksgiving dinner—I wouldn't miss that if both hips popped out of their sockets."

Not for one minute had I been concerned that Cheese Puff might not get his daily exercise and idolization. I was,

73

however, concerned that Mrs. B might try to do more than she should. "And who's going to take care of you?"

She fluttered her lashes and turned the full wattage of those sapphire eyes on me. "I hoped you might help with that, dear."

That's what a selfish little part of me had been afraid of. Don't get me wrong, I was delighted to help—my fear had to do with the time factor. I had lessons to plan and reams of pages to read for the classes I was taking.

"I'd be happy to," I said, trying to sound like I was. "What would you like me to do?"

Mrs. B held out her martini glass, empty except for a three-inch pink plastic saber. "A refill would be nice. There's a pitcher in the refrigerator and a jar of olives right next to it. I like two of them."

"Or three or four."

She flashed a conspiratorial smile and patted a tummy so flat it verged on concave. "It's my appetizer, dear. And they say olive oil is good for the heart." She tapped her chest as if to check the condition of that organ and nodded as if confirming all was well. "And then perhaps you could find my husband's old cane—it's up in the spare bedroom, I believe—and after that, it won't be too long before I'll be ready for dinner." Cheese Puff's ears perked up and she gave them a scratch. "And so will this handsome little devil."

I got to my feet and gave them a bow. "And what would you and the prince like for dinner?"

"Mexican. From that little place by the library. I'll have the enchilada plate with a side order of chips and guacamole." She paused and put her ear to Cheese Puff's muzzle. "And he says he'll have a taco with just chicken and lettuce—no hot sauce. But tell them to put plenty on mine."

"Will do," I said with a grin. Mrs. B liked her food hot and spicy and her liquor cold and plentiful enough to take her deep into a cloud of happy and comforting memories so could face the nights without Marco. I set her empty glass by the sink, took a fresh one from the freezer side of her enormous refrigerator, skewered four olives with a fresh plastic saber—this one neon green—and floated them in a generous sloshing of gin cut with a whisper of vermouth. After I handed it off and received a couple of folded bills and a spare key to her condo, I went in search of the cane.

Her unit mirrored Myra and Nelson's. The spare bedroom at the back was crowded with boxes, but they were neatly labeled and stacked. "Marco's hats. Marco's shoes. Marco's suits. Marco's golf outfits." Even counting hand-me-down baby togs from Iz, I'd had fewer clothes in my entire lifetime.

I recalled the four boxes I'd filled with Albert's shirts, slacks, shoes, and socks and carted to a homeless shelter. Knowing they would do some good gave me comfort, but perhaps Mrs. B got more comfort from keeping Marco's wardrobe. I wondered if she went through these boxes when she was feeling blue, if she relived the nights out on the town when he wore the red silk vest or the pleated shirt with the French cuffs. Photos of him displayed on walls and tables could have been dictionary illustrations for the word "dapper."

"Try the closet, dear." Her voice floated up to me. "The left side. Behind the garment bags."

Following her directions, I dove between two translucent plastic bags stuffed with glittery garments and retrieved a gnarled cane made of dark wood with a rubber covering at the bottom and a silver handle shaped like porpoise leaping into a hoop. It was far heavier than I expected, two pounds at least.

"That's it," she said when I presented it. "I had it made for him the year before he . . . had his accident."

Her hesitation made me wonder, yet again, if there was more to the story of Marco Ballantine's death than the version she'd shared with me—that he lost his footing getting onto the escalator at a casino outside of Seattle and tumbled to his death. I'd heard speculation that Marco had been connected, that he managed money for less-than-legitimate groups, and may have been promoting partnerships between gaming organizations here and in Las Vegas. All Mrs. B ever said was that he "invested" in a lot of businesses.

"I found this piece of driftwood on the beach and designed the handle and, you see, it worked out perfectly." She stroked the cane, then leaned it against her chair and took a long swallow of her martini. "Now I can get up if I need to while you're gone. And if there's any trouble, I've got the rapier."

There was a word you didn't hear every day. "Rapier?"

"She doesn't know that this is a sword cane," Mrs. B whispered to Cheese Puff, her words slurring faintly. "There's a little catch on the fishie's tail. If I flip it back, I can pull the blade out and run the intruder through."

I sighed, hoping she didn't self-medicate so much she'd decide to get in a little fencing practice while I was gone. "I'll go pick up dinner."

She raised her glass. "You'll let me know if I'm taking advantage, won't you, dear?"

"Not while you're armed and dangerous I won't."

She laughed and took another long swallow.

As I drove, I considered Mrs. B's lifestyle. If I lived to be her age—and for the record, I had no idea exactly what that age was—I hoped I'd be as independent.

Independence. That was crucial. If I found myself as broke as I was now, tethered to a regimented facility, and surrounded by people like Iz—or worse yet, Iz herself—I doubted I'd want to go on living.

"So make sure that doesn't happen," the little voice nagged. "Get those courses done and get a teaching job so you'll have a pension. Set goals."

Reality bites, doesn't it?

As if to underline that point, a rain squall coupled with end-of-rush-hour commuters turned a five-minute trip into fifteen and it was going on six when I passed the library and pulled into the packed parking lot of *Vaya Con Queso*, my favorite restaurant. Along with fast service, moderate prices, and generous portions, it also managed to deliver variety and taste. So what if the décor was Spartan and the service mostly self?

I located a spot by the row of plantings marking the edge of library property, parked, and jumped out, my mouth watering at the thought of a nest of tortilla chips filled with guacamole, sour cream, grated cheddar, and zesty salsa. As I hitched my purse on my shoulder, I heard a faint mewling.

A kitten?

Stooping, I peered beneath the low dome of a Japanese maple. Its dense, red-orange leaves shed the rain, creating a dry cave near the trunk. A trickle of light from a street lamp revealed a huddled figure in dark clothing.

"Are you okay?"

The answer was another sob.

I was about to ask if I could do something to help when I had second thoughts. As a public building with heating and air conditioning, the library was a magnet for those living on the streets. For all I knew, this person could be drunk, hallucinating, overdosed, psychotic, or trying to lure me closer and grab my purse. Or worse.

Even if none of that was true, by offering assistance I could find myself sucked into a vortex of neediness and problems too complex for me to resolve. Besides, Mrs. B was waiting for dinner. And then there was all that reading and grading I had to do.

The figure sobbed again, the sound setting off echoes of loneliness and hopelessness in my own heart. With a grip on my purse strap and my trailing foot pointed outward to launch a getaway, I inched closer. "Are you okay? Is there anything I can do?"

"No," the figure sobbed. The voice was that of a girl, and vaguely familiar. "My dad doesn't care about me. I'm gonna run away. And I'm never coming back."

Quiz Answer:
Really? You need me to tell you the answer to this one?

Too many of today's kids don't know much about
a) respect
b) carbon paper
c) discipline
d) rotary-dial telephones
e) a loving, complete family unit

CHAPTER TEN

I unzipped my purse and grasped my cell phone, then hesitated. Should I call the police? A crisis line? Her father? Who *was* her father?

"He's always working," the girl sobbed. "Or else he's with her."

Where had I heard that voice?

"He'd never miss me." She gulped back another sob. "If no one likes you, no one misses you when you die. You get cremated and sent to your cousin in a box like they say they're gonna do to Mr. Stoddard."

Bingo. This problem had a face—the little Goth girl from Susan's class who put forth the theory that Henry had been abducted by aliens planning to clone him. I dropped to my knees and decided to skip over Henry Stoddard and deal with the living. "Of course your father would miss you. And your friends would, too."

Her sobbing increased and I gave myself a mental boot. If she had close friends, she'd probably be with them instead of under a tree in the rain. I grasped at a straw. "Mrs. Mitchell would miss you."

The sobbing abated. "She's nice," the girl sniffed. "When everyone was hogging the colored pencils she let me make my map all in black and white and gray and didn't take off any points."

A Goth map of the world. I gave Susan points for flexibility. "She'll help if you tell her about your problem. So will your counselor. How about I meet you at the counselors' office before school and make sure you get an appointment?"

She sniffled and raised her face to the light. Hair obscured her eyes, and mascara streamed down her cheeks. She wiped at it, drawing the smudges toward her ears like bat wings. "Really?"

"I promise."

I gave myself another mental boot. Why hadn't I said I'd try? Kids often had far more strict rules about promises than many adults—Jake, for example, had broken that forsaking-all-others promise without a qualm.

"You have no idea what you're doing," the little voice in my head insisted. "You're just making things worse."

Have I told you lately how much I hate that nagging little voice? Especially when it's right?

I stretched out a hand. "Come out and we'll get a soda." My stomach rumbled out a complaint—a soda alone wouldn't cut it. "And a taco."

"Really?" Her voice was filled with awe.

It's only a soda and a taco, I thought as she crept through the branches, shook out the black cape she wore over a black sweater, leggings, and boots, and scrubbed at her face with the tissues I handed her. The mascara blended to a uniform gray tint that looked like makeup for a low-budget vampire movie.

"I didn't think teachers were allowed to do stuff like this," she said as we walked to the low-slung restaurant.

I felt a frisson of fear and had a vague memory of a rushed training session about contact with students. "Stuff like buying you a snack?"

She shrugged, pulled her hood up and flitted ahead, a darker shadow in the murky night, then a slender silhouette against the heavy glass door as she opened it. A burst of scents drew us in—grease, corn chips, onions, beef, peppers, cinnamon. The sounds of clattering pots, crinkling paper bags, and orders trilled in rapid-fire Spanish washed over us like a warm tide. Hunger trumped my concerns about appropriate behavior.

"The menu's up there." I pointed above the heads of those standing in line and stood a careful eighteen inches from her. "And I'm paying. Pick out what you want."

She chewed at the remains of smeared white lipstick and studied a series of colorful photographs accompanied by numbers and captions. "A taco, I guess. And some water."

Her voice was whispery and hesitant. Fearful of asking for too much?

"That's not enough," I said firmly. "You've been out in the cold. You need at least two tacos and some chips and a shake. Beef or chicken?"

She chewed her lip again. "Vegetarian?"

"No problem."

"Chocolate, strawberry, or vanilla?"

"Chocolate."

"Done. Go splash some water on your face. Then get us a table and round up napkins and silverware."

She darted off and I dialed Mrs. Ballantine and explained the situation.

"That child is more important than an old lady's dinner schedule. What's her name?"

I sighed. "I can't remember. I see a hundred and fifty kids every—"

"You'd better ask," she said in a voice as crisp as new money. "She won't think you give two hoots and a handshake if you address her as 'hey you.'"

As if I'd ever do that. I opened my mouth to protest, remembered the thirty-year gulf between us and her devotion to Cheese Puff's welfare, and clamped my teeth.

"Buy her dinner. And don't worry about us. Cheese Puff has a biscuit and I have two olives left. Perhaps we'll catch forty winks."

I rolled my eyes. They'd be snoring in harmony in no time. I'd get their dinner when I was ready to go home. Whenever that might be. How would I know when it was safe to leave her on her own? And what if it didn't appear that I could?

From the corner of my eye I saw the girl give me a full-arm wave from a table across the room. That seemed too demonstrative for a Goth, but what did I know about that, either? I was a walking black hole of non-knowledge.

I waved back—just from the elbow—put my conscience on hold, and ordered her tacos and a chimichanga for myself. With a tray filled with chips, salsa, and guacamole, I headed for the table, noting that she'd anchored the napkins with our plastic forks and lined up the water glasses to the right of the knives, just the way I used to do it when I was young and my family wasn't fractured.

"Here we go." I set the bowls on a scarred green table, parked the red plastic service tag—number 27—at the edge, slid the tray to the far side, and smiled to ease what I had to say. "I'm sorry, but I've forgotten your name."

She shrugged as if that happened all the time, and grasped a chip in fingers tipped by glossy black nails. "It's Allison Martin." With a turn of her wrist she swiped the chip through the guacamole and tipped her head back to look out from beneath a thick fringe of hair. Her eyes were light brown with flecks of green. "But my friends call me Arachne."

"Arachne?" The sound of it made me shudder and I squeezed my arms against my sides. "That's, um, unusual."

"It's from a myth. Athena got mad at her for weaving pictures of the gods screw—uh, fooling around—and turned her into a spider."

I covered another shudder by reaching for a chip. Spiders were among my least favorite creatures—number five behind Jake, his redheaded friend, Myra, and Jessica. "How did you get a nickname like that?"

"I picked it."

She raised her chin and I wondered if she was demonstrating pride in her choice or preparing to defend it. I felt a pang of remorse and then wished I could turn back the clock and pick my high school nickname instead of being called Fish Lips. What can I say? When you break up with a boy, you have to be prepared to deal with the fallout. But it could have been worse. If our relationship had continued he might have gotten a glimpse of the birthmark on my hip—the one shaped like a waterfowl. I could have been called Duck Butt.

No way could I share that with Arachne. "Do you read a lot of mythology?"

"Oh yes. Especially Norse legends." Her fingers twined, nails flashing in the bluish tint of the fluorescent lighting. "They're so . . . dark."

I crunched down another chip and decided to steer the conversation away from "dark." I had a vague memory that Norse gods lived with the knowledge of how their world would end and the manner in which most of them would perish. Not a life-affirming topic for here and now. "Do you have a lot of friends at school?"

She raised her chin again. "A few. You know. The ones like me."

I nodded. Like any school, this one had its share of cliques— jocks, geeks, Goths, student government leaders, intentional misfits, the pretty, and the popular. "Do you talk to your friends about what's bothering you?"

"Sometimes." She dipped her finger into the condensation from her glass of ice water and drew a wet line parallel to her knife. "But they have problems, too, so . . ."

"So you listen to them more than they listen to you?"

She gnawed off the last smear of white lipstick. "I guess."

"I'll bet you're the kind of friend who listens all night. Sometimes people take advantage of friends like that."

She frowned, but I went on before she could defend her caring nature or her friends' self-involvement. "I have friends who treat me like a landfill. They dump on me and leave."

I raised my glass, took a quick swallow, and felt a chill that had nothing to do with the icy water. "That can make you feel really lonely." Especially if you had no close family—or if that family included a sister like Iz. But this chat was about her problems, not mine.

A boy in a green apron trotted over with a brown tray loaded with two steaming plates and a tall glass with a swirl of whipped cream on top. He slid them onto the table, plopped down a pile of extra napkins, and aimed a shy smile at Arachne. I slipped him a dollar and he grinned and trotted off.

"I think I'm a pretty good listener." I used the tines of my fork to cut a hole in the top of my chimichanga. "Want to see if I'm right?"

She gave me one of those I-see-right-through-you smiles but then, between bites of taco, unloaded.

With a few variations and modern updates, it was a tale that went back to Hansel and Gretel, Cinderella, and beyond. Departed mother—run off to Miami with a boy toy—hardworking but overwhelmed and occasionally oblivious father, potential stepmother, resentment, perceived unfair demands, rule-flaunting, and revenge. The running-away threat, I guessed, fell in that last category. Which didn't make it any less real.

When she wound down, I summarized the latest paternal offense in the most neutral tone I could manage. "So you weren't *where* you said you'd be *when* you said you'd be, and when you got home he was annoyed."

"Not *annoyed*." She stabbed the air with a corn chip. "*Furious*."

"Noted." I tapped my fork on my plate. "He was *furious* because he rearranged his work schedule to pick you up in front of the school and take you to the dentist. But you went out another door and—"

"Because I *forgot*." She managed as much of a glower as anyone with hair in their eyes can.

"Right. You forgot." I tapped the plate again, noting that point. "And you turned off your cell phone. So he went to the dentist's office, but you weren't there and he had to pay a fee because you missed the appointment without sufficient notice."

She dropped her shoulders. "It was only a checkup."

"But he still had to pay."

"But not that *much*." She pouted, dropped her defiant gaze, and picked at a shred of cheese. "Only thirty dollars."

I glanced at the kid who'd cleared our table and felt a flash of anger. How many hours did he have to work to make that much? I drew in a breath and set my fork on the edge of my plate. "Thirty dollars won't break your father's budget. But if anything happened to you it would break his heart."

I spread my fingers over my sternum—high school theater class stuff. "I bet he imagined you'd been kidnapped or worse."

She ducked her head and I let her twist in the wind for a moment. "When I get scared I want to run, but when men get scared they often lash out. It's called the fight or flight response and it's the way all animals are wired— rabbits, deer, dogs, and people."

She looked up and, although her lips were still pushed into a sullen pout, I spotted a spark of interest in what I could see of her eyes.

"So when you got home, your dad was relieved and then all his fear turned into anger and, even though he loves you, he lost it and yelled and you ran. Right now he's probably even more worried than he was before. And as sorry as he can be."

She shook her head. "He's not. At least he never says he is."

I waved that aside. "That's the way guys are, especially fathers. Because they work hard and pay the bills and fix the flat tires, they think we want to believe they're tough. So they act that way. But inside some of them are like this." I grasped my fork and poked the cheesy-ricey center of my chimichanga. "Soft."

I forked off another bite and waited, hoping I hadn't undersold it or, worse, oversold. What did I know about fight or flight besides what I'd read in waiting-room magazines? I was no expert on emotions or, as you've already concluded, much of anything else. The aroma of the food on my fork made me queasy.

Arachne picked the shred of cheese from her plate and stretched it like a rubber band. "So they get mad so we don't know that?"

I sighed to the bottom of my lungs. "Right."

86

She smiled. "I shouldn't tell him about the fight or flight stuff, should I?"

I made a show of peering around at the men seated nearby, then whispered. "Guys hate to think we've figured them out."

She gave a most unGothlike giggle. "I wish my dad had a girlfriend like you, Ms. Reed. You're awesome."

I brushed that aside. "My dog thinks so, too."

"You have a dog?" She bounced on the bench seat—definitely too animated for a Goth. "I love dogs. I wish I had one. But we live in an apartment." She bounced again, hands fluttering. "If you ever have to go out of town, I could come over and walk and feed her."

"Him. It's a boy. Cheese Puff."

She giggled once more. "That's so cute. Does he look like a cheese puff?"

"That's how he got his name."

"Does he like walks?"

"Sure." If it wasn't raining and there were plenty of people out to adore him, otherwise it was all about getting it done and getting back inside.

"Maybe I can take him for a walk with you. Maybe over Thanksgiving?"

"Now you're really crossing a line," the voice in my mind carped. "You can't do that."

And slap her back into runaway mode? I passed the buck. "You'll have to clear it with your father."

She pouted again. "He probably won't let me."

"You're right. He might not. After all, he has no idea who I am, does he?"

She nodded.

"And it's his job to keep you safe, right?"

She nodded again and I dug a pen from my purse and wrote my number on a spare napkin, recalling the agony of youthful requests turned down for what seemed like no reason. "If he wants, he can check me out."

Frowning, she tucked the napkin into a pocket in her cape, and drew out a skinny phone—black, naturally. "I guess I better tell him where I am."

But she didn't flip the phone open, just turned it in her fingers like a worry stone. "He's gonna yell."

I shrugged. "You bet he is. But now you know why he's yelling, right?"

She hung her head. "Yeah. But what do I say?"

"Do you love him?"

She nodded.

"Then tell him right away." I gave her an encouraging smile. "And wait until he's done yelling and apologize for everything and take responsibility and then tell him again."

I piled our used plates and utensils onto the tray and carried it over to a pass-through window, then placed the order for Mrs. B and wandered down a short hall to the restroom where I killed a few moments doing things you don't need to read about. When I returned, she had the wrung-out look of someone recovering from stomach flu.

"He's coming to get me." She chewed her lower lip. "I didn't tell him that I said I was gonna run away. I didn't really mean it. I was being a drama queen."

"Don't you think you should be honest and take responsibility for *everything*?"

She chewed her lip again, then nodded, raised her chin with determination, and headed for the door.

"See you in the morning," I called. "At the counseling office."

When I returned home after watching her scamper to a dark SUV, Mrs. B and Cheese Puff were deep into an old James Cagney movie. They dug into their dinners like food was about to be rationed while I brought her toothbrush and nightgown downstairs and made up the sofa bed.

By the time I got home, I was feeling pretty good about my skills as a counselor, nurse, and delivery service. Then I pushed the button on my blinking answering machine and heard Detective Atwell's voice. "I have more questions. Be at my office at 2:30 tomorrow afternoon."

No "please." No "are you available?" And no "thank you." When you have the power to toss people in jail, apparently you can dispense with etiquette.

Quiz Answer:
All answers have some merit but, sadly, I'd pick *e*.

A substitute's wardrobe should:
a) allow for expansion due to stress eating
b) be washable and durable
c) not reveal too much
d) be able to repel gum and ink
e) be loose enough to allow armpit air circulation

CHAPTER ELEVEN

If you're addicted to criminal investigation shows like I am, then you've heard it a hundred times—in a murder case, the first 48 hours are critical. Even by my math-challenged calculations, it had now been 144 hours since history teacher Henry Stoddard became, well, history. That probably explained why Detective Atwell looked like he'd been on a steady diet of broken glass.

Not that I was the poster girl for the benefits of a good night's rest. Wondering how to make your paltry bank balance cover legal fees can cut into your beauty sleep. And I was already thirty-some years behind on that. Thanks to my personalized chromosomal/DNA lineup, I'd escaped Iz's double-wide frame and facial features, but no one would ever tap me to strut a fashion runway in Milan. Spout all the platitudes you want about beauty being skin deep, the right genetic gifts translate into a lot less trouble picking the locks on the doors life leads you to.

Atwell ushered me into a room that had "sweatbox" written all over it. I planted my cheeks on a chair with about as much padding as a granite tombstone and inhaled the sour odor of unsupported alibis. Glands responsible for spewing out perspiration went into overdrive.

"Let's go over it again." He slapped a sheaf of papers on the narrow table between us, thumbed through it, pulled out a stapled chunk, and paged through that. I wiped my hands on my slacks and thrust my elbows out to aerate my armpits. For the record, this technique works well only in a high wind or if you're willing to flap your arms like chicken wings. Within moments my antiperspirant gave up the fight and sweat trickled down my sides.

Atwell positioned a microphone, flicked it with a ragged thumbnail, then cleared his throat. After setting the scene with time, date and names, he got down to it. "Why did you try to stop the assistant principal from entering Mr. Stoddard's room?"

Crap.

That came out of left field. Had Jessica told him? Had a passing student or teacher seen us? "I thought, you know, because it was a crime scene, the fewer people who went in there the better."

"And what made you so sure it was a crime scene?"

Duh. There was a dead body?

While I swallowed that sarcastic answer, Atwell snorted through his beaky nose. "You watch a lot of TV crime shows, right?"

I nodded, making yet another mental note to get a life.

"And that was the only reason? There wasn't something you didn't want her to find?"

Yikes, a two-parter. Would anything I said plunge me deeper into the black hole of suspecthood? My mouth didn't wait for my brain. "Wouldn't I have hidden that something instead of calling Miss Frost to tell her Henry Stoddard was dead."

91

Atwell did his pouncing tiger routine, hands slapping the table. "But you didn't tell her he was dead, did you?"

"Only because I couldn't get a word in edgewise," I yelped. "She assumed I was calling because Henry wouldn't let me have the atlases and hung up."

He shook his head and I played the highest card in that suit. "You talked with her. You know how she is."

Fear flickered in his eyes. "Let's move along. You said everyone knew that Henry Stoddard was 'sometimes a little cranky.' Is that correct?"

Was he asking if the statement accurately reflected Henry's character or if indeed I had spoken those words? Both choices were fraught with peril, but number two seemed marginally safer. "Is that what you recorded?"

He nodded. "How do you know that everyone knew that?"

"Well, I don't really know. I guess that's a figure of speech. I mean, not *everyone* knows *everything*, right?"

Atwell waved that aside. "Who did you hear that from?"

Here we go, I thought, plunging into Hearsay Evidence Swamp. Could I emerge without naming names? "Lots of people."

He skewered me with a stare worthy of a pit viper. "Be specific."

Not a chance. "Students, teachers . . . everyone."

"Be *more* specific."

"I can't be."

"Can't? Or won't?"

This time choice number one seemed the safest. "Can't. I sub in several schools. I hear lots of things. I don't keep a log."

He scowled. "You can't remember even a few names?"

"Not for sure. Besides, what does that have to do with anything?" The little voice in my brain told me to shut up, but my mouth kept going. "Henry Stoddard *was* cranky. What does it matter who commented on that?"

His scowl darkened. "What matters to this investigation is not your concern."

I squirmed in my chair, rocking it away from the table. "I think I should get an attorney."

He rolled his eyes. "That's up to you."

I waited, but he didn't add anything like, "Oh, there's no reason to do that," or "You're not a suspect." Instead he flipped pages, watching from the rims of his eyes. Could I get a second mortgage or a line of credit? Would any bank anywhere pony up for someone whose income swerved back and forth across the poverty line like a driver three drinks over the limit?

Atwell folded back another page and smirked. "Did you fail to report him for shoving you because you had been led to believe that nothing would be done about his behavior?"

Whoa!

I struggled to keep my face still. Was Atwell just fishing or had he heard the blackmail talk?

I thought back to yesterday's lunchtime conversation and how everyone except Susan seemed concerned about the extent and whereabouts of Henry's dirt. But that was just a gut feeling, not proof. And I could have misinterpreted their expressions.

And then there was Jessica. She was frightened. And desperate enough to corner me.

A snowflake of fear drifted down my spine. What if she killed Stoddard and searched his room but found nothing, then went to his house and found more nothing? That would explain her desperation.

But if I told Atwell, she might get revenge. Who knew what the extent of that might be?

My head pounded like a kettledrum marking out the beat in the background of a science fiction film. Boom. Boom. Boom. I longed to press my hands to my temples to make it stop, but knew that would look suspicious.

"Was that why you failed to report Mr. Stoddard?" Atwell prompted. "Because you believed no one would take disciplinary action?"

I tried to remember what I'd told him last week, but now there were more snowflakes of fear and a vast, cold, looming whiteness. Like a blizzard, it covered my thoughts, slowing them, freezing them, until my brainscape resembled the setting for one of those bleak Russian movies.

Atwell stared at me with his snaky eyes. A snow snake. Were there such things? Did snow snakes kill with venom or by crushing? Should I give up Jessica or keep floundering on?

"No," I squeaked. "I didn't report him because he didn't really 'shove' me."

Atwell's reptilian gaze dropped to the papers on the table and he pressed his lips together, then blew air between them. "That's it? The only reason?"

"Yes. Of course," I burbled.

He kneaded his chin. "You didn't decline to report him because you intended to bypass approved channels?"

Bypass as in strangle him?

I shook my head, thinking that my substitute training hadn't covered the "approved channels" for reporting an incident like that. I was willing to bet, however, that such reporting would have required filling out forms, talking with honchos, and wasting countless hours on something he would have denied and I still saw as no big deal.

Atwell sighed again. "Then I guess we're done." He shuffled the papers into a heap and nodded to the door. "For now."

Struggling to hold my feet to a walk, I escaped to fresh air and freedom—however temporary that might be. As I unlocked my car, I realized that Atwell still hadn't asked the question I found most obvious—did I have any idea who killed Henry Stoddard?

I drove home pondering that. Rumor had it that Henry traded in job security and favors, not money, and his wardrobe and house seemed to bear that out. Over the years he must have scraped up dozens of secrets and made a slew of veiled threats. And yet no one killed him until last week. That, I assumed, meant he'd been extremely careful—or extremely lucky—about picking his targets and making demands. So either he put the squeeze on for more and the worm turned, or he lined up a new victim and found he misjudged his mark.

What kind of a secret made someone kill? What had the killer been trying to save? A reputation? A marriage? A career?

As I pulled into the condo complex, my mind was churning ideas like a blender, but a flash of white caught my eye. Peering into a pocket of November gloom, I spotted Myra and Jake corkscrewed together beneath a dripping maple tree beyond the trash containers. His hands cupped her bony butt and a white plastic shopping bag—what else?—dangled from her elbow.

A familiar fury tightened my muscles. Then I laughed and my rage and pain shattered. This was no betrayal, no tragedy; this was farce, satire, travesty. Myra had the softness and sex appeal of one of those minimalist chrome faucets. She wasn't Jake's type. Or at least not the younger and curvier type he pursued in the past.

This might be less about attraction and more about self-preservation. Jake might be desperate to find

someone to underwrite the next place he hung his hat—
and the rest of his garments.

As I turned off the engine, I wondered if he knew
Myra was married and had no cash to spare.

No, he wouldn't have his tongue on her tonsils if he
suspected he'd get nothing for his efforts. She, on the
other hand, would get more than forty-two seconds worth.
If he had nothing else, Jake had staying power.

I glanced at my watch. 5:27. Perhaps the only reason
he wasn't demonstrating that right now was Nelson's
imminent arrival.

Chuckling, I hefted my purse and briefcase and slid
out. Although they were only a dozen yards away, Jake
and Myra seemed oblivious, but Trash Guy II, lounging
against the bin and cradling a brown paper sack, was more
vigilant. Like one of those creepy paintings, his gaze
tracked me as I opened the trunk and took out the bottle
of gin I'd picked up for Mrs. B.

As I crossed the parking lot, I glanced back and noted
he was still staring. Was he interested in me or the bottle?

Skin crawling, I scuttled to my tiny porch, unlocked
the door, and thumbed the deadbolt into place when I got
on the other side.

By arrangement, Cheese Puff had been delivered to
Mrs. B's unit after his afternoon walk, so my place was
quiet. I dumped my purse and briefcase on a chair and set
the gin on the counter. After a moment's hesitation—the
last few messages hadn't been all that positive—I pushed
the button on the blinking message machine that
indicated I had three calls.

"Babs, Babs, Babs." My gut coiled and crimped as Iz's
smug voice repeated the nickname I loathed. "Guess
you're out preparing students for a life of conformity
much like your own. My lecture was so well received
they've asked me back to fill a cancellation. And don't

forget I refuse to sanction a holiday where women do the bulk of the work and then worship the mall gods."

Meaning, don't call her on Thanksgiving. I opened the refrigerator and got out a carton of key-lime-pie yogurt to counteract the acid my stomach produced at the sound of her voice. The irony of Iz's claim lay in the way she interpreted the word "sanction." She wouldn't cook or shop, but if others wanted to go all out, she'd drink their wine and gobble their food. She'd been skewing reality so long she didn't notice the hypocrisy.

I pushed the button again. "Hi, Barbara." Susan's voice, tired and tentative. My stomach delivered another shot of acid. Had they found a long-term sub? Was I getting the boot? Had I screwed up my part of the grading?

"First, I got a call from Arachne's father and I gave you a gold star. And second, um, I know this is late and I'm sorry, but would you like to come over for Thanksgiving dinner? Some of the teachers can't get home to their families or don't have— Anyway, it's in the evening, at 7:00. Let me know tomorrow. I've got the main dishes covered—turkey, stuffing, potatoes, gravy, cranberry sauce, green bean casserole—but everyone will bring a specialty dish. After those eels I told Brenda to bring wine—it should be hard to mess that up."

Hard, I thought as Susan wound up with another apology, but not impossible. Brenda might make the wine herself, from rhubarb or sauerkraut—or leftover eels. Shuddering, I noted the event on my mostly blank calendar.

Mrs. B and the Committee were gathering at her condo at noon for drinks and appetizers—appetizers she'd asked me to shop for and prepare. If I made extra, I could contribute those to Susan's dinner. And the timing should work. The Committee was dining at two at a hotel buffet and then returning to Mrs. B's for another round. Even given the extensive collection of after-dinner offerings Mrs. B had accumulated—everything from banana to violet liqueurs—they should be dozing off by 5:30. 6:00 at the latest.

After the questions Atwell's interview sparked, I wanted a closer look at my colleagues. And it would be good to have the day filled with activities, to avoid brooding about how my life might look if Bryce and Albert hadn't died, if my parents had gotten therapy, if Jake hadn't cheated, if Iz—

"Stop it."

I swallowed a spoonful of yogurt and punched the button a final time. "This is Dave Martin. Thank you for helping my daughter Allison."

A male voice, confident but not overbearing, as strong and warm and smooth as good brandy. A sexy voice but, unlike Jake's, one with substance.

"She wants to walk with you and your dog. I've checked you out with Mrs. Mitchell and Allison has my permission as long as she keeps her cell phone on and is home by dark. Allison can be . . . flighty and unpredictable . . . touchy. She's at a difficult age and our family situation is . . . well, fractured. My work schedule is intense and irregular so I'm not always there when she wants to connect. I appreciate your interest. I hope to meet you soon."

A man who hoped to meet me soon! I almost played the message again, then told myself to get real. He was seeing someone. Besides, there must be a rule about getting involved with a parent of one of your students. Not that Allison/Arachne was technically my student, but—

"Cut it out," I ordered myself.

I finished the yogurt, took the gin to Mrs. B, and set off to pick up the Thai food she had a craving for. As I wheeled past the end of the complex, I spotted Jake lowering himself into that low-slung car beside his redheaded "landlady." As I waited for a break in the traffic, I studied their reflections in the rearview mirror. She sat upright and gripped the wheel with both hands. Jake canted to his right, up against the passenger window.

I swiveled my head, spotted traffic gaps looming, and eased out. Just before I gunned it, I glanced in the mirror again and noticed a dark sedan pull in behind them. The man behind the wheel was wearing a yellow slicker.

If Trash Guy II had a car and money to fuel it, why was he hanging around here?

Quiz Answer:
f – all of the above (And yes, I know f wasn't a choice. I wanted to see if you were paying attention.)

Subs think of school holidays as
a) a welcome relief
b) days without pay
c) a chance to reassess their careers
d) mental health days
e) opportunities to get a life

CHAPTER TWELVE

In an effort to avoid the day-before-Thanksgiving crowds, I set my alarm for six, slapped a ball cap on my head, hustled Cheese Puff through a walk, and was at the 24-hour supermarket with a gigantic go-cup of coffee by seven. I was armed with the list for Mrs. Ballantine's appetizer trays and two hundred-dollar bills peeled from a stack wrapped in aluminum foil and stashed beneath three bottles of vodka in her freezer.

"I read an article that said you should always keep cash on hand for emergencies," she said. "So I have little packets here and there."

Allowing for at least three other packets, Mrs. B had cash on hand equal to what I'd make subbing between now and, say, the end of the next decade. As for my own set-aside stash, it once held a whopping sixty dollars, but I'd already borrowed back forty for gas and dog biscuits.

"Don't bother with change," Mrs. B said as she pressed the bills into my hand. "Buy the little guy some treats or toys."

Toys, hell. Five long days loomed before my bank account got a financial transfusion from the school district and other than standby PB&J ingredients, I was down to last-ditch food choices—packages of noodles, bran-flake cookies, soy milk, limp broccoli, spongy potatoes, and freezer-burned chicken thighs. Mrs. B's bank account, however, seemed both substantial and recession proof, and I detected no concern about the mob or the government moving to siphon it off. Perhaps Marco had laundered his takings into legitimate investments. Or stashed the loot in an off-shore account.

"None of your business," I reminded myself and hustled into the store.

The aisles were nearly empty so I made good time past wine and soft- drinks displays, to coolers of specialty meats, cheeses, and olives, and to shelves stacked deep with crackers and jars of nuts, artichoke hearts and marinated mushrooms. When faced with a question of which brand to choose, I picked the one with the highest number on the price tag. Mrs. B had money to burn; she wouldn't quibble about tossing a few more dollars into the flames.

By the time I reached the check-out counter, women with the determined scowls of linebackers were charging through the automatic doors. As I loaded my car, a van crowded to within a foot of my bumper and a man who looked like he wrestled alligators for a living burped the horn. His wife, who could have been Bernina Burke's sister, rolled down the passenger window and drummed the heel of her hand against the door.

A week ago I would have been intimidated and tossed my environmentally correct cloth bags of gourmet goodies into the trunk like dirty laundry. But being interrogated by the police, rescuing Arachne/Allison, staring down Jessica Flint, and watching my ex-husband come on to every woman in the vicinity had fostered a strange kind of confidence—like that numb and disembodied feeling you

101

get when you brake two inches short of plowing into the car in front of you. So I made sure the jars and bottles were upright, and braced the bags with cartons of soft drinks.

"Hurry up," the woman growled.

I loaded a bag of dog food and pointed my chin toward the rear of the parking lot. "There are plenty of spaces back there."

"I don't like to walk."

I wedged the dog food in beside the sack of wine. "Obviously," I muttered.

"What did you say?"

I opened my mouth to repeat the word, complete with snide tone, but self-preservation kicked in. All the confidence in the world wouldn't keep my ribs from splintering if she got me down and sat on me. "Works for me."

She frowned. I shrugged, set a sack of chips and crackers on top of the dog food, and slammed the trunk shut. "Then hurry up," she said with a snarl.

Talk about motivational speaking. Technique like that could halt glacial retreat.

I dawdled to a cart-return pen in the next aisle while Alligator Wrestler burped the horn. A week ago, guilt would have made me hustle, but today I saw this as their problem. Finally, after wiping a smudge from my glasses, I settled into the car, checked belt and mirrors, turned the key, and slipped the shift into reverse.

As luck—mine, not theirs—would have it, they had to back up so I could squeak out of my space. Grinning, I took every inch they gave me, lingering against their front bumper long enough for a burly man in a car not much larger than a wheelbarrow to zip into my spot from the other direction.

102

Alligator Wrestler leaned on his horn making it bleat like a castrated lamb. His wife howled like a banshee on uppers. I shot forward, pausing at the end of the row to look back. Alligator Wrestler jumped from his van, fists up. As if emerging from quicksand, Burly Man oozed from his car. Unfolded, he towered over Alligator Wrestler. Mrs. Alligator Wrestler avalanched out and lurched toward them.

Store-bound shoppers about-faced, clearly recognizing a great fight when they saw one shaping up. With the right music and a little editing, I could post this on the net and get thousands of hits.

If I had a video camera. If I didn't have to get to the bakery. If Mr. and Mrs. Alligator Wrestler wouldn't turn their wrath on me if I stuck around.

I was still priding myself on my sprouting self-esteem when I shucked off my shoes and flopped on my bed for a little assigned reading followed by a lot of napping in preparation for a paper due next week. Cheese Puff crawled up on my stomach, wagged his orange flag of a tail, and licked the tip of my nose.

"Begging for a rubdown, are we?"

He nudged my chin, the signal that he wanted a full-body massage—my fault for reading him the article about how kneading your dog's muscles can improve your own physical and emotional health. So far, he seemed to be getting all the benefits, and I found that once you start a routine your dog enjoys, you better be prepared to continue—especially if your dog is a small one.

"A small dog gets up every day with just one thought in its mind," my vet had cautioned. "And that thought is, 'I will bend you to my will.'"

I smiled and ran my fingers along Cheese Puff's sides. "So, we're doing this to prove I'm your slave, not because you really want it."

"I want it," a voice said. "I really want it, baby!"

Cheese Puff opened his eyes. I twisted my neck. We both stared at the wall behind my bed.

That was Myra's voice. Had she and Nelson gotten a new script?

"If you want it, then you're gonna get it," a man's voice answered. "Every glorious inch."

"Every glorious inch?" From what I'd overheard in previous weeks, glorious wasn't an adjective she'd let Nelson apply to his male appendage.

"Ooohhh," Myra moaned. "Aahhhh. Give me more. Give me all of it."

"Jake Junior is at your service," the man said.

Jake Junior?

I sat up, dumping Cheese Puff to the bedspread and earning a look of betrayal. Granted, my sexual experience hadn't been encyclopedic, but I knew—in the biblical sense—only one man who'd given his penis a name. That man was my ex-husband. And that name was Jake Junior.

Something bumped the wall. "Oooohhhh," Myra moaned again.

"What have I done so wrong," I asked the ceiling, "that I have to listen to my ex-husband boinking the bimbo next door?"

Cheese Puff shot me another withering look, jumped off the bed, and headed for the door.

"You're right," I told him as the bumping grew in frequency and volume. "I don't have to listen. We'll take a walk."

I toed into my loafers, and glanced out the window for a weather-check. The rain and wind of recent days had stripped most of the leaves from the trees that shielded the parking lot, so I had a clear view of Nelson's car just before it rolled into his spot beneath the canopy.

My heart gave a little flutter. "OMG. Nelson's home. What should we do?"

Cheese Puff blinked, then bounced to the bed, and sat on my pillow.

"Stay here and listen? We can't. He's going to barge in on them and—"

And I'd have a front-wall seat. I planted myself beside Cheese Puff, took the gold hoop earring out of my right ear, and leaned against the wall. It was vibrating with their rhythm, making me wonder about construction standards.

"Faster," Myra moaned.

"This bed is like a trampoline," Jake panted. I can't get traction."

The thumping speeded up, then slowed.

"Harder," Myra commanded. "Faster."

"I can't," Jake wheezed, "I'm getting friction burns."

I slapped a hand over my mouth to contain a vengeful chortle.

"Shut up," Myra ordered. "If I wanted excuses, I'd screw my husband. He's—"

"Right behind you," Nelson's voice boomed.

The thumping ceased.

"Oh shit! You said he was at work."

"What are you doing home?" Myra squawked. "You never leave work before 5:30. Never."

"I do now. The bank went belly-up."

"He's got a camera in his phone," Jake howled.

Springs squeaked and I heard what I guessed was the thud of feet hitting the floor and a scrabbling that sounded like a man gathering up clothing tossed aside in the heat of passion—or the thrill of conquest. Jake was far too controlled and calculating to experience let-yourself-go

105

passion. Nor did his concept of sex have anything to do with intimacy. He probably thought of it more as closing a sale.

"Put that phone away, Nelson," Myra ordered in her most imperious tone. "Don't you dare take pictures of—"

"Of what looks like grounds for divorce?" Nelson laughed. "Say cheese."

Cheese Puff's ears perked up.

"Cheese, not Cheese Puff," I whispered. "Who knew Nelson had a sense of humor?"

"You won't divorce me," Myra said. "I'll take you for everything you've got. This condo, my car, support payments."

"Good luck." Nelson laughed again and this time there was a maniacal edge to it. "The condo's in foreclosure, the cars are about to be repossessed, and you can't get blood out of a stone. Smile for the camera."

"You told me he was loaded," Jake complained. "You said you'd—"

"You bastard!" Myra screamed.

"Which one is she calling that?" I asked Cheese Puff.

As if she'd heard me, Myra clarified. "You can't do this to me, Nelson. How will I live?"

"Maybe you can get a job as a personal shopper." Nelson guffawed and I heard a repeated slapping sound. Was he applauding himself?

I nodded to Cheese Puff and gave Nelson a thumbs-up.

"But where will I go?" Myra sobbed.

"Obviously you can't move in with your pal here. His redheaded girlfriend would throw you both in the river." Nelson laughed again, viciously. "Maybe she'd like to see these pictures."

"No," Jake howled. "Don't do that. Please don't do that."

"I don't know what she sees in you. You're limp. As shriveled as a prune. Myra, I thought you wanted a man with staying power."

"I've got plenty of staying power," Jake protested. "If you hadn't walked in on us I would have—"

I shook my head. Only Jake would boast about endurance at a time like this.

"Shut up, Jake, no one cares," Myra screamed. "Just shut up and get out. I never want to see you again."

"But he said I was—"

"I don't care if he said you were hung like a gerbil, get out!"

"One more photo before you go, Prune Boy," Nelson said.

"Prune Boy," I whispered to Cheese Puff. "I love it."

I heard a wet smacking sound and the scuffing of feet on carpet. Something heavy slammed against the wall.

"Give me back that phone!" Nelson yowled.

"Nobody calls me limp," Jake said, his voice fading out.

A moment later I heard the downstairs door slam. "Exit Jake," I said.

"Nelson, are you okay?" Myra mewled. "Your nose is bleeding."

"Don't touch me, Myra." Nelson's voice had real authority, not the hollow kind from previous confrontations. "And don't think that because Prune Boy took my phone I lost the evidence. I e-mailed the best pictures to my attorney."

"But Nelson, honey, you're my life, my love. Jake was just—"

"Just the last straw, Myra. The last straw in an enormous bale accumulating on my back since the day I married you."

"I'll make it up to you, I promise. I'll get a job, I'll—"

107

"We're done, Myra. Pack up and get out."

"But . . . but I have nowhere to go."

"Neither do I," Nelson's voice deflated like a balloon. "But if we're not out by noon on Monday we'll be evicted."

"But what will I live on?"

"That's your problem."

I heard shuffling footsteps and then only muffled sobbing.

"Show's over," I told Cheese Puff, holding out my palm for a high five—or as high a five as you can get from a dog with three inches of ground clearance. "That mean old witch who complained about you is on the way out." I leaped from my bed and gathered him into my arms. "Let's go tell Mrs. B the news."

On the way downstairs that damn little voice chided me for gloating. "They're victims of the economy, too, you know."

"But they're still predators," I insisted.

Cheese Puff licked my nose in a show of support. "Predators who don't like dogs," I added. I'd pity them exactly the way an impala might pity a lame cheetah.

Quiz Answer:
That depends on the sub.

The worst lunch a sub can bring
a) is loaded with garlic
b) is in a container larger than the microwave
c) needs twenty minutes of prep time
d) sticks in the teeth
e) produces enough gas to fill a blimp

CHAPTER THIRTEEN

At 6:06 Thanksgiving evening I left Cheese Puff snuggled into a chair beside Mrs. B, stashed two platters of appetizers on the back seat of my car, and headed to Susan's house. After an afternoon of being referred to as "the baby," or "Cheese Puff's mommy," I was looking forward to hanging with people in my own age bracket— and to having conversations that didn't include cures for constipation or the opposite problem.

Beyond that, I wanted to learn more about the career I hoped to pursue. After three days in Stoddard's classes and my success with Arachne/Allison, I'd convinced—or perhaps deluded—myself that I could establish rapport with teenagers.

Susan's house was a brick ranch set back from a winding street in a group of spreading maples. It had wide windows and a veranda screened by wisteria vines. A chaise, two wicker chairs, and a table clustered in one corner of the porch and I imagined her sitting there in the summer, sipping a frosty drink, reading a thick book about the Civil War or the New Deal, and sharing pithy paragraphs with her husband of seventeen years. He was an engineer who worked from home, and I'd created a mental image of someone good with his hands, precise, meticulous, and soft-spoken.

As I pulled the platters from the back seat and balanced them on my arms, I thought about the aspects of marriage I missed—familiarity, company, and emotional support. I'd had two out of three. Albert, bless his heart, had been too preoccupied with birding to notice much about my mental state, and Jake— Well, I don't need to tell you what he's preoccupied with.

Before I plunged into another relationship I had to confront the qualities—uncertainty, guilt, and the desire to be liked—that kept me from getting what I needed. Otherwise, I'd have a leading role in another marital disaster movie.

Standing sideways and balancing the platters, I rang the doorbell with my elbow and waited. After a moment I heard indistinct shouting, a thud, more shouting, and then stomping footsteps.

A man in a bright orange sweatshirt with the word "Texas" in bold letters flung the door wide and scowled as if I was the latest in a long string of converts proselytizing for a religious sect worshipping that de-planetized chunk of rock known as Pluto. "What do you want?"

Even frowning, even with a three-day growth of beard, he was gorgeous. I felt a stab of jealousy. Susan had it all. "Uh, sorry. Uh, Kevin? Susan invi—"

He spun toward the rear of the house. "Susan," he bellowed. "One of your school people is here."

A door slammed in the distance. "I'll be right there," Susan called in a voice as tight as a guitar string.

"Come on in. I'll take one of those." Kevin snatched the platter from my left hand, and strode through an archway halfway along a narrow hallway.

I hesitated, then stepped across the threshold and nudged the door closed. I set the second platter on a pie-crust table, took off my raincoat, and hung it on a wooden rack with curving arms.

As I moved, the soles of my shoes chuffed in a layer of grit on the worn oak planks—not what I expected in Susan's house. The sandpapery sound made me itch all over and yearn to get my hands on a broom or vacuum cleaner.

"It's tough to juggle a career, housework, and a home life," that little voice lectured. "And it's not like you're doing such a bang-up job."

My conscience had a point, and I forced a wide smile as Susan shot down the hallway, wiping her hands on an orange and yellow flowered apron that shielded a black sweater and slacks. "Sorry, sorry, sorry. I was basting and had to get the bird back in the oven."

As she came closer, I saw that her eyes were swollen and bloodshot. A cold? Allergies?

"That's okay." I picked up the platter. "I brought two of these. Kevin took the other one."

Susan's lips crimped, then she nodded. "Let's go back to the kitchen. I'm running behind and could use some help with the potatoes if you don't mind."

"I'd be happy to." I offered the polite lie that was expected of a guest, even if that guest would rather scrub grout with a toothbrush.

Susan didn't so much as glance at the archway through which Kevin had disappeared, but I peeked at a boxy room that reminded me of wartime shelters where people waited out bombings and firestorms. There were no paintings or posters on the gray walls, no carpet on the floor. Utilitarian. On one side of the room a battered slab of plywood balanced on cinder blocks held an array of computer equipment. Nearby, Kevin and a man with a strong family resemblance hunched on a sway-backed green sofa, gripping controls and staring at the video game displayed on a hulking TV screen.

I noted that he'd yanked back the plastic wrap and set the platter on a slanting drift of books and newspapers, sending a cascade of appetizers to the floor. I felt a pang of regret for the time spent stuffing mushrooms and mixing spreads for tomato slices and wrapped my arms protectively around the remaining platter.

Susan turned left and we entered a huge kitchen where the air was redolent of sage and onions. A vast clutter of figurines crowded a narrow shelf circumnavigating the room level with the top of the doorway, but the rest of the kitchen was all business. The countertops were clean and clear—except for a few pots and bowls and an industrial-sized bottle of gin.

"The potatoes and the knife are there." Susan pointed to a ten-pound bag beside the double sink and then swooped to a low cabinet and came up with a tall pot. "Peels in the colander for the compost, please."

"How many?" I asked as I rolled up the sleeves of the glittery dark green blouse I bought to wear to dinner last Thanksgiving—a day spent instead mourning the demise of my marriage. Lest I dwell on that, I replayed the scene I'd heard through the wall and felt my lips slide into a grin.

"It seems I'm always running behind." Susan slapped a can of yams into an electric opener and zipped off the top. "I even made a checklist so I'd stay on target, but . . ."

"Things always take longer than you think." I seized the paring knife and flayed my first victim—the runtiest potato in the bag. My strategy was to start small and "reward" myself with the large ones last. Pathetic, huh? When the reward for staying on-task is stripping the skin from a full-pound monster, you *really* need a life.

112

Susan drained the yams, dumped them into a square glass dish, tossed in marshmallows and raisins, and topped that off with dollops of peanut butter.

I blinked. Peanut butter wasn't part of yam recipes from my Thanksgivings past, but I reminded myself that Susan was creative and competent, that I should be open to new experiences.

"The first batch of bread was a disaster. Too much salt. The second didn't rise." Susan fitted foil over the yam dish. "The vacuum broke and half an hour ago I discovered that my brother-in-law ate the onion rings for the green bean casserole and I was elbow-deep in stuffing and couldn't go to the store."

I nodded, surprised that Susan, the most organized teacher I'd ever run into, hadn't checked her ingredients before she began to cook.

She raised a glass of iced clear liquid and took a huge swallow. "I had to improvise with breadcrumbs and crumbled bacon."

Call me a traditionalist, call me inflexible, but bacon instead of onion rings just wouldn't cut it. "I'm sure it will be fine," I lied.

"And then I discovered the cranberries were all soft and mushy—a cucumber went bad and leaked all over them—so I made relish with marmalade and raspberry jam."

Was she joking?

I skinned potato number three, waiting for her to laugh. Instead she swallowed more of her drink, hauled out a cutting board and a knife that would have made Jim Bowie envious, and began to chop turkey organs. "And the dryer went on the fritz and baked wrinkles into the only tablecloth that fits when the leaves are in. But that doesn't matter because Kevin is using the leaves for shelves in his den."

113

She gave the liver such a vicious whack that the knife stuck in the board. "We'll be crammed in like sardines." She wiggled the blade loose and blotted her eyes on her sleeve.

"It will be fine." I wished I meant that. Menu substitutions and make-dos were minor issues if the mood was festive. Susan's was well below bleak. And sinking.

"Do you really think so?"

I drove the point of the knife into the sprouting eye of my seventh potato, noting that my own mood barometer had slipped to the low end of determined and now hovered just above desperate. "It will all work out," I mumbled, hoping to convince both of us.

"Will it?" Her voice was that of a woman headed for the gallows.

"Sure," I babbled. "Squeezing in will make it seem more like family."

"Family." She flailed at the innards with zeal that would have won her a promotion during the Spanish Inquisition. Bits of giblets went airborne, then plummeted to the countertop with soft slapping sounds. "Family's a wonderful thing, isn't it?"

Susan's tone, bitter as hemlock, brought a picture of Iz to my mind. Resplendent in her satin blouse with smears of chocolate in the corners of her frowning lips, she pointed a reproachful finger. I shook my head. Enough with being a cheerleading Pollyanna, maybe what Susan needed was commiseration. "Um . . . well, I guess it can *be* wonderful, but it kind of depends on who's in your family and . . . what their agendas are." I hoped I managed to imply that I was sympathetic and that my own situation was less than wonderful.

"That's so right." She aimed the knife at me. Light shimmered from a strip of blade unsullied by turkey guts and the stench of raw liver clogged my nose.

"That's so, so right," she repeated, jabbing air inches from my eyes. Ordering myself not to flinch, I gripped the next-to-last potato and my stubby paring knife.

She dropped her knife on the counter. "Want a drink?"

Like you wouldn't believe. "Sure."

She snatched a tumbler from a cabinet, tossed in ice cubes, and sloshed gin over them, filling the glass to within an inch of the rim. "Tonic?"

"Please."

She grabbed a bottle from the refrigerator and splashed in maybe two tablespoons. I tossed the potato aside, seized the glass, and drank, gin flaming down my throat and scorching my stomach lining.

"For example," Susan continued, "there's *my* family, and then there's *Kevin's* family."

I nodded and attempted a breath while she took another swallow from her tall glass. "*My* family goes skiing and snow tubing over Thanksgiving. We play charades and put on plays. We have traditions." She set the glass down with a snap. "Traditions."

"Traditions are good." Like onion rings in the green bean casserole.

She nodded. "But Kevin's family—and that's Devin, period—thinks tradition means sitting on their duffs, drinking beer, and punching buttons on those stupid games."

She bent, opened a cabinet, brought out a cast-iron frying pan, and slammed it on a back burner. "I should have said no way when Kevin suggested that Devin move in. But he'd been laid off and his unemployment wasn't much." She dumped the massacred giblets into the pan. "You know how that is."

"Yes." I started on the last potato, challenging myself to make one endless peel and failing within six seconds. I do better with apples. The fact that I knew that further signified my lack of a life.

"But you've got hustle. If Devin had the least bit, I'd get you two together."

I flinched. Talk about dodging a bullet. I'd dodged a cannonball.

"Kevin said it would be for only a few weeks. He said I'm at school so much and so tired when I'm home I'd hardly notice we had a roomer. Roomer! As if Devin ever choked up a dime for anything besides beer!"

Devin had a lot in common with Jake.

"And I *do* spend a lot of time on school work, but Kevin used to understand. He was proud when I was named department head; he said he knew how much it meant to me to build a great program."

Dumping the cutting board and knife into the sink, she opened the refrigerator, pulled out a stick of butter, and aimed it at me. "And I *am* tired. I'm exhausted from September until June. Teaching isn't the cakewalk some people think it is."

"Those people should be required to sub for a week," I suggested, trying to lighten the tone and change the subject. "That would be a wake-up call."

Susan waved that aside. "Devin's not looking for work and Kevin hasn't had a paying project for months. They've reverted to adolescence." She sliced off a chunk of butter, tossed it on the pile of mutilated giblets, and fired up the burner. "Playing games half the night. Merging into one parasitic unit." She seized a wooden spoon from a green glass vase and jabbed at the butter. "They're bleeding me dry."

I patted her shoulder, feeling off balance, dizzy. The placid image of her life I'd conjured up on the porch was 180 degrees off. Shows you how finely honed my powers of observation are.

116

"I stopping being their maid and I moved into the guestroom." Snatching a dish towel from a hook beside the sink, she buried her face in it. "Kevin didn't even notice."

An attempt at subject changing here would be callous, so I winnowed my brain for a response. Should I suggest she buy a sexy nightgown? Nope. I'd tried that when Albert got involved with a new bird book and been humiliated. Should I offer my futon sofa and help her pack?

The frying pan sizzled and the odor of scorching turkey heart assaulted me. Leaping to the stove, I turned down the flame, yanked the spoon from her fingers, and plowed furrows in the smoking turkey innards.

"I wish I could walk out," Susan wailed into the towel. "But my grandmother left me this house. It's mine. He's not getting it. He's not!"

I felt a surge of selfish relief. I wouldn't need to share my cramped condo.

"Thank goodness I have my career." Susan blew her nose in the towel and tossed it aside. "I'd go crazy if I didn't. And I can finally build a model social studies program now that Henry's not standing on the air hose. That needs wine."

She spun and plucked a dark green bottle from the refrigerator, twisted the cork loose, and splashed liquid into the frying pan. It bubbled and hissed, releasing an acrid cloud that fogged my glasses. "Deglazing," she said. "Keep stirring."

Choking, I batted at the cloud with one hand and stirred with the other.

"Oh, damn it all!"

Peering through condensation-covered lenses, I saw Susan hurl the bottle against the wall. "Vinegar," she screamed. "The wine turned to vinegar."

A metaphor for her marriage. Not to mention this dinner. The bottle, unbroken, pinwheeled to the floor, spewing soured wine.

Just then the doorbell rang.

"I'll get it." I thrust the spoon into Susan's hand and ran to admit Brenda and Aston with a bottle of rhubarb wine and a jar of something pale and slimy he said were pickled wild boar knuckles. Gertrude, carrying two cans of beets, came close behind, and Doug trailed after her with a box of doughnut holes and a can of squirt cream. By the time Phil Benson arrived with a bag of barbecue potato chips and a CD of his guitar class attempting the greatest hits of the 60s, the fictional headache I'd planned to plead as an excuse for leaving early had become the real deal.

Thirty minutes later I was home munching leftover appetizer ingredients, digesting a couple of aspirin, and reassessing my life. On the one hand, my two less-than-perfect marriages now seemed about par for the obstacle-strewn course. On the other hand, if Susan was an example of how teaching could strangle my life, maybe— even if I had to move to Boise or Fresno or Hackensack—I should get another job in radio.

Quiz Answer:
f – all of the above

The worst subs
a) don't follow lesson plans
b) have no sense of humor
c) have no classroom management skills
d) hate the job and the kids
e) quit in the middle of the day

CHAPTER FOURTEEN

Friday morning, after an hour browsing websites in vain for jobs in an industry undercut by newer technologies, I tamped out last night's pipe dream of a return to radio. A teacher's audience was far less tuned-in, but the job offered decent pay, a pension, and summers off. And, like any job, it consumed your life—or lack of a life—only as much as you let it.

Decision made, I brewed a pot of coffee, and spread my textbooks and notes on the dining nook table. With Cheese Puff on my lap, I settled down to work through the afternoon. That, of course, was the cue for the phone to ring.

"Dad said I can come walk your dog with you," Arachne told me without preamble. "He'll drop me off in a few minutes. I'll ride my bicycle home after."

Granted, much of my childhood is a blur and to say parental involvement was minimal after Bryce's death would be stretching it, but I know I learned to ask permission. I also learned that adults—notoriously unreliable and caught up in their own lives—seldom agreed to plans I hatched without their input.

"I mean," Arachne amended, "if that's okay with you."

I gazed at my stack of work, then through the window. As if on cue, a ray of sunlight glazed the few leaves still clinging to the maple. Sunshine wasn't something to be trifled with between the end of September and the middle of April in this soggy neck of the woods.

"Sure," I said, telling myself she had permission and vowing to do or say nothing even remotely inappropriate, especially not the F-bomb I'd dropped so casually as a radio producer. "I live at the—"

"Dad says he knows."

She hung up, leaving me to wonder how Dave Martin knew the address I'd withheld from the phone book. Had Susan given it to him? I frowned at Cheese Puff, certain I'd told her only that I had a condo by the river. Well, I'd ask him when he dropped Arachne off.

Flipping on the television, I discovered that it was a whopping 56 degrees and the sunbreak was expected to stretch through the afternoon. A vision of the appetizers I'd finished off for breakfast loomed in my mind and I decided a bike ride would keep the new fat cells on my hips from getting too comfortable.

Cheese Puff circled and whined when I wiggled my ancient wide-tired bicycle from among stacks of boxes in the closet under the stairs.

"Of course you're going." I leaned the bike against the side of the futon, ducked back into the closet and got a basket, harness, and the components of the jury-rigged safety apparatus that kept him from leaping out should we come across a foxy female of his species—whatever that species might be.

He trembled with anticipation as I fastened the harness. "Now wait right there while I get a jacket and your sack."

The fundamental rule of living in the Northwest is "never trust the forecast" and I'd been drenched too many times to ignore it. I clipped the basket to the handlebars, folded my jacket to form a cushion at the bottom of the basket and covered it with a waterproof sack. Should we get caught in a shower, I'd pop Cheese Puff inside and cinch it so only his eyes and snout were exposed.

Just as I shrugged into a bright blue sweater, the doorbell rang. Arachne, wearing black jeans, a black sweater, and her black cape, stood alone on my miniscule porch, a white paper sack thrust toward me. "Dad bought pastries."

My fat cells jiggled with joy. Cheese Puff barked.

"Oooohhhh." Arachne tossed me the bag and dropped to her knees.

I made a two-handed catch while Cheese Puff pranced up to her, swooped his head beneath her reaching hand, and grunted with contentment when she rubbed his ears. "Cheese Puff," she cooed. "You're a snuggle bunny."

Not, I thought as I set the pastry sack on the table, what I considered Goth-like language. "I thought we'd go for a ride on the river trail," I told her. "Do you want a snack now or when we come back?"

"Later." She cradled Cheese Puff like a baby and pressed her nose against his. "I'm not hungry, but Dad said it's polite to bring something."

A man with manners. This I had to see.

I peered past her, but spotted only Nelson Bancroft stuffing an armload of banker suits into the trunk of his car. "Where *is* your father?"

"He had to go to work."

"Oh." I closed the door. "How did he know where I live?"

"I don't know." She nuzzled the top of Cheese Puff's head. "Oh, you smell so sweet. Like roses and violets." Her nose wrinkled. "But your breath smells like . . . pickles? No. Olives."

I chuckled. She'd sniffed out perfume from members of the Committee and Mrs. Ballantine's martini garnish. Had Mrs. B let him dive to the bottom of her glass for the olives?

I smiled at that image, then caught myself. Were olives bad for dogs? What about pimiento? And that salty brine? Not to mention the gin. Mrs. B and I were overdue for a chat about his diet.

Speaking of which. I peered into the sack and spotted a chocolate éclair, a square of baklava, a triangular tart shell stuffed with blueberries, and two giant cookies bursting with nuts and chocolate chips. Dave Martin wasn't just a man with manners, he was a man who understood that most women like choices—especially when those choices involve food. Too bad he was taken.

I set the sack on the table, filled two water bottles, and snagged my keys. "Let's put Cheese Puff in his basket and get him locked down."

Arachne scooped him up and placed him on the folded stuff sack and I wove four short bungee cords across the basket to retard his efforts to jump out, then hooked the retractable leash to the ring on his harness and shoved the handle over the grip on the handlebar. The theory—as yet untested—was that if he managed to escape the potholder weave of the bungee cords, the leash would allow me to reel him back in.

"That's so neat," Arachne gushed. "It's like he's inside a pie crust. Like he's a Cheese Puff pie."

That sounded like something Brenda would cook up, and a vast improvement on eel anything. Smiling, I locked up and wheeled out across the porch and down the walk, Cheese Puff periscoping up through the central square of the cord grid. We passed Nelson Bancroft stowing a carton of what looked like appreciation plaques in his back seat. I nodded to be polite, and got a glare in response.

Arachne threw a leg over a bicycle far newer than mine, secured her cape by knotting it around her waist, and rode a figure eight in the parking lot. Watching her, I caught a flash of yellow and spotted Trash Guy II ducking behind a shrub. Arachne rode a longer eight and, far down at the end of the complex, I spied Jake, scuttling along, talking into a cell phone, and peering over his shoulder as if he'd escaped from prison and bloodhounds were baying on his trail.

I mounted up and pedaled that way in time to see him slip through a gap in the hedge that screened the condos from the street. A few seconds later I heard a car door slam. Pedaling faster, I reached the gap just as a black sedan accelerated away.

I blinked. Was that Jessica Flint's car?

If so, Jake hadn't wasted time between the derailment of Myra's gravy train and launching Plan B. Or was this Plan C? Or D? For all I knew, he had a complete alphabet of back-up schemes involving women and money.

Arachne zipped past. "Which way to the trail?"

I pointed, she took off, and I fell in behind, feeling my thighs chafe inside my jeans. Too many appetizers. I felt a wave of disgust at my lack of willpower, then told myself extra poundage deflected the phony charm of men like Jake. Following that line of thought, the calorie-packed sack from Dave Martin was a shield for my battle against bogus boyfriends.

We turned right on the sidewalk at the end of the complex, cut through to the river trail, and went left, aiming at the snow-topped pyramid of Mount Hood and pedaling into a sharp, steady breeze. Clear skies this time of year usually meant a high pressure system channeling the Coho Wind through the Columbia Gorge. For a moment I thought of suggesting we ride in the opposite direction, then realized we'd have to buck the breeze on the way back.

We wove our way through a stream of runners and walkers, then whizzed past a couple of restaurants, a park, another condo complex, and an area of light industry. A plane roared overhead, outbound from the airport on the Oregon side of the river, and Cheese Puff raised his snout and growled. With its engine clattering, a motorboat churned up the river, a photographer with a tripod balanced in the bow. The wake rippled against a steep rocky beach that last week had been wider than my futon sofa but now was the width of a throw pillow. Another few days of pounding rain and water would be lapping at the roots of the trees and vines clinging to the bank that dropped a sharp twenty feet from the base of the knee-high stone wall at the edge of the trail.

Arachne slewed her bike across the trail, planted one foot on either side, and pointed upstream. "Is that Mr. Marsden?"

I braked, wheeled in beside the stone wall, dismounted, and shaded my eyes with my hand. Coming toward us was a trio of canoes—two long, wide, and built of dark wood, and one shorter, stubbier, and painted white with a forest of green trees and a mountain along the side. I'd seen that picture up close many times—the canoe was usually stashed under a deck at the downstream end of the condo complex.

In what Aston had complained about as a breach of historical accuracy, all three canoes were stuffed with piles of mock fur, but the men paddling were clad in what appeared to be genuine buckskin. One wore a coonskin cap. The sight of it picked the lock on a mental door and brought forth lyric fragments from a song about Davy Crockett, something about Tennessee and a bear.

I shook my head. If that got embedded, I'd have to take extreme measures and sing something truly insipid to drive it out. I won't tell you what that might be because I'm sure you have your own techniques for rebooting your brain. I'm also sure you know you'll be stuck with the reboot tune for hours. The cure may be worse than the ailment.

"What's he doing?" Arachne asked as the canoes swept past and the photo boat turned to follow.

"They're re-enacting the way the trappers used to come down the river to trade their furs back in the 1800s."

She laid a hand on Cheese Puff's head. "Furs from little animals?"

She seemed genuinely surprised. How had she managed to sidestep this knowledge? "Uh . . . yeah."

She planted her fists on her hips. "Well, I hope their boats tip over and all those furs fall out."

"They're not real—"

"Hey, move it. I'm running here!"

Cheese Puff growled and I turned to see Jake's redheaded friend bearing down on us, leg muscles bunching with each long stride, elbows pumping as she raised and lowered a set of hand weights, hair flying like a flag of war.

"Get that damn bike out of my way."

"I am," Arachne cried. With one leg on either side of the bike she crimped the wheel and shuffled backwards. The hub of her rear wheel caught in my spokes. I bent to work it loose with my left hand, steadying the bike with my right.

The redhead had plenty of clearance—five feet at least—but she didn't swerve from the center of the trail. One weighted fist angled out and jabbed Arachne's shoulder, shoving her across the stone wall.

Arachne's weight and momentum pulled the bike along with her, pinching the fingers of my left hand between the wheels, dragging me and my bike behind her across the wall. The wheels broke apart with a wicked twist that flayed skin from my knuckles and ripped a scream from my throat.

I somersaulted twice and landed with a lung-emptying thud against a stump. Gasping, I watched Arachne's bike wedge itself between two saplings, pinning her beneath it.

But my bike, with Cheese Puff on board, rolled straight for the river.

Quiz Answer:
d, e, c, a, and *b* – in that order, and in my opinion.

The fire alarm almost always goes off
a) on cold and rainy days
b) in the middle of a test
c) when you're in the restroom
d) on a scheduled basis
e) when there's an actual fire

CHAPTER FIFTEEN

I scrambled around the stump and rode the embankment like a slide, feet up, hands fending off branches and brambles.

Cheese Puff's head swiveled and he looked back, eyes bugging. The bike bounded over a rock, ricocheted off a tree, wobbled across that scrap of beach.

Arachne groaned, then shrieked. "Cheese Puff."

The front wheel hit the water. The bike swayed. Yipping, Cheese Puff struggled out of his bungee-cord cage and clawed at the handlebars.

The back wheel rolled into the river. The bike toppled. Wheels spinning with the flow, it drifted deeper. Cheese Puff, tethered by his retractable leash to the handlebars, paddled with tiny paws to stay afloat.

"Hang on. I'm coming." I pushed off with my hands, lurched to my feet, staggered downstream through a maze of ankle-twisting rocks, got ahead of him, and belly flopped into the river.

Cheese Puff clawed his way up my arms to my shoulder, ripping my glasses from behind my left ear. "You're okay." I shoved my glasses into place and got my feet under me, water lapping at my thighs. "We're okay."

I wrapped my left hand in the leash to create a bit of slack and, with the numbed fingers of my right, scrabbled to unclip it from Cheese Puff's harness. The current shoved the bike deeper into the river, tightening the leash wrapped around my hand, jerking me along. Cheese Puff whined, claws catching in my hair. My feet slid on smooth rocks and slick sand, water reached my hips. I jerked at the leash, hoping to free it from the handlebars.

It didn't budge. Neither did the clip on Cheese Puff's harness.

Giving that up, I went for the harness itself, groping for the fasteners. Cheese Puff nipped at my fingers, perhaps thinking I was trying to push him off my shoulder.

"It's okay," I said, my voice more of a yelp.

The leash tightened around my left hand, dragging me another step away from shore. The current clasped my waist. I swayed and dipped in its ruthless embrace.

And then Arachne was in the water behind me, one hand clutching my sodden sweater, her strength surprising. She slapped my fumbling right hand from the harness and grappled with the leash clip. Cheese Puff pawed at my forehead, yelping.

"He's loose. I got him," Arachne panted.

From the corner of my eye I saw her face, tight with concentration. She draped him across her shoulder and clamped her teeth on his harness to hold him.

My left hand throbbed as the noose of the leash tightened even more. Arachne grunted and jerked hard on my sweater, swinging me about so she could get a grip on the cord below mine. I laced my right hand in beside hers and we leaned toward shore, drawing in the slack until one handlebar emerged and I seized it and dragged the bike to the bank.

"You poor little thing. You're freezing." Arachne kissed Cheese Puff's nose and stuffed him inside her black sweater, tucking it into her jeans to keep him from slipping out. Trembling, he peered out of the neckline at me.

I touched his nose. "We'll get you home and give you a treat as soon as we can." Yanking my sweater off, I wrung it out, then ran my hands down my legs to remove excess water from my jeans.

"Only my legs are wet." Arachne snatched up the cape she'd shed on the beach and offered it. "And I don't get cold easy."

I hesitated, but that Coho Wind sifted through my blouse and wicked heat from my skin. "Thanks." I wiped my glasses, then swaddled myself in the cape, got the bike onto its wheels, and peered around for the path of least resistance to the top of the embankment.

"That woman pushed me on purpose." Arachne dug her cell phone from her pocket. "We should call the cops."

For a moment, that seemed like a good idea, and then I let the tape run in my mind. The witnesses were a Goth teen and the woman who used to be married to the alleged perpetrator's live-in boyfriend—never mind that said boyfriend was scum and the alleged perpetrator might not yet be aware of that fact or of my severed relationship to said toxic algae bloom. She'd deny doing anything or say we were mistaken or it was an accident or I was jealous and out to get her. At best, she'd get a warning. At worst, a cop might charge me with endangering Cheese Puff by having him tethered to the bike. Even worse, the redhead might manage to arrange other accidents in the future.

I shivered and drew the cape tighter. "Let's get home first."

With me pulling and Arachne pushing, we got my bike to the top of the embankment, bucked it over the wall, and then did the same with hers. All four tires were still filled with air and, although my front wheel was bent, by cheating the handlebars to the right it rolled in an almost-straight line

I wrung out the jacket and stuff sack and piled them back in the basket with my sweater. When I tried to put him on that soggy cushion, Cheese Puff howled and shot his legs out to the sides as if he was a flying squirrel.

"I can carry him." Arachne slid him back into her sweater. I was about to argue that she might hit something and crash against the handlebars when Cheese Puff gave me a look that said he'd almost drowned thanks to *my* safety precautions and was thinking of transferring his allegiance permanently.

Although it took only about ten minutes, the ride back was teeth-chattering, goose-bump-inducing torture. I pedaled hard to get my blood moving, but the wind stripped away any core warmth I built up.

As we wheeled around the side of the condo, I spotted Mrs. Ballantine, wrapped in a pale gray cashmere coat, sitting on the bench in the little garden sheltered by the curving brick wall. Sun silvered her hair and glinted off the diamonds in her ears. As I rode closer, I saw her mouth drop. She planted her cane and wobbled to her feet. "Why are you wet? What happened?"

I braked beside her and glanced over my shoulder. Arachne was a hundred yards back. "We fell in the river."

"Fell in the river? How did you do that?"

"Just about the same way you fell on the sidewalk," I said through chattering teeth.

Her eyes widened and her gaze slid toward the unit opposite the garden. "That horrible woman?"

"Yeah."

"Well, it's time she was dealt with." Her matter-of-fact tone was the same one she used to tell me the proportions of gin and vermouth in her martinis.

Dealt with?

"Never you mind," she said as if she'd read my thoughts. "She'll be taken care of."

Not just dealt with, but taken care of. Yikes. Did that mean fitted for a pair of cement boots and taken on a one-way cruise? "It could have been an accident. I don't think you—"

"Never you mind," she repeated. Leaning on the cane, she tottered onto the path for a better view. "Is that the child you found in the shrubbery?"

"Right. Listen, about the rcd—"

Mrs. B flipped that aside with a snap of her wrist. "The one who's infatuated with myths and heroes and love and death?"

"Yes. But about the—"

Mrs. B clasped her hands. "I was the very same as a girl."

I was tempted to say I doubted she'd been the very same as anyone, but just then Arachne wheeled up and Cheese Puff peeked out of her sweater.

"The little prince was with you?" Mrs. B shot a lethal glare at Jake's condo. "He went into the river too?"

"Yes, but Arachne saved us." I nodded to the girl. "This is my neighbor, Mrs. Ballantine, head of the Cheese Puff Care and Comfort Committee."

"I'm delighted to meet you." Mrs. B offered a pale and slender hand that showcased a diamond and sapphire ring worth more than the equity in my condo. A matching bracelet and a jeweled watch encircled her wrist.

Arachne's eyes widened and she touched Mrs. B's hand with her fingertips. "It's nice to meet you," she said in an awe-filled voice. "My real name is Allison."

131

Mrs. B withdrew her hand and brushed Allison's hair from her eyes and up off her forehead. "Would you prefer I call you that, dear?"

Arachne glanced at me, then nodded. "Yes, please."

"Then Allison it is," Mrs. B decreed. "Although I may slip and call you 'Vera.' You remind me of a friend from my showgirl days; she was a heart-stopper and you're every bit as beautiful."

Allison blinked and Mrs. B's hand dropped to Cheese Puff's head. "Let's get the little guy inside before he catches a cold. I'll heat up some dog food."

Seizing her cane, she headed for her door in a three-beat march calling over her shoulder, "I have some imported hot chocolate. I'll get the kettle on. You get changed."

"She's like a queen," Allison whispered. "A snow queen."

A monarch of the mob, I thought as I stood on a pedal and propelled myself to the parking lot. We rolled under the canopy and swung off as Myra Bancroft came toward us, platinum hair yanked back into a bun so tight her eyes slanted, arms wrapped around a box brimming with shimmery lingerie. She gave me a Medusa-like glare and I responded with a prom-court fingertip flutter and bumped my bike up the steps and inside with Allison right behind.

"And that was a witch." Allison leaned her bike beside mine against the futon, untucked her sweater, and set Cheese Puff on the floor. "*Another* witch." She peered at me from beneath her fringe of hair. "You need a spell to get them to back off."

I conjured up a mental image of Iz. She claimed to practice witchcraft. Wouldn't she enjoy it if I came begging for a protective spell? And wouldn't kids at school—not to mention teachers and administrators—

132

have a thousand questions and comments if word got around that I agreed with Arachne's assessment of my neighbors and her suggested course of action? I forced a laugh that sounded like a cat about to kack up a hairball and moved on. "Take off your shoes and socks and set them by the heat vent in the kitchen."

I draped her cape over a chair and dug out a couple of treats for Cheese Puff. "I've got sweat pants and spare slippers upstairs." A gift from Iz, they were black and furry and had cat faces, complete with whiskers, on the toes.

Trembling from cold and a receding tide of adrenalin, I dragged myself upstairs, tossed the sweats and slippers over the banister, then peeled off my soggy clothes and dumped them in the bathtub. My legs were blotched red and purple and rippled with goose bumps. After turning on the ceiling heat lamp, I rubbed my skin with a bath towel, and used the hair dryer alternately on my thighs, toes, and hair. Cheese Puff nudged the door open and I turned the dryer on him until his hair fluffed out so far he appeared twice his normal size.

The heat lamp glowed a dull red and the top of my head blazed, but my heart felt cold and still. If the bicycle had rolled another few feet into the river, Cheese Puff might have been swept away.

I scooped him into my arms and pressed him against my chest, his hair silky against my skin. "What would I do without you?"

He licked my chin and snuggled against my neck. My heart seemed to thaw and I felt it beat in my fingertips, hands, arms, and throat. Then it pounded in my temples. That woman! That horrible woman! She could have killed us all.

Mrs. B was right. Something had to be done. But what? Revenge would be sweet, but could I live with a mob hit on my conscience?

133

Quiz Answer:
Let's hope it's *e*.

If you arrive late at a school you should
a) blame the secretary for giving you bad directions
b) claim you couldn't find a parking spot
c) insist your alarm didn't go off
d) say you had a flat tire
e) take responsibility, apologize, and move on

CHAPTER SIXTEEN

Except for trotting Cheese Puff around the complex—while keeping a wary eye out for Jake's redhead—and making a pizza run for Mrs. B, I buckled down for the next two days. By Sunday evening I was caught up on work for my courses and, with the help of materials Susan e-mailed, had prepared with a week's lesson plans for Henry Stoddard's students. When I presented myself before Big Chill on Monday morning, I felt almost ready to teach about the Renaissance.

"Did you have a nice holiday?" I asked.

"Right up until 6:15," she grumbled, shoving a sub form at me. "Jerome's at a conference and Jessica was supposed to cover an early meeting, but she must have overslept."

My mind generated a hot and sweaty image of Jessica and Jake doing everything *but* sleeping.

"Had to call for an administrative sub." Big Chill scrunched her face as if she'd been force-fed a spoonful of castor oil. "Lord knows who we'll get. And we'll have to pay even if Jessica shows in the next two minutes." She tore the paperwork from my hands and slapped it on the desk.

Leaving Big Chill fuming, I scuttled into the mailroom to pick up the week's bulletin of activities and assorted memos, then darted to the attendance office for new roll sheets. From there I hit the copy room and found just one person ahead of me—Aston Marsden copying a recipe for wolverine chili. Repressing a shudder, I slid the ten pages of my packet into the machine, set it to copy back-to-back, collate, and staple 170 copies, crossed my fingers, and pushed "start."

Perhaps as a reward for my ordeal in the river, the machine didn't jam, overheat, or mangle my originals.

Lugging my ten-pounds of worksheets, I dropped off my lunch—leftover pizza with feta cheese, spinach, and tomatoes—in the teachers' room refrigerator, and headed to my next destination.

Stoddard's room was still off limits and rumor had it that condition wouldn't change soon. Everyone agreed that putting students in a room where a man died was a recipe for disaster, so corollary rumors had the space becoming a teachers' planning room or conference area. In the meantime, his students shuttled to temporary classrooms, and I shuttled with them—if the definition of shuttling is beating feet at a dead run.

I started the day at the far end of the math wing, trucked to the rear of the media center, then hurtled downstairs and across the width of the school to the photography classroom. After lunch I careened from a health room back up to the math wing with fifth period off for planning.

Susan—who seemed to do as much problem-solving as she did teaching—had choreographed a group of muscular upperclassmen with free periods to roll a cart of textbooks to appropriate destinations, but I lived in fear they'd be diverted or decide to skip out and leave me shoving the cart. In the fine tradition of carts everywhere, it had one sticky wheel and a brake that keep slipping to the "on" position.

Plowing through clusters of shuffling students, I reached my first room, dropped the copies and my briefcase on a chair, and cleared an area on a front table littered with protractors, rulers, and worksheets.

Like many other creatures, teachers tend to be territorial and few are delighted about sharing a room. So I was careful to clear no more space than I absolutely needed, to use only my own dry erase markers, and to wipe out all traces of what I'd written on the board before I left.

While I waited for the computer to boot up, I skimmed the weekly bulletin. Like many schools, this had daily televised announcements, but most kids zoned out or used the time to goof off. To increase awareness and grade point averages, I'd pondered weekly quizzes on school-related events.

With that in mind, I dug in my briefcase for a marker and found the bright yellow pen Josh had gathered up with the atlases the day I found Stoddard's body. Yanking off the cap, I drew the felt tip across a notation about spring sports. It left not a trace of a mark.

"Damn."

Stoddard's pen was as defunct as he was.

I glanced around for a trash can, didn't spot one, noted that I had only five minutes to load my presentation into the computer, and tossed the pen back in my briefcase. No time to dawdle. I'd learned the hard way that sophomores are a tough audience. And sophomores just back from a five-day vacation would be even tougher. I hauled in a few cleansing breaths and mentally went to my happy place—an all-you-can-eat buffet line featuring

137

jumbo cashews, fruity rum drinks, hot artichoke dip, linguine with pesto sauce, coconut shrimp, and chocolate mousse. Salivating, I ran through my computerized slide show, then planted myself beside the door with what I suspected looked like an undertaker's idea of a smile.

Carpooling home from class in Portland that night, I watched through bleary eyes as a relentless wind ripped the final clouds of the latest storm system to tatters. A bulging moon shouldered its way above the fray and lit a path along the rippling black water of the Columbia. I shivered, remembering the deadly embrace of that cold current.

After my initial attempts to persuade Mrs. B not to "take care of" the redhead, I'd tried to establish a head-in-the-sand distance from the problem. But desire for revenge and anxiety about the shape of that reprisal tumbled through my mind, locked like yin and yang inside their circle. The result was paralyzing exhaustion.

When I reached the condo, I longed to crawl into bed and pull the puffy comforter over my head, but Cheese Puff did the full-bladder dance beside the door. With a sigh, I belted him into his harness, and stuffed a plastic bag in my pocket along with a small canister of pepper spray.

I waved at Trash Guy III when he popped from behind the bins in his blue tarp, and set out downstream, away from Jake's condo and along a well-lit path that skirted another condo complex and a cluster of shops and restaurants. Here and there the trail spread like an apron to make space for benches or picnic tables.

Even though it was almost 10:30, there were enough people out that I felt secure. Still, the bank was steep here and there was no shelf of beach to give me purchase in case the rampaging redhead struck again, so I hugged the inside edge of the trail and kept my ears tuned for the sound of pounding feet.

I set a fast pace, on the lazy side of a trot, to the border of a downriver park and turned around. That made the round trip a full mile—enough to loosen my muscles, but not so much that I'd be too geared up to sleep. As we approached the condo complex, I slowed to give Cheese Puff time to sniff shrubbery and check his pee-mail.

Ahead of me, moonlight glimmered on the water and frosted a row of rotting pilings that stretched ten yards into the current. They looked like the masts of a spectral ship rising from the river. A wisp of cloud feathered the moonlight and a chill slithered down my spine.

I glanced around, but saw only a couple strolling hand-in-hand well ahead of me. I hauled in a calming breath; the air was clean and damp with a faint aroma of fried fish that made my mouth water. "You had a muffin during the class break," I reminded myself.

Cheese Puff looked up from sprinkling an azalea, nose twitching. "But it was a bran muffin," I clarified. "So we deserve a treat when we get home."

At the word "treat" he lowered his rear leg and dug in with his front feet, tugging at the leash, towing me toward that magic canister full of dog cookies. I envied his excitement over a chunk of dried . . . something or other. I'd never read the list of ingredients. I should compare brands and nutritional values. A responsible dog owner would. Maybe over Christmas break.

Cheese Puff tugged harder and I picked up the pace. Ah to be so pleased and excited by such a small thing. I tried to imagine what kind of treat would make me run and decided food alone wouldn't do it. A chocolate truffle wrapped in a thousand-dollar bill, now, that might—

Cheese Puff made a tight right and stopped at the edge of the trail, lips drawn back, ruff rising, tail low and quivering.

I stumbled to a halt, fingered my pepper spray, and peered around. No one behind me and only that same couple ahead. Empty benches to my left, and a gray wedge of shadow under the lip of the steep bank. "What is it?"

Cheese Puff growled and lunged toward the river.

"No." Left-handed I reeled him back, remembering the article I'd read about coyotes making their way into the city along streams and greenbelts, devouring cats and small dogs as they went. "Come."

He ignored the command, growled again.

Using both hands, I reeled in the rest of the leash. "Come on, coyote bait." I jerked him off the ground and pressed him tight against my chest. He squirmed around to keep watch on the river, still growling, body stiff.

I stared into that wedge of shadow. Saw nothing. Heard nothing. Walking backwards, I retreated toward the condo complex. "What do you see?"

Cheese Puff wrinkled his lips, and shook his head the way he did when he didn't like the food he was offered. Mrs. B had thought that routine was cute and indicated his good taste. Until he scorned beluga caviar.

"What is it? A dead gull? A fish?"

He growled again.

I spotted a pale gleam and a slow turning movement out on the water. There was something caught against the pilings. Something white. Something with a hand.

Quiz Answer:
e – the best answer
b, c, d – might work once each
a – the sure way to burn your bridges

According to some students, a perfect day for a sub involves
a) sending half the class to the discipline office
b) marking the other half absent
c) finding a box of chocolates in the teachers' lounge
d) leaving a long note filled with specific names and offenses
e) handing out extra homework

CHAPTER SEVENTEEN

A scream tearing at my throat, I ran, Cheese Puff squeezed against my chest. Without slowing, I sped past the darker path that branched off to the rear of the condo unit and pounded along the riverfront trail until Mrs. Ballantine's deck loomed above me.

A security light flickered on as I bolted up the stepping stones among rose bushes screening the deck supports. I mounted the steps, shoved through the gate in the railing, and skated across planks beaded with water. A second light flashed on, one I knew was controlled by a switch in the living room beside the sliding glass door. The curtain twitched and I caught a glimpse of feathery white hair. Then a latch clicked, the door rolled wide, and I stumbled into warmth and light.

Cheese Puff whimpered and pawed at my cheek. I realized my fingers had dug deep into his flanks. "I'm sorry, sweetie." I thrust him at Mrs. B who gathered him against a fuzzy green bathrobe.

"Are you okay, dear?" She pinched at my clothing. "Did you go in the river again?"

"No." Flexing throbbing fingers, I staggered to a deep red loveseat and sank into its plushy cushions. "But someone else did."

"How dreadful." Mrs. B's eyes widened and she put her fingers to her lips. "Who is it?"

"I—" An image of Jake's redheaded friend bloomed in my brain and a Richter-scale tremor shook my core. Was Mrs. B feigning surprise and lack of knowledge? Had she had the redhead "dealt with"? I studied her, reminding myself she'd been a showgirl, been married to Marco, was probably an expert at counterfeiting emotions, especially shocked innocence. "I don't know who it is."

She squinted at me for a second, then hobbled to a brown and gold striped wing chair. "You didn't see that person fall in?"

Did she want to know how much I'd witnessed? Because she might need to have me dealt with too? I crossed my arms to squelch a shiver. "All I saw was something white in the water. It had a hand."

My words emerged in a squeaky rush. Did that sound like a lie? I took a breath. "Cheese Puff growled. Otherwise I never would have noticed. It's—the body is mostly underwater." I pointed toward the downstream end of the complex. "Up against the pilings."

She nodded, stood, and retrieved the cordless phone from the table beside her favorite chair. "You'd better call the police. I'll get the brandy."

I took the phone in a trembling hand. Surely if Mrs. B was responsible for this crime she'd find some excuse to kill time, hoping the current would work the body loose and carry it away. Glass clinked on glass and I watched her pour generous tots of expensive brandy. She capped the bottle and replaced it on the shelf—neat and efficient

142

as always. Wouldn't she have made sure the body was disposed of far from here? My tight muscles loosened just a bit. Of course she would have.

I punched 911 and accepted the brandy snifter. But I didn't have more than a sip. A woman who discovers two bodies within two weeks needs all her limited wits about her when the cops come calling.

Wrapped in quilts, with Cheese Puff tucked between us, Mrs. B and I sat in a swing on her deck and watched a patrol boat spotlight the pilings as two divers freed the body. We weren't the only spectators. Every deck and balcony was crowded and whenever the breeze shifted I caught whiffs of popcorn, beer, or hot chocolate. As if this was New Year's Eve.

"Do you suppose it's some poor soul who jumped from a bridge?" Mrs. B mused.

Was that a genuine question or an attempt to divert my suspicious mind? I shuddered and pulled the quilt tighter around my shoulders. Had the redhead been dumped from a bridge? While she was still alive?

Stop it, I ordered myself. You don't know that's the redhead. You don't even know if it's a woman. Maybe it's some poor homeless man. One of the Trash Guys. Or maybe it's someone like Nelson who painted himself into a financial corner and couldn't face the consequences.

I pondered walking down on the trail and looking up. If the redhead was on her deck with Jake, then Mrs. B was harmless. But if Jake was alone—

"Looks like they got . . . it," Mrs. B said.

I heard no trace of anxiety in her voice. Either she hadn't been involved in this person's demise or this was an Academy Award performance.

She'd supplied us each with a pair of binoculars and, although I felt like a ghoul, I lifted mine when the divers brought the body alongside the boat and hoisted it aboard. Adjusting the focus, I strained my eyes. The body, shoeless, wore a long-sleeved blue dress. A woman. I sucked in a sharp breath, leaned away from Mrs. B, and tweedled with the focus knob again.

A mat of hair covered the face, but it wasn't long and it wasn't red. Not Jake's friend. I let out a long breath, lowered the binoculars, and eased back toward the center of the swing.

Mrs. B patted my arm. "You're still shivering, dear. Are you certain you don't want more brandy? The policeman who took the report didn't say they'd want to talk with you again."

"No, no more brandy, thank you. I've got to get home to bed. " I stood, folded my blanket, and carried it inside, almost skipping with relief. The redhead wasn't in the river. Mrs. B hadn't dealt with her.

"Yet," pointed out that little voice in my brain, always a stickler for detail.

That three-letter word insured that sleep, like my dream of squeezing into a size 6, eluded me.

So, tail dragging, I slumped into school at 7:02 the next morning. Protocol dictated that I check in with Big Chill, but as I approached her office I heard her speaking in a voice with enough acid to etch glass. "I don't have time for stupid questions. Jessica isn't here AGAIN. And If I get stuck with the same administrative sub they sent yesterday I'll retire before lunch."

I reversed course, ducking into the mailroom and snatching up my attendance sheets without drawing her wrath. Or so I thought until second period when the classroom phone rang.

"I don't need this stress," Big Chill seethed. "I could retire. I *should* retire. Right this minute."

I gulped air. "I'm sorry I didn't check in. But you were bus—"

"He wants to see you ten minutes ago."

Another swallow. My throat burned. "Mr. Morrow?"

"No! That detective. Atweed. Or whatever he calls himself."

My heart swelled against my windpipe and the kettle drum in my brain started thumping Atwell's theme song. "Why?"

"I don't know. He wouldn't say," Big Chill's frustrated tone implied that she'd attempted to pry that information from him, gotten nowhere, and would mete out punishment in time. "He's cooling his jets in the conference room while I find someone to cover for you. Officious little man. Acts like he's my boss. I wouldn't work for him if he was the last—"

She hung up in mid rant and, stomach flipping, I replaced the receiver. What did Atwell want now?

Sixty eyes stared at me instead of at their textbooks or Renaissance packets and I knew that sixty ears had been listening. I'd uttered darn few words, but thirty reality-TV-fueled teenage brains would explode the syllables into a conflict-filled script before I got downstairs. "In a few minutes I'm going down to the office," I announced. "While I'm gone, keep working on your packets. I'll be back soon."

They nodded, but exchanged "yeah, right" glances from the edges of their eyes. For once I knew what they were thinking. This morning Allison had attached herself to my side as I trekked to my first classroom. "Everyone's saying that you were the one who found Mr. Stoddard. Is that true?"

I'd considered evasive action, then nodded.

"Why didn't you tell me?" she'd wailed. "I pulled you out of the river. I thought we were friends."

145

That's how friendship is measured?

"The police didn't want me to talk about it," I said, trying to remember if Atwell had ordered me to keep my lips zipped and deciding we'd discuss the definition and boundaries of friendship at some future date.

"Yeah, cops do that," she said as if she'd had many brushes with the law. "But you didn't kill him, did you?"

I'd halted and brushed back her bangs so I could look into her eyes. To my dismay, they'd been dark with doubt, the green flecks almost invisible. "Of course not."

The doubt faded, the green flecks glowed like emeralds, and she'd grinned. "I knew it. Some kids say you did and some say if you didn't you should have because he was a total jerk. But I told them you would never because you love your dog so much and even if someone was totally cruel you wouldn't hurt them back— like that witch that pushed Cheese Puff in the river."

While I processed that, she'd peeled off and joined a group of girls dressed in—what else?—black.

Maybe, I thought as I straightened the materials on the cart, if Atwell accused me of killing Stoddard, I'd call Allison for a testimonial.

After a quick circuit of the room in a vain attempt to get kids focused on their work, I wrote and printed out a note for whomever Big Chill found to cover for me. I taped two copies to the textbook cart, put one on the table, and stuck another in my briefcase to cover my butt—a reflexive action I'd learned in the radio business. Five long minutes passed before Aston Marsden appeared carrying a couple of rocks, a plastic bag of wood shavings, and a spray bottle of clear liquid. He smelled of smoke and perspiration. "I'm practicing starting a fire with flint," he explained. "In the rain."

A mop-haired tough-guy wannabe by the door rolled his eyes and plucked a cigarette lighter from his backpack.

No. No. No.

I snatched it from him. He frowned and made a "give it back" gesture, but I mouthed the magic words "I'll call security," and he ducked his head and went back to doodling chickens juggling chainsaws.

"I'll be back as soon as I can." I tucked the lighter in my pocket and picked up my briefcase. "They're working on their packets. At the end of the period they should put the textbooks on the cart and someone will roll it to the next class."

"No sweat." Aston dumped his gear on the table, covering my note.

Mop-head laughed and mimed applying antiperspirant. Aston, who was building a pile of shavings, didn't seem to notice.

When I got downstairs, Big Chill was doing sentry duty, pacing in front of the administrative offices. "Jerry's concerned because this Atwedge is back again to talk with you."

I didn't blame him. Principal Morrow was responsible for the welfare of 1500 kids. But if he interpreted Atwell's demand for more quality time with me the wrong way, and if he bounced me from the school, the concept of presumption of innocence wouldn't stand a chance against rumor and innuendo. I'd have a shadow over my career the size of Rhode Island.

"I'm sure it's just regular police procedure," I told Big Chill in a trembling voice. "They haven't made an arrest so they're going back over everything."

I peered into her tired eyes. If I could convince her, she'd convince Jerome Morrow. "All I did was find the body," I said in the firmest voice I could manage. (For the record, about as firm as your average bowl of pudding.) "I didn't kill Henry Stoddard."

147

"Of course you didn't," Big Chill said with a snort. "You didn't work with him long enough to be on killing terms."

Talk about back-handed support. Picture *that* statement on a resume.

"Jerry never does anything rash." She leaned close and whispered, "Especially anything that might make someone think about hiring a lawyer."

She dusted her hands together, advice given, subject closed. "I've got a good mind to tell this Atweird to stop doing his job on our dime," she fumed in a loud voice. "Waltzing in whenever he feels like it, expecting me to drop everything and rearrange schedules to suit him."

I nodded, waiting for her battery to run down. It took a few minutes and her diatribe covered the years she'd been with the district (thirty), the sick hours she'd accumulated that she ought to take (hundreds), the fact that she could retire whenever she felt like it (and do just fine on her pension, thank you very much) but Mr. Morrow needed her so she put up with crap like this (day in and day out without a single complaint) for his sake.

It was almost refreshing when Atwell greeted me with a grunt and then silence. He let that play out as I took the same seat I'd sweated in a dozen days earlier. Telling myself that detectives in books always used silence as an interrogation strategy didn't keep me cooler and dryer.

Atwell switched on his tape recorder and slipped a black pen from his pocket. It had been gnawed at so often that one end was gray and flattened out like a tongue depressor. I wondered what his dentist thought of this habit and whether he'd need his teeth capped before he closed this case. He opened a little spiral notebook and cleared his throat, but said nothing.

He was silent for so long that, pathetic as this sounds, I was daydreaming about my lunch—tomato soup, cheese, crackers, and a carrot—when he finally spoke. "Do you find it as odd as I do that there have been two murders in the past two weeks and both times you discovered the victim?"

Even if I knew anything about the laws of chance, this wasn't the place to cite them. And mentioning that this had never happened to me before was an explanation/excuse more pathetic than my lunch. I settled for a shrug.

"And do you find it as odd as I do that you knew both victims?"

I flinched as if he'd dropped a noose around my neck. The body in the river was someone I knew? My mind popped up an image of it hoisted aboard the boat last night. I hadn't seen the woman's face. But it *had* been a woman.

Atwell popped his knuckles. "And do you find it extremely odd that you fought with both victims shortly before they died?"

That imaginary rope tightened across my trachea.

Fought? I hadn't fought with Henry Stoddard. He'd shoved me and I'd walked away. But if Atwell was using the word "fought" to cover that incident, then I'd also fought with—

Quiz Answer
f – all of the above plus giving a pop quiz

A sub's best friend is
a) the school payroll clerk
b) almost anyone who's been there/done that and
  understands
c) her masseuse
d) the clerk at the liquor store
e) the teacher who assigns a video she hasn't seen
  before

CHAPTER EIGHTEEN

Jessica Flint!

Her name lit up my mind like a flashing neon sign.

"That was Jessica Flint they pulled from the river," Atwell said in a smug tone.

And she was murdered, or Atwell wouldn't be delivering the news. I remembered the mat of hair covering the face of the woman caught against the piling, the bare feet, the blue dress. I'd seen her wearing a blue dress, maybe that same one, in late October. It had French cuffs, a high collar, and a matching belt cinched tight around her narrow waist.

I hadn't liked her much, but being liked wasn't part of her job description, and no one deserved to be killed, dumped in the river, then fished out while strangers gawked and hoisted a few. I wondered whether she'd drowned or been dead before the current took her.

I chewed at my lower lip. Ask those questions and the suspect meter needle might swing closer to my name.

"You knew her." Atwell leaned toward me. "Is that correct?"

"Yes." Was her murder linked to Henry Stoddard's? Had she killed him, found the information he'd hidden, attempted to use it, and been killed by her intended victim? Or had she been working with someone—the other half of that "we" she'd mentioned? And had that someone turned on her?

I felt cold and small and frightened and wanted to blurt out everything. But what did I have to blurt? The theory, based on gossip and rumor, that Henry Stoddard was a blackmailer. Atwell might laugh and tell me to stop wasting his time. He might suspect me of trying to cast blame elsewhere. Worse yet, he might accuse me of withholding evidence and charge me with something. Dithering, I picked at the cuticle on my thumb.

"Tell me again," Atwell ordered, "about the fight you and Assistant Principal Flint had outside Henry Stoddard's room the day you found his body."

Even though I'd seen this coming, sirens went off in my brain. Danger. Proceed with caution.

I sat up straight and met his gaze. "I never described it as a fight. It was more of a . . . discussion." I tried what I hoped was a casual flip of my wrist. "I explained that I was trying to keep her from contaminating the crime scene."

"Right. I forgot that you were helping our overworked crime scene technicians." He smiled like a crocodile spotting a small furry animal struggling in an eddy. "She shoved you for doing your civic duty."

Rage roiled in my gut, but I tightened my muscles and held it back. "That was my intention. And she *didn't* shove me."

"She didn't?"

"No. She kind of bumped me with her hip."

151

He rubbed a patch of stubble along the blade of his jaw. "Have you noticed that our discussions of what did and didn't happen always disintegrate into a dialogue about the definitions of verbs?"

I let that bit of bait stay on the trigger of his trap. "She didn't shove me." I folded my arms across my chest. "We didn't fight."

"Did you ever see her in an argument with another staff member?"

I squirmed, remembered hearing she'd chewed out Aston about the stench of his buckskins and unloaded on Doug for being two minutes late to a staff meeting. But Atwell asked me what I'd seen. "No. I never saw that."

Atwell rolled his eyes, then made another note. "When did you see her last?"

I thought back, remembered the car that picked up Jake on Friday. Had it been Jessica's? Should I mention it if I wasn't certain? Would he think I was making it up? Better stick to what I knew for sure. "Last Monday."

"Here? At school?"

"Yes. I saw her in the hallway." I hesitated. Telling him she came to my condo would open a speculative, hearsay-evidence-crammed can of worms. But not telling could set me up for more trouble. People saw us there. Jake, for one.

My gut clenched like a fist. If Atwell learned I'd introduced Jessica to my ex-husband he might assume I had a motive to kill her—jealousy.

As if. I wanted Jake back the way I wanted swine flu or an IRS audit.

I felt like I was again on the edge of a swamp filled with sinkholes, quicksand, and unknown perils. Every step took me farther from firm, safe ground, from my dull, depressing, downsized, but relatively stable excuse for a life. If I made it back to firm ground, I'd be grateful for every minute spent cleaning the oven, dusting behind pictures, or reorganizing my sock drawer.

But I couldn't leave Jake out of the story. Because, again, there was a witness—one of the versions of Trash Guy.

I took a deep breath and plunged into the swamp. "I also saw her later. At my condo."

Atwell raised those jutting brows. "Oh?"

The word hung there, fat and round, like the Hindenburg seconds before it burst into flames.

He examined his pen, seemed to find a spot less gnawed than others, and marked it with his index finger. "Was that a social visit?"

"No." I sucked in another breath and told him how Jessica set the meeting but hadn't been in her office, how I waited and then left, how she'd been parked in my spot when I got home, and that she wanted to know what I took from Henry Stoddard's room besides the atlases.

Atwell's brows crept higher, like twin caterpillars inching away from rising water. "And what was your answer?"

"That I didn't take a thing except the books." Heart pounding, I spilled more of my story. "I asked her what she was looking for, what was missing, and she said, 'That's what we're trying to find out.' I thought, because she said 'we,' that maybe she was working with Mr. Morrow. Or with you."

Atwell blew air through his lips and shook his head just a millimeter. "What else did she say?"

Editing out Jessica's not-so-veiled threats, I gave him most of the rest. "If I had something that belonged to Henry Stoddard I'd better give it to her."

"And did you? Do you?"

I spread my hands. "No. I took only the atlases from his room."

He rolled his eyes. "That's right, Miss Don't-contaminate-the-crime-scene walked off with those, didn't she?"

I felt myself flush, bit the edge of my tongue.

He pinched the knob of his chin. "What do you think Jessica Flint was looking for?"

"I don't know." And I didn't, not exactly. But if gossip was accurate, and if someone had killed Stoddard because he was a blackmailer, and if the murders were linked, then I had an obligation to tell Atwell. Didn't I? No matter what he thought of my motives for doing so? No matter how many innocent people he grilled to get at their secrets?

As if he could sense my indecision, Atwell leaned closer. "You have no idea at all?"

I gave my tongue a break and chewed on the inside of my cheek. Let's say I told him about the rumors. He'd want me to name names. "Do it," that voice in my head insisted. "You can't take care of everyone else."

A trickle of sweat ran behind my right ear. I slipped my hand into my pocket for a tissue and felt Mop-head's lighter.

"Not even a guess?" Atwell prompted.

"Just rumors," I muttered, fingering the ridged wheel, thinking of Aston and his flint and wood shavings, of the fire I was about to start. "That's all. Rumors."

"Tell me about those rumors," he ordered.

I hesitated for two more seconds.

And then I did.

Atwell's expression remained bland—as if I was telling him about how to make modeling dough or steam off wallpaper instead of how Stoddard was suspected of dealing in dirt—but his lips twitched into a faint but satisfied smile and his pen tapped his notebook like he was beating out a drum solo for some dope-fueled rock

154

group from the late 60s. The beat set off a sympathetic throbbing in my bladder and I crossed my legs.

"Who did you hear those rumors from?"

"Lots of people," I equivocated. "The teachers I eat lunch with. Others."

He pointed at the tape recorder. "Names."

"It could all be myth, legend."

"Names."

"You won't tell them I told you, will you?"

He rolled his eyes and snarled. "Names."

Not sure whether that eye roll meant he would or wouldn't, but getting the message that his patience was as thin as the profit margin for the last guy in on a pyramid scheme, I reeled off a few names. Aston because I figured he could fend for himself, Susan because I figured she had nothing to hide or to fear, Gertrude because she'd driven to Henry Stoddard's house claiming simple curiosity, Doug because of the way his voice squeaked with what I took for fear, and Brenda because she seemed edgy and the thought of that eel Alfredo still made me gag.

"Anyone else?"

I shook my head. "That's all I can think of right now."

"You've got my card. Let me know if you 'remember' any more."

"I will."

He rolled his eyes once more as if to say I was about as trustworthy as the CEO of a bogus hedge fund, then told me not to discuss any of this with anyone and pointed to the door.

I scuttled out and was halfway to my classroom when I realized he'd sidetracked the interview before I told him about introducing Jake and Jessica.

Ducking into a ladies room, I took care of business while I considered whether I should go back and dump that tidbit in his lap. Jake was many things—a tomcat, a con man, a chronic liar—but I couldn't see him as a killer. I especially couldn't see him killing a woman he appeared to be lining up for his next string of free lunches. And then there was the jealousy card I knew Atwell would play to try to fit the square peg with my name into the round hole labeled "killer."

The bell rang, making up my mind for me. I ran, briefcase slamming against my leg, to my third-period class.

Aston wasn't in the teachers' room for lunch.

"Probably out on the grounds hunting down a squirrel with a slingshot," Doug joked. "Or digging up a mole with a pointed stick."

Cold, greasy guilt filled my gut. The soup I'd slurped down turned to acid and the cheese and carrot to lumps of lead. I knew exactly where Aston was—across that conference room table from Detective Atwell. And I knew the others would be next.

"Aston's so serious about recreating the past I think he's missing out on living in the present." Susan stabbed her fork into what looked like soggy turkey hash with a hint of gangrene around the edges. To my relief, she pushed the container aside and opened a bag of peanut-butter-filled pretzels with trembling fingers. Her skin was pasty, her eyes dull, and her cheeks sunken. Strain from her marriage? Or was she coming down with something?

"He doesn't have other interests and he doesn't date." She gave me a glance that could have been an attempt to size me up as mate material for him, or an apology for mentioning Aston's lack of assignations given that I had none of my own. "I worry about him."

I was worried about Aston, too—worried about how he'd react to Atwell's questions, and how Atwell would react to him. Aston, in role-playing mode, was a man of action capable of taking the law into his own hands. And Aston was almost always in role-playing mode.

But if I shared my concerns, everyone would know who was responsible for opening the Stoddard-as-blackmailer can of worms. They might pretend to understand the position I'd been in when I coughed up their names, but they'd still think I ratted them out. The bottom line was clear: If they found out, I could never eat lunch in this room again.

Quiz Answer:
a – but I'll accept arguments in favor of other choices

If a teacher's room looks like the aftermath of a tornado, the sub should
a) clean it up
b) mention it to the teacher
c) make jokes about it to others
d) complain to the principal
e) do and say nothing

CHAPTER NINETEEN

By the time I got home I was thoroughly depressed about the bleak state of my future. Rocking Cheese Puff while he licked my chin didn't lift my sagging spirits. Neither did wolfing down a bowl of French vanilla ice cream with caramel sauce and chopped nuts. And my mood plummeted farther into Dumpsville when I finally got the nerve to push the button on the answering machine and heard Iz's voice.

"The hotel isn't included in my fee for the presentation so I'll be staying with you."

"Note the lack of 'may I?' in that sentence," I said to Cheese Puff.

"I can't get any rest on that tortilla you call a futon, so I'll use your room. Put on clean sheets and vacuum up the dog hair so I don't sneeze my head off."

I smiled, imagining Iz's magenta Mohawked head bouncing down the stairs after a ferocious sneeze.

"And buy some chocolate I can eat."

I glanced at the candy dish I hadn't gotten around to filling since she demolished its contents nearly two weeks ago. "Nah." I bounced Cheese Puff onto my shoulder. "I'll clean the bedroom, but that's as far as I go—no special treats for her. Iz is like a plague of locust. She eats anything in her path."

But I'd give up my bed. After all, she'd made a lot of sacrifices for me when we were kids and it was easier than listening to her complain.

I wandered into the kitchen, got out my bottle of cheap rum, ascertained that there was nothing to mix it with except soy milk or coffee, and went to visit Mrs. B and her liquor cabinet.

"The TV says that woman in the river was the assistant principal at the school where you're working," she said as she let me in.

"Unfortunately." I set Cheese Puff on the wing chair and kept going to the kitchen.

She trailed behind. "And isn't that where a teacher was killed before Thanksgiving?"

"Even more unfortunately." A bottle of gin as big around as one of my thighs hunkered at the front of the cabinet. Standing on tiptoe, I spotted the rum behind it.

"You never told me that, dear."

I hadn't. Not intentionally. We hadn't crossed paths until she took her fall, and that was four days after I discovered Henry Stoddard's body. Then there had been so much drama with Allison, Jake and Myra, the plunge into the river, and finding the body I now knew was Jessica's.

"You know you can tell me anything, don't you, dear?" She reached past me, grasped the gin, and lowered it to the counter. "After the life I led, I'm not easily shocked or offended."

I nodded, wondering if that life included helping her husband rub out the competition.

"Did you know that teacher?" She uncapped the gin.

159

I seized the rum bottle with a shaking hand. "To know him was to loathe him." The cap fought my numb fingers.

"Let me do that." Mrs. B laid a hand on my arm. "You're twitching like a pole dancer with a yeast infection. What's wrong?"

"Nothing."

She cocked her head and studied me. "Well, it's a pretty weighty nothing. Sit down. I'll make you a drink."

While she mixed, I dropped onto a pale blue fainting couch and stared out at the river. 'What else did they say on the news? About that woman?"

"Just what I told you. They don't know much besides her name and where she worked, but they repeat that every half hour and remind us to watch at five or six or whenever." She hobbled to my chair, handed me a tall blue-green concoction, and pinned me with a steely stare. "Is she part of the nothing that isn't bothering you?"

I shrugged and took a long swallow. It was orangy and tangy with a powerful finish. Heat pulsed down my arms and legs.

"If you want to stew in it alone, I can't make you share." She sighed and picked up a glass from the table beside her favorite chair, plucked the olive from the bottom and popped it in her mouth, then went for a refill with Cheese Puff at her heels. "But I hate to see you all worked up. You've become like a daughter to me, and I want to help if I can."

"I know. And I appreciate that—and all you've done for Cheese Puff."

I drank more, felt my toes and fingers tingle. I *was* tired of stewing in it alone, but I was afraid she might decide that my problems should be "dealt with." Maybe if I asked for advice, not help. Maybe if I made it clear I'd handle things myself.

Mrs. B set a bowl of jumbo cashews on the table beside me, limped to her chair, sat, and patted her lap in invitation to Cheese Puff.

I eyed her black wool slacks and royal blue sweater as I nibbled a cashew the size of my pinkie. "I haven't brushed him for a week. You'll be covered in orange hair."

"And the dry cleaner will take care of it," she said with a smile. "Life is too short to worry about a few little dog hairs."

If dogs can smirk, that's what Cheese Puff did just before he bounced onto her lap. "There's my little prince," she cooed, kissing the top of his head. "What a precious little thing you are."

I took another long drink. At least if I went to jail, Cheese Puff would be well taken care of. Heck, he'd probably do better without me—eat gourmet food, wear a top-of-the-line leather collar with his initials set in diamonds, have a professional grooming service come to call instead of being clipped with a nail scissors and popped into the kitchen sink when he got whiffy. But going to jail was the last item on my bucket list. It was time I got proactive.

"Do you know a good lawyer?" If I took out a second mortgage and pawned the diamond I got from Albert, I might have enough to pay for . . . him to advise me to get a public defender. "A good lawyer who works cheap?"

Mrs. B's brow furrowed. "It's been my experience that good and cheap are rarely the same, dear."

That called for another swallow.

She held up a hand. "But it's also been my experience that if what you need is advice of a legal nature, there are often other ways to get it that don't cost a dime. For instance, we could call a meeting of the Committee."

I gawked. "The Cheese Puff Care and Comfort Committee?"

161

She nodded.

I almost laughed out loud. The last time they'd gathered, on Thanksgiving, the conversation centered on the merits of various antacids and laxatives, Cheese Puff's possible parentage, and proposed condo regulations governing wind chimes. Granted, they'd all been tipsy— Mrs. B poured with a liberal hand for which I was grateful at this moment—but I'd seen little evidence that this group was a think tank. I might as well call a meeting of Trash Guys I, II, and III.

"Verna was a court clerk," Mrs. B said. "She's seen it all and then some. Sybil's son is a prosecutor in Idaho. And Jim did time."

Whoa!

I sat up straight, eyes wide. Jim, the man who wouldn't kill a spider, who had a face and beard like Father Christmas, who collected aluminum cans for the Humane Society? "Did time? For what? Jaywalking?"

Mrs. B sipped her martini. "For drugs and assault and all manner of things."

Double whoa!

"He became a counselor when he got out. He's helped a lot of people through some horrendous problems."

"Including murder?" I clapped a hand over my mouth. Too much rum.

Now it was Mrs. B who sat up straighter. "Surely the police don't think you—"

I glared at my nearly empty glass of tongue-loosening liquid, knowing it hadn't made me do anything I really didn't want to do, that I'd come looking for an opportunity to spill it all. "I don't know what they think. But it seems everything I say gets me in deeper. Detective Atwell twists my meanings."

I gobbled another cashew. "And I'm afraid to tell him about Jake and Jessica because they might think I was jealous and killed her because I wanted Jake back. Which I don't. And I could lose my job and I don't have any money for a lawyer and I might lose my condo and even if I wanted to go home and live with my parents they wouldn't let me."

Out of breath, I lurched to a halt, then hiccupped the last of my woes, "And my sister . . . is a lesbian with a magenta Mohawk who practices witchcraft."

Mrs. B blinked twice, lifted Cheese Puff from her lap, sat him on the cushion beside her, and headed for the kitchen once more. "This calls for something more substantial to eat. And another drink."

Two hours later, a golf umbrella held high to protect Cheese Puff from a relentless drizzle, I walked around the condo complex, wondering if I'd made things better or worse. Mrs. B had been fascinated by Iz, exasperated by Jake, and distressed to learn the dire facts of my financial situation. She offered to loan me money and, to my surprise, accepted my refusal without protest or argument. Finally she instructed me to tell Atwell that I introduced Jessica and Jake and assured me that the Committee would review the options and come up with a plan.

Not once had she said that something would be "dealt with," so I assumed, perhaps naively, that said plan would be within the law.

"What's done is done, right?"

Cheese Puff looked back at me and hunched to lighten his load by a mail box post.

"Do you think I should have kept my lips zipped?"

Canine to the core, he dug at bark dust with his hind legs. Plastic bag in hand, I stooped to collect his donation.

"Hey, Barbie."

Crap. Not Jake again.

163

I tied a knot in the bag while pretending I hadn't heard.

"I need to talk to you," he called.

Sticking to my pretense, I reeled in the leash and hustled for home, skirting the puddle that always formed at a dip in the sidewalk. From the corner of my eye, I spotted Trash Guy II shambling along on a parallel course, headed for the trash containers. I wondered again about his backstory and whether I would manage to escape his fate.

Shoes pounded on asphalt and splashed through the puddle, then Jake hauled up beside me wearing a brown leather jacket over a tight white T-shirt and jeans. He insinuated himself under the umbrella and slung a damp arm around my shoulders. The pungent scent of his cologne made my sinuses shrivel.

"Haven't seen you around much."

Cheese Puff bared his teeth and growled.

Jake poked out his foot. "He won't bite, will he?"

"Not unless you try to kick him. Or I tell him to."

Jake pulled his foot back. "Why would you do that?"

"Why wouldn't I?"

While he puzzled over that, I shook off his arm and went on my way. He caught up in two strides and tried to squeeze under the umbrella again, but I canted it, exposing him to drizzle, silvery in the glow from the lamps around the parking lot. "What do you want, Jake?"

He finger combed hair off his forehead and gave me his boyish and sincere smile, the one with top teeth caught on the inside edge of his lower lip. "What makes you think I want something? Maybe I thought it would be pleasant to take a stroll with someone I care for."

I'd need a lot more liquor before I swallowed that line. "Then go get your redheaded friend."

Jake winced, then covered with his misunderstood-but-willing-to-forgive pout. "She's out."

"At her anger management class?" I asked in a tone syrupy enough to put a diabetic into a coma.

He gave me a puzzled frown. "No, at the fitness center she manages." He flashed the intimate smile. "She'll be gone for hours. And to tell the truth, things aren't going all that well between us."

I put my hand over my heart. "Really? I'm stunned."

"Me, too," he said with such sincerity I knew my sarcasm had bounced off his bulletproof ego. "I thought we really clicked. But she changed after I moved in."

Meaning she noticed his idea of being *into* a relationship meant getting *into* her wallet, and *into* the neighbor's pants. "Well, you know what they say, proximity is the mother of reality."

He squinted, lips in a half pout. "Huh? Who says that?"

We reached the short sidewalk to my porch and I turned my back on him. "Good night, Jake. As always, talking with you has been an experience. But I've got to go to work tomorrow."

"Uh, yeah. That must suck. Jessica says you're not cut out for teaching."

I felt a flash of fury. What did she know? And how dare she tell— Wait a minute. I replayed the last sentence. Jessica *says*? Present tense. Did Jake not know that Jessica was dead?

"She says you're opinionated and have a problem with authority." His smug tone and smile implied he agreed with that assessment.

I wanted to slap his smile until his lips came loose, but instead I clutched the umbrella handle and Cheese Puff's leash. "Jake, Jessica—"

"She's in the market for a larger house and I've got just the place," he crowed. "3,000 square feet with a 360 view. It's a steal, but she's got to act fast."

"Jake, she's—"

"She's not returning my calls." He slid a cell phone from the front pocket of his jeans and checked the screen. "Is she at some big school meeting?"

"No." I took a deep breath, halfway feeling sorry for him and halfway hating myself for that. "She's dead."

"Huh." He shook his head. "What are you talking about?"

"That was her body they fished from the river last night."

Jake glanced toward the river, tapped his phone as if that might change the past, then slid it back in his pocket. "But what about that house I found?"

I blinked. What part of "dead" didn't he understand?

"What about my commission?" He held out his hands, palms up.

I sighed. It wasn't that Jake didn't understand death, he just didn't understand why it should inconvenience him.

"I was counting on that money," he whined. "What am I going to do now?"

I placed the bag of poop on his open palm. "Frankly, my dear, I don't give a dump."

Quiz Answer:
e – unless you never want to cover for that teacher again

Choose the best response to the question "Did you ever smoke marijuana?"
a) Not since the 60's, dude.
b) No, I prefer it baked into brownies.
c) Not without a prescription.
d) The war of 1812.
e) What's marijuana?

CHAPTER TWENTY

Allison and Josh caught up with me on the stairs as I rushed to my classroom the next morning. In breathless voices punctuated by the thudding of the guitar case against his back, they gave me the speculation summary about Jessica Flint's demise: she fell off a yacht during a wild party, lost control of her car, or tumbled down the embankment while jogging.

Although this was milder stuff than I'd heard when Henry Stoddard died, I knew more about Allison and her emotional state now and her fascination with death concerned me. "Maybe you should go talk with a counselor. They have a special room set up down by the theater."

"Good idea." Josh nodded. "I heard they have snacks there."

Snacks? Well, whatever it took.

"But the weirdest thing," Allison panted, unfastening her cape and revealing a deep purple T-shirt, "is that they found Miss Flint right by your place. It's like you're a magnet for murder."

167

I winced at this echo of Detective Atwell.

"Probably just coincidence," Josh assured me in a tone that implied he didn't buy that and neither would anyone with an IQ above that of an avocado.

I winced again, thinking of Principal Morrow and the pressure he might be under to rid the school of a "murder magnet" if word got out to the general public. In the "small mercies" category of my mind, I filed a memo to myself to be grateful that police hadn't released my name or a reporter hadn't dug it up.

"Yet," amended that smug little voice in my brain.

"Just coincidence," Allison echoed Josh, gazing up at him in the same way Cheese Puff gazes at the jar of dog cookies.

"Come on." He wrapped one hand around hers. "We gotta meet Courtney and Zach before class. We'll go to the counseling room after first."

"Right." Allison blushed as he towed her back the way we'd come. "See you later, Ms. Reed."

Were they a couple? When had that happened? How long would it last? And how would her mental state be affected if they broke up?

As I unlocked the room and got set up, I wondered if I should have a talk with her about the possibility of heartache or whether I should alert her father.

I recalled his strong, smooth voice. I wouldn't mind hearing it again—not one bit. Then I reminded myself he had a girlfriend, and got to work.

Teachers had warned me that teens have few boundaries and sooner or later a student would ask a question that would make me sweat, squirm, and wish I could be beamed elsewhere. Since I use the title Ms., I'd already fielded questions about my marital status. It's an unfortunate fact that too many teens come from fractured, spliced, or just plain broken families, and not much in the way of relationship malfunction surprises them. After I explained that I divorced one husband and lost the other at sea (so to speak), the usual follow-up question was whether I had a boyfriend—a line of inquiry easily quashed with a torturous description of my schedule.

I'd also been asked my age, if I had any children and why not, my choice in music and TV programs, and which slasher movie was my favorite. Now I expected I'd be fielding questions about my "murder magnetism."

With no time to come up with something better, I decided to go with the coincidence card that Josh had dealt me. As theories go, it was as lame as a political duck, but I knew how to give it credence. The Internet. If you read it on-line, it has to be true, right?

I powered up the computer, entered the search words "famous coincidences," and printed out the results. If all else failed, I'd read a few, and divert the attack.

The enemy however, outflanked me, and opened a new front.

It was Mop-head who, after demanding to know when I was going to return the lighter I'd confiscated (short answer to that—never, it was now in the possession of a security officer), asked, in a voice that carried to the far reaches of the room, "Hey, Ms. Reed, you ever done a doobie?"

In the past two weeks I'd crawled into a bottle of rum a couple of times, but even with all the stress I'd been under, the thought of scoring grass to unwind never crossed my mind. When I'd been offered joints in high school and college I'd weighed the pros and cons and been paralyzed by indecision and uncertainty more powerful than peer pressure to get lit up.

But saying "no" wouldn't fly. Mop-head would see it as a knee-jerk reaction, a brush-off, a flat-out lie.

169

Answering the question with a question—What do you think?—was also a bad idea. Mop-head, and the twenty-nine others hunched forward in their seats like Middlesex farmers listening for the hoof beats of Paul Revere's horse, would decide the answer was "yes" and spread the word across the school.

I opted to play dumb, raising my voice so they'd all hear. "What's a doobie?"

Mop-head's jaw dropped. "You don't know what a doobie is?"

While other kids rolled their eyes and shook their heads in disbelief, I played dumber. "Is it one of the guys from that singing group that had a bunch of hits in the 70s?"

He squinted. "Huh?"

"I think 'China Grove' was one of theirs." I gave him wide eyes and a smile. "Oh, and 'Listen to the Music.' And something about a train."

Mop-head smacked his forehead with the heel of his hand. "That's lame. You don't know what a doobie is?"

I shrugged. "I guess not."

"Well, it's—"

The bell rang, cutting off both his answer and my charade.

I intended to poll the lunch group for advice, but the mood was angry and sullen, and the topic was murder, not marijuana. Every one of them had spent quality time with Detective Atwell, and every one was livid—except Susan, who appeared even more wrung-out than yesterday.

"And then he had the nerve to ask me what I had to hide that Henry Stoddard might have discovered," Brenda fumed as she opened a square plastic container and unleashed the smell of wet dog and fennel. "And whether Jessica Flint knew my secret—the secret I don't have!"

In the silence that followed her outburst, Aston excavated a lumpy biscuit from the bottom of a greasy leather pouch and gnawed at it. "Did you tell him about the oven explosion?"

"No." Her cheeks flamed. "Officially that was an accident. And I paid for what the insurance didn't cover—voluntarily." She aimed her spoon at his nose. "And if you open your mouth, I'll tell him about the student who sliced his arm open with your skinning knife. I'll bet you didn't share that bit of bloodshed."

"He shouldn't have been snooping in my car." Aston glowered. "Besides, it was listed as a cut on the official report."

Gertrude turned to me and cupped a hand around her mouth. "A cut that required a dozen stitches."

"Eleven," Aston said with a snarl. "And eight of them were pretty damn small."

Gertrude raised her hands in surrender. "I stand corrected."

"It's not like your closet has no skeletons. Like that missing money."

Gertrude blanched and opened her mouth, but Susan slapped the table. "Enough. This is ancient history, all common knowledge except to newbies." She hooked a thumb at me. "I'm sorry, but if it's no secret, there's no leverage."

Aston frowned and folded a limp strip of fatty bacon into his mouth. Gertrude and Brenda exchanged uncertain glances. Doug rolled his lower lip between his teeth and coughed. "Um, I suppose everyone know—"

"How you transposed the numbers on a bunch of grades and caused a stampede of screaming parents into Mr. Morrow's office?" Susan asked.

Doug blushed prom-dress pink and ducked his head, but I noted that he looked relieved.

171

"Could have happened to anyone," Aston mumbled.

"So could the money thing." Gertrude thumped the table with her fist. "When kids count the concession-stand receipts in a hurry, it's easy to make mistakes. But I was supervising and, if you remember, I took full responsibility and made up the difference." She glared at Aston. "You know I did."

"That's the point," Susan said. "We *all* know about *all* of this. And it's *all* piddling stuff—tempests in teapots. I'm sorry, but there's no foundation for blackmail."

One by one the others nodded. Aston took another bite of his grimy biscuit and spoke around it. "Well somebody here must have a nasty secret and old Henry must have dug it up and Jessica must have got her claws into it. Otherwise they'd still be among the living."

With that prompt, the conversation veered off into speculation about the nature of that huge secret. No one eyeballed me and wondered aloud who had given them up to Atwell, no one hinted that I had any secrets, and no one seemed to have any inkling that I had spotted Jessica Flint in the river. I finished my microwave pasta and scuttled out before conditions changed.

I kept on scuttling for the rest of the day—from class to class, out to my car when the final bell rang, to the grocery store for a carton of milk and a jar of peanut butter, and home to face up to fifty pages of graduate-program reading and the long-delayed phone call to Detective Atwell to tell him about introducing Jake and Jessica.

My conversation with Jake last night had convinced me he had nothing to do with her death, but even without consulting an attorney I knew I could be in deep doo-doo if Atwell discovered I'd withheld evidence.

172

Cheese Puff lifted the edge of his lip at the pelting rain when I opened the door then hopped up on the futon, so I didn't waste time getting him into his harness and attempting a walk. Instead I brewed a cup of tea, then got out my text and notebook and dug into my briefcase for a pen. My grasping fingers came up with a sticky butterscotch candy, the nub of an eraser, a bent paperclip, and that worthless dried-up yellow marker pen I'd been toting around since the day Henry Stoddard died. I opened the cabinet beneath the sink and tossed it all into a brimming garbage pail.

The marker slid from the heap, bounced onto the floor, and broke into two pieces. I bent to pick them up and discovered a flash drive hidden in the marker's shell.

Quiz Answer:
Whatever you say, kids will draw their own conclusions.

If students weren't allowed to use cell phones in school

a) they'd complain bitterly
b) they'd claim First Amendment violations
c) they'd pass notes
d) they'd use their phones anyway
e) more learning might take place

CHAPTER TWENTY ONE

I reached for the flash drive with quivering fingers. Was this where Henry Stoddard stored the dirt he dug up?

I remembered how some of the teachers argued that Stoddard wouldn't have the skills to use a flash drive. Wasn't it Aston who said that would be like a dinosaur using toilet paper? Yet here it was, stuffed inside the marker that had fallen from the stack of atlases I took from his room. I felt a perverse respect for Stoddard's skill at misdirection.

"Don't touch it," carped that little voice in my brain. "Call Detective Atwell right now."

That voice, as always, was conscientious, cautious, and correct. But if there was something on that flash drive that concerned me—although I couldn't imagine what that might be—I wanted first-hand, detailed, pre-knowledge of it. I wanted to be prepared for the worst when Atwell hauled me into his interrogation room.

On the other hand, this tiny storage unit might belong to someone else—a student or even another teacher. If that was the case, why should I waste Atwell's time?

Telling myself I would definitely hand over the flash drive if it was Henry Stoddard's—no matter what might be on it—and that I would merely look at the contents and certainly not tamper, I snapped on a pair of yellow rubber gloves, plucked it from the floor, and trotted upstairs to my computer.

There, I discovered things about Henry Stoddard I never would have suspected. One, he was writing a novel—a steamy, erotic novel set during the French Revolution—a novel entitled *Let Them Eat*—

"Wooo!"

Cheeks flaming at the fourth word of that title, I skimmed the first chapter. Who knew you could do those things in a cart on the way to the guillotine? Who even suspected you might want to? If I quoted from this, I'd be the star attraction in the teachers' room for weeks.

"Except you shouldn't be reading it," that little voice reminded me.

"Damn."

I closed the file and opened one titled "Substitutes." There I found a series of notations stretching back years and chronicling Stoddard's efforts to bully subs in order to "separate the sheep from the goats." His crusade was founded on the belief that most teachers, and all subs, were inferior. I found the entry for the day he confronted me at the restroom and noted he described me as "intimidated but not convinced" and intended to badger me again.

"That jerk!"

I closed the file and browsed to one titled "Flint." Here he'd noted that he intercepted her in the parking lot, told her he knew all about what she was up to, and left her to stew. Like a laboratory researcher, he described her reaction: "color fading from her face, shifting eyes, trembling hands."

175

A week later he intercepted her again and said her secret was safe unless she made trouble for him. Again he described her reaction: "a glance over her shoulder and a slight sigh of relief" before she told him she had no idea what he meant and wouldn't give anyone special treatment. Then she'd walked away, in Henry's words, "her hips gyrating like a stripper's, her high heels tapping out an invitation to tear off her clothes."

"Eek!"

But that was the sum of it. There was no mention of the nature of her secret or how Henry learned of it. Being careful to make no accidental additions that might leave a record of my prying, I scrolled through the other files, starting with administrators and teachers I knew, and made the biggest discovery of all—Henry had nothing on anyone.

It appeared he banked on the fact that most of us have embarrassing experiences we'd prefer to keep private. All he had to do was pretend to know. His victims filled in the blanks, braided their own ropes, and tied their own nooses. They stepped into space and twisted in the breeze of their own fears while Henry laughed at their pain.

A horn tooted in the parking lot. Startled, I raced to the window and spotted my ride to class in Portland.

"Drat."

I turned off the computer, jogged downstairs, seized my text and notebook, tossed Cheese Puff a dog biscuit, and shot out the door.

Rationalizing that disturbing Detective Atwell at a late hour wouldn't enhance his personality, I didn't call him when I got back from class. I *did* browse the rest of the files on the drive and found more of the same and notes for a second racy novel, *Hannibal's Hard Hunger*. Ugh.

Thanks to my late-night research, I overslept and didn't have time to call Detective Atwell before school. I spent every free minute between classes hatching a plan and here's what I had when I picked up Cheese Puff from Mrs. Ballantine's and unlocked my front door—place the drive back on the kitchen floor and pretend I had just discovered it.

"Pathetic," snarked the little voice in my brain. "You don't have the acting ability to pull that off. You're going to pay for this stupidity."

"All true." I climbed the stairs to retrieve the flash drive.

"They'll know you looked at it," the little voice shrieked.

I halted, two steps from the top, heart pounding. "How?"

"They have experts," the voice said with smug certainty. "They'll know."

Would they? My knees wobbled and I sat down hard on the top step.

The little voice chanted like a bratty kindergarten kid who wore a frilly dress, had naturally curly hair, and never colored outside the lines. "You're. In. Trouble."

"I'm aware of that," I said with a snarl.

Cheese Puff appeared at the bottom of the stairs and cocked his head. "It's okay," I told him. "There's no one here."

He raised a front paw and rested it on the first step.

"I told you to call Detective Atwell as soon as you found that thing," the voice sniped.

"Shut up."

"Well, I did. And you know it."

"Shut up right now," I yelled. "Or I'll get a frontal lobotomy and put you out of my misery."

177

Barking, Cheese Puff charged up the stairs and leaped past me into the bedroom. He darted into the closet, checked out the bathroom, and sniffed under the bed.

"There's no one here," I told him again. But the hair on the back of my neck prickled.

Don't be silly, I told myself. No one knew about the flash drive, and no one could have gotten up here without Cheese Puff intercepting them.

Gooseflesh puckered the skin on my arms.

Cheese Puff stared at me with his beady eyes as if trying to telepathically remind me he'd been with Mrs. Ballantine most of the day.

Had someone broken in to steal the flash drive? Was that person still here?

I bolted to my feet. But instead of hurtling downstairs and calling for help, I scrambled to my computer. I needed that flash drive. It could help me get off of Atwell's hook. I'd fight for it if I had to.

Cheese Puff yipped and darted out of my way.

I hurled myself at my desk, saw the flash drive still in the computer port, stumbled to a halt, my heart pounding against my sternum.

"Imaginary issue resolved," I told Cheese Puff when I could breathe again. "Real problem still looming—a charge of tampering with evidence."

Clearly, there was only one thing to do—go back to Mrs. Ballantine's and spill my guts once more.

That's why she was ensconced on my futon with Cheese Puff on her lap when I heard Detective Atwell's steps on my walk forty-five minutes later. It had taken me just five minutes to blurt out my story, but it took twenty-five for her to dress for the encounter—sleek black slacks, teal sweater, chunky diamond rings on each hand, a pearl necklace, and pearl and diamond earrings. "Twelve carats of diamonds says money," she'd told me as she dressed, "but a string of perfectly matched pearls says a woman is a force to be reckoned with."

"And Detective Atwell knows that?"

"Maybe not." She fluffed her hair. "But he'll figure it out soon enough."

I scuttled to the door the second I heard Atwell's footsteps on my miniscule porch. "Wait until he rings the bell, dear," Mrs. B cautioned.

He knocked instead. My clammy hand slipped on the knob. I turned it with my wrists and jumped back.

Atwell looked like he'd been living on a steady diet of beer, raw dough, and lard. His face was puffy and mottled, his nose red and porous like those mammoth strawberries that are all show and no taste. "What have you got?" he growled.

"Detective." Mrs. B set Cheese Puff on a cushion, stood, and extended her hand, diamond flashing. "I'm Barbara's neighbor and friend, Muriel Ballantine."

Atwell jerked as if her hand was a live wire. "Ballantine?"

"Marco was my husband." She twisted the diamond on her ring finger. "Perhaps you knew him."

Atwell's eyes narrowed. "Only by reputation."

She smiled as if he meant that in a positive way. "He was very active in the business community."

Atwell glowered, then turned to me. "Where's the thing you found."

"Upstairs," I squeaked. "In my computer."

Mrs. B pointed to the broken marker on the kitchen floor. "It came out of that pen that may have been in Mr. Stoddard's room."

Atwell turned the glower up a notch and toasted us both. "*May* have been?"

Cheese Puff echoed his tone with a snarl.

179

Atwell took a step back "Is that a dog?"

"Yes." Mrs. B beamed. "Isn't he the cutest lit—"

"I'm allergic to dogs. Especially rat dogs. Where did you find the pen?"

I swallowed to clear my throat, no easy task with muscles tight from fear. "It might have been in among the atlases. But it might have been on the floor where I dropped them when I realized he'd been strangled." Sucking in a breath, I raced on. "Josh—the kid I told you about—scraped the atlases together and found the marker. I tossed it in my briefcase and—"

"She forgot all about it until a few minutes ago." Mrs. B stepped to the table and tapped the textbook I'd opened. She'd demanded accuracy in the small details because the large ones—the time shift and the fact that she hadn't been here—were bogus.

"*Forgot* about it," Atwell repeated.

"Well, it was only a marker pen," Mrs. B said, "It wasn't the Hope Diamond or a thousand-dollar bill."

"And I didn't know there was anything inside," I insisted. "It looked just like any other marker. You thought so too when you first saw it."

Atwell's eyebrows shot toward his hairline. "When was that?"

"When you searched my briefcase the day I found Henry Stoddard's body. I'll bet your fingerprints are all over it."

Atwell glared, shuffled his feet, then snorted.

"Anyway, I came over to borrow some peanut butter," Mrs. B continued, mentioning one of the few things found in my refrigerator but not in hers, a vital detail should anyone check the validity of her statement. "Barbara was just about to start a reading assignment and she set the marker on the counter while she was getting the peanut butter and it fell to the floor and broke open and we saw that . . . computer thing."

"Flash drive," I supplied.

Atwell curled one edge of his upper lip and studied the pieces of the marker and the textbook. "And it didn't occur to you to call me right then?"

"Of course it did," Mrs. B said in a honeyed voice. "But we know how busy you must be investigating two murders and how much pressure you're under. We didn't want to waste your time, so I suggested we make sure that this flash thing belonged to Mr. Stoddard."

Atwell rolled his eyes. Mrs. B twinkled, all innocence and diamonds. "We were very careful." She pointed to the yellow gloves on the counter. "Barbara wore gloves."

"Oh, she wore *gloves*." The acid in Atwell's tone could have stripped paint. "And that made it okay to tamper with evidence?"

I quivered, but Mrs. B fingered her pearl necklace. "But we didn't *know* it was evidence until Barbara got it into her computer. So *legally* I don't believe that we actually could be charged with tam—"

"Enough." Atwell raised his palm. "We'll let the prosecutor hash that out. Show me where it is."

I led the way upstairs and pointed to my computer.

Atwell bent, squinted at the flash drive, then torqued his neck and peered at me. "What's on it?"

"I didn't—"

"Spare me the story." He chopped air with the edge of his hand. "What's on it?"

"A pornographic historical novel and a log of his attempts to intimidate almost everyone by claiming he knew things he didn't," I blurted.

"But no list of dirty little secrets." Mrs. B raised her eyebrows. "Unless he mixed them into the novel. We read only a few pages." She dismissed Stoddard's writing with a flip of her hand. "I prefer literature with deeper meaning, more character development, and a plot that doesn't depend on gratuitous sex. Of course, as a detective, it will be your job to read it all. And probably more than once."

Atwell's nose and cheeks grew even ruddier. He frowned, perhaps trying to decide if he'd been insulted, then snapped open his cell phone. "I'm calling someone to collect that marker. And your computer."

My stomach lurched. "You can't. I have a paper due on Monday."

He gave me a smile without a shred of sympathy. "You should have thought of that before you opened those files."

"You can use my laptop," Mrs. B said. "It's brand new."

"But what about my research? All my sources are in there. And my notes."

"Guess you'll have to take new ones," Atwell said with a smirk.

"Can I copy them to a flash drive?"

He shook his head, his smirk becoming a grin. "I can't take a chance on you corrupting evidence more than you already have."

"The Committee will help you," Mrs. B said. "They love a challenge."

I nodded numbly, thinking this wasn't a challenge, this was a catastrophe. What did the members of the Committee know about how to teach reading or assess your success at doing that? How would they know which Internet sources were valid? And how could they make sense of obtuse "educationalese" language that often left me shaking my head?

Mrs. B nudged me and whispered, "Did you tell him about Jake?"

"Who's Jake?" Atwell growled.

"My ex-husband," I squeaked. "Jake Stranahan."

"He lives down at the end of the complex," Mrs. B added.

"And why should I care?" Atwell skewered me with a glare.

"I introduced him to Jessica Flint," I yipped. "The day she came to ask me what I took from Henry Stoddard's room. But I don't think Jake killed her. He didn't know she was dead until I told him last night."

Atwell added more wattage to the glare. "He's your ex, but you're introducing him to other women and keeping him informed of current events?"

"No, I—"

"Barbara is completely done with him." Mrs. B came to my rescue. "She'd prefer it if she never had to see him again. But she bumped into him while she was out walking her dog." She squeezed my arm. "I would have snubbed him cold, but Barbara's too polite for her own good."

A sigh erupted from Atwell's lips and he turned the glare up to flame-thrower setting. "And you didn't tell me this earlier be—"

"Because she knew you'd think she was jealous and had a motive to kill Jessica Flint." Mrs. B aimed a finger at his nose. "You'd get more information out of witnesses if you put more effort into listening and less into intimidation."

Atwell's face turned the color of molten lava and his hands curled into fists. I cowered behind Mrs. B. She stood her ground, fingering her pearls until he shook the kinks out of his hands, laughed out one explosive "Ha," and pointed to the door.

"Go walk that sorry excuse for a dog. But don't go too far. And don't even think of telling anyone about this." He aimed a finger at Mrs. B and smirked. "And I'll need your fingerprints. Unless they're already in our files."

"They're not." With a proud toss of her head she spun on one heel and ushered me to the stairs.

"He's just trying to make things tough because he's mad," Mrs. B consoled me as I got Cheese Puff into his harness. "He doesn't have an ounce of evidence against you that isn't circumstantial. Not one bit."

"I guess," I muttered. "But what if he finds something that isn't circumstantial?"

"There's nothing to find." She wrapped her hands around my forearms, her grip stronger than I imagined it would be. "Is there?"

"No. But I can't prove that I *didn't* kill them. What if the killer plants something to frame me?"

She chewed at her lower lip, considering that for a few seconds. Then she smiled. "We'll worry about that if it happens. Trust me. It will all work out."

She wrapped me in a hug and I inhaled the faint scent of lemon soap and a perfume I couldn't identify but knew was far beyond my budget. She hadn't said the problem would be dealt with and she hadn't told me to never mind. So perhaps she didn't intend to resort to extreme—and illegal—measures to resolve things. That was cold comfort, but all I had.

Quiz Answer:
All answers are valid, but *e* has my vote.

The best response to "I hate this lesson" is:
a) It hasn't killed anyone yet.
b) It doesn't think much of you, either.
c) It's in the curriculum and we have to get through it.
d) What could we do to make it more interesting?
e) Why don't you take a nap instead?

CHAPTER TWENTY TWO

The next week passed in a blur of grading quizzes and worksheets, and plowing through research-paper-related articles tracked down and highlighted by members of the Committee. Sleep eluded me and I walked with head bent, neck stretched, waiting in numb anticipation for Atwell's axe to fall.

Why had Henry Stoddard imagined that prisoners could boink like crazed weasels in a tumbrel rolling along a cobblestone street toward the guillotine's bloody blade? Was that his idea of a turn-on? If so, it was another reason not to miss him.

On Friday, Atwell called me in after school to make an official statement about finding the flash drive and needle me with questions now so familiar I answered by rote. He gave up within a few minutes, delivered the usual warning about not leaving town, and showed me the door. I zipped through it and headed straight to Mrs. Ballantine's condo.

"He's got nothing," she insisted for the twentieth time.

"Or he's taking his time." Sharpening his axe. Gloating in anticipation.

"Try to think about happier things," she advised. "Like the holidays."

Yeah, the holidays. Two weeks without school or a paycheck. Two weeks of alone time or tagging along with the Committee, shopping, driving around to look at the lights, or gorging at all-you-can-eat buffets. I wasn't making much progress toward getting a life.

"And isn't your sister coming soon?"

Pangs of anxiety shot through my gut. I'd forgotten that Iz was descending on me in five days.

Mrs. B locked me in a hug and patted my back. "I'm sorry, dear. Let me mix you up something to take your mind off of . . . well, everything."

"Not until I get my paper written," I moaned.

"I'll have a drink waiting for you," she said. "And a tin of those giant cashews."

With fat, salt, and liquid relaxation at the end of the trail, I burrowed into the stack of articles and pounded away at the borrowed laptop. Thanks to the Committee's encouragement and the meals they delivered, I finished up on Sunday evening with time to spare for an intensive proofreading session and a tall glass filled with a frothy drink.

By the time Wednesday rolled around, I'd had many sips of the potions Mrs. B mixed, but the suspense of waiting for Atwell's next move kept eating at me. The bags under my eyes ballooned, the tiny lines across my forehead and around my mouth deepened, and nothing settled my churning stomach. All I could keep down was chicken noodle soup, fruit juice, and rum.

"I'm worried about you," Susan said at lunch. "You look frazzled."

"I'm fine," I lied, thinking that in her case frazzled would be an improvement. Her clothes hung from her shoulders, her hair lay flat against her head, her eyes were bloodshot, her nose was raw, and her mouth had a permanent pinch as if she'd just gargled with vinegar. I wondered whether her marriage had disintegrated even further, if long-simmering resentment had flared into confrontation. Had Kevin hurt her? I made a surreptitious survey of her face and arms, but saw no bruises or marks.

"Well, you look like you're exhausted." She stabbed at limp green peppers and carrots swimming in a fishy-smelling sauce at the bottom of a soggy takeout box. For the past week she'd brought nothing from home. It appeared she'd stopped shopping and cooking in an attempt to starve Kevin out and was starving herself as well. She set her fork aside and shook her head. "It's too much, too big a load, your graduate classes and then subbing every day."

"For the dead guy," Aston added in a sepulchral tone.

Susan's lips pinched tighter and she shuddered. "I'm sorry. This is all my fault."

"Why is that?" Brenda asked.

Susan pushed the takeout box aside. "I shouldn't have agreed that Barbara take on Henry's classes. It's just too difficult for someone without much experience."

A wave of nausea engulfed me and the few sips of soup I'd swallowed rose in my throat. If Susan expressed her concerns to Jerome Morrow, he might find another sub and leave me scrabbling for jobs to keep my financial house of cards standing. "I'm keeping up with it," I insisted. "I'm doing okay."

"You are in my book," Gertrude said. "Kids have stopped trying to transfer out of those classes."

"And I've heard a few say they hope you'll stay," Doug added.

"That's high praise in these circles." Aston snagged Susan's takeout box, sniffed at it, then dumped the contents on top of what looked like a blackened cornmeal pancake. "Stop worrying about what you don't need to, Susan. And stop apologizing for what isn't your fault."

Susan gnawed at her lower lip. "Well, if you think you can manage . . ."

"She'll manage." Aston forked in a load of soggy vegetables. "If she has problems she'll come to you. She's no dummy."

"Talk about high praise," Doug said with a laugh.

Susan nodded and, relieved, I plunged through the remainder of the day, staying after school to grade 150 worksheets and make out detailed lesson plans for the next two days. It was dark when I got home and found reality, in the substantial shape of Iz, planted in my porch swing.

For a few glorious seconds I teetered on the brink of telling her I had to rush off to Portland, even though tonight's class was cancelled. Then I decided to stand my ground. "Is it Wednesday already?"

"Don't give me that innocent act," Iz ordered. "I see right through it."

I shrugged and unlocked the door. After grousing about my failure to consider her comfort and send her a key, Iz lugged her gear up to my bedroom and rummaged around while I changed into jeans and a flannel shirt. She'd barely gotten into a full-throttle rant about the contents of my refrigerator—nothing made from the milk of goats sacred to a goddess, nothing plucked from trees grown on an east-facing slope, nothing harvested from vines planted under a full moon—when the phone rang. I dove for it as if I'd fallen off a cruise ship and it was a life preserver.

"Some of the Christmas ships are practicing out on the river," Mrs. Ballantine said in breathless voice. "The Committee's coming over. I'm making snacks and hot toddies. Bring the little prince."

I glanced at Cheese Puff, barricaded behind the throw pillows on the futon; he looked like a condemned man hoping for a stay of execution. I slid my gaze to Iz's derriere as she bent to search the crisper drawers. "Uh, I'd love to," I told Mrs. B, "but my sister is visiting."

Iz straightened and fixed me with a stony glare your average basilisk would envy. The implication, I knew, was that but for her visit I'd be involved in some illicit activity, probably with a male.

"I remember, dear," Mrs. B said. "Bring her along."

"I'll try," I said, wondering what Iz would make of Mrs. B and vice versa.

"Do you know that nothing in your crisper is crisp?" Iz closed the refrigerator door with a snap. "Try what?"

"Try to get you to visit Mrs. Ballantine, my neighbor. She invited us to watch . . . uh, ships out on the river preparing for a winter tradition." Emboldened by the quick thinking that allowed me to avoid mention of a particular holiday, I went on to defend the condition of my lettuce and carrots. "I lowered the thermostat to help stop global warming."

Iz's frown lines smoothed out. "Is this a solstice celebration?"

"I'm not sure," I lied. "Mrs. B will have snacks. She makes wonderful appetizers."

I could almost see Iz's fat cells doing the pig-out polka. "Well, if it's a solstice celebration I suppose I should attend."

I held back a smile, got an all-weather jacket from the closet, shrugged it on, and popped Cheese Puff into his harness.

Iz's frown lines returned with reinforcements. "That mangy dog is coming?"

Cheese Puff bared his teeth and I scooped him into my arms and stroked his head. "Mrs. B loves him."

189

Iz rolled her eyes, but stuffed herself into her shiny black faux leather coat. It made her look like a sea lion and I almost expected her to bark as she followed me out the door. "Quite a museum," she said a minute later as we threaded our way through Mrs. B's living area toward the sound of clinking cups and excited voices.

I didn't respond. I'd never seen Iz's place, but my best guess was that her taste ran to . . . well, to be honest, I didn't want to think about it.

Mrs. B, armed with a bottle of quality rum, greeted us at the door to the deck and skewered Iz with her sapphire eyes. "This must be Iz." She offered a hand, palm down, fingers slightly curved. "I've heard *so* much about you."

For a few seconds they stood like two powerful magnets, repelled by their own force fields. I didn't breathe. Having met someone who couldn't be bullied, would Iz stalk from the field of battle with a caustic comment in an attempt to save face?

But, no. With the speed of a striking snake, Iz grasped the offered hand and squeezed. Mrs. B raised her imperial eyebrows and crimped her glossed lips. Her knuckles whitened as she returned pressure. Iz's eyes tightened and her arm trembled as she did the same. They held that pose like statues for long seconds, then Mrs. B jerked Iz's hand up and toward her. Thrown off balance, Iz staggered, released her grip, and clutched at the doorjamb.

"I'm so sorry," Mrs. B simpered, tossing me a wink. "It seems the closer I get to seventy the clumsier I become. Can't even shake hands without half killing someone." She pressed the bottle of rum into my hands and took Cheese Puff in return. Draping him against her shoulder like a baby in need of burping, she sauntered out to join the Committee, leaving me with Iz.

My sister massaged her fingers, her basilisk glare back with a vengeance. "Pushing seventy, huh?"

"She was a dancer," I babbled, setting the rum on the counter as I recalled that my last evening with Iz had ended with a world-class hangover. "She stays in shape. Walks and lifts little weights and squeezes a rubber ball."

Iz grunted and flexed her fingers. "Is her food worth eating?"

"See for yourself." I skittered onto the deck and found Mrs. B had provisioned as if expecting a platoon to drop by after an all-day forced march. A table, sheltered from the chilly mist by a striped awning, was crammed with bowls of nuts and candy, platters of tiny sandwiches, carafes of mulled cider and hot cocoa, and two fondue pots, one filled with cheese sauce and the other with melted chocolate so rich and thick I longed to use it as a facial.

Iz grunted yet again and staked out a chair in the lee of the privacy panel screening the deck that once belonged to Nelson and Myra. Filling a plate with chunks of bread and sponge cake, she got busy with a fondue fork. I poured a mug of cocoa and joined the Committee at the railing.

The black river spread before us, swells spangled by the flashing lights of a dozen ships festooned with garlands of tinsel and strings of blinking bulbs strung on wire shaped into angels and reindeer, bells and trees. Mrs. B turned so that Cheese Puff could get a look and cooed to him, "Isn't it lovely? It's like a little bit of Vegas right here on the river."

I sipped my cocoa and decided not to mention that dogs didn't see colors. She'd only protest that Cheese Puff was no ordinary dog and could, in fact, detect distinct variations in shade. So I listened to the sucking sound of Iz dipping into the fondue pots, watched the ships crisscrossing the channel, and checked out the crowd gathered on the packed walkway along the riverbank.

191

Many held drinks, binoculars, and cell phones. Even Trash Guy II had turned out, lurking up near the end of the condo complex, the lights from the ships reflecting off his yellow slicker.

"The little prince is squirming, dear," Mrs. B whispered. "I think he has to go potty."

"His wish is my command." I set my cocoa mug on the railing, took Cheese Puff from her arms, and snapped on the leash I'd stuffed in my jacket pocket. Committee members parted and we made our way down the steps, my slick-soled loafers sliding on the wet wood.

When we reached the stepping stones in Mrs. B's tiny rose garden, I set him down. "How about right here?"

He sniffed the trimmed canes of one bush, then lowered his haunches to within a centimeter of a stepping stone and gave me a put-upon look.

I sighed. This was going to be one of those nights when he'd inspect and reject shrubbery until I longed to pick up his scrawny body and squeeze the yellow stuff out of him. "Okay, let's go down the trail."

His ears perked up and we eased along behind the spectators toward the end of the complex, Cheese Puff considering a variety of foliage en route. "You'd think that stuff was perfume instead of pee," I groused.

Cheese Puff glanced over his shoulder, then tugged his way past the last of the onlookers and around behind a dripping rhododendron marking the top of a narrow paved trail that plunged down the bank to a scrap of pebbly beach. The weathered trunk of a tree lay on the upriver side of that beach; on warm afternoons I often sat there and, if there were no other dogs around, let him off his leash. Spooked by lapping ripples and shifting pebbles, he never ventured more than a few yards. For all his feigned bravado, he was little more than a nerve ending with legs.

192

"No." I worked my way around the rhody, untangling the leash, and squinting into the shadows. "We're not going down to the river tonight. And there's no way I'm letting you run around on your own in the dark."

Cheese Puff stuck out his lower jaw in an expression of stubborn disdain and ran out the rest of the leash.

"No." I stomped toward him, reeling in the cord. "Forget it. No way."

"You could at least wait until I ask before you turn me down," a male voice said.

Cheese Puff growled, but I kept tugging at the leash, the soles of my shoes slipping on fallen leaves littering the steep, mist-slick trail. "I'm saving us both time," I said.

"Ha. Ha." Jake left lots of space between the words to indicate a lack of amusement. "Your sister's back there digging into a fondue pot with both paws. Looks like she's gained twenty pounds since I saw her last."

Spoken in a sly knife-between-the-ribs tone he probably thought would annoy me—and would have if I gave a fig about Iz's weight problem or his opinion. "Thirty," I corrected. "At least."

"She looks like a killer whale in that coat. A killer whale with a Mohawk."

Damn. I liked his image better than the sea lion one I'd come up with.

"She here to try to borrow money?"

With a yank that almost took my feet out from under me, I dislodged Cheese Puff, pulled him close, hit the lock button on the leash, and faced my ex. "Like you aren't?"

From the corner of my eye I spotted the parade of bedecked ships approaching. In the flickering light, Jake held out his hands, fingers spread wide, and gave me his best ingratiating smile. "Hey, I'm just trying to make conversation. You don't have to be so crabby."

Oh, but I did. Crabby was the best defense against Jake and his smarmy charm. It worked against Iz, too. Someday maybe I'd evolve to the point where I could defend myself in other ways, but for now— "There are dozens of people out watching the ships," I sniped. "Go talk with them."

"I want to talk with you." He laid a hand on my arm and leaned close. I smelled cinnamon mouthwash and beneath it the juniper scent of gin. In the faint red and green light from the boat passing us, I saw he'd missed three whiskers in the center of his left cheek and a pimple had erupted on his chin.

"Listen, I've got a deal cooking," he said in a throaty whisper. "I guarantee a five-hundred-percent profit."

I heard a faint trickle and glanced down to see Cheese Puff leaving his mark on Jake's high-end jogging shoe. "My financial advisor says I shouldn't even listen to you, let alone invest with you."

"But it's a killer deal," Jake wheedled.

Cheese Puff lowered his leg and scuffed at the trail with his hind feet, tossing leaves onto the shoe. "It's *no* deal," I informed Jake.

He grasped my other arm. "You can't afford to walk away from it."

"I can't *afford* a lot of things, Jake, because you ripped me off." I turned the gripe-o-meter dial to high. "I can't *afford* new clothes or dinners out or a vacation. I certainly can't *afford* one of your deals."

"But this one will make you rich."

I shook off his grip, bent, and scooped Cheese Puff into my arms, releasing the lock button so the leash would retract into the handle. "No. Way. No. Deal." I attempted to inch around him, shoes sliding.

194

"Come on, Barbara. Don't blow me off until you hear all the details." He seized my shoulders and shook. My teeth clicked together. Cheese Puff snarled.

"You're drunk, Jake. Let me go." I twisted in his grip, holding Cheese Puff tight against my chest. My shoes were like ice skates and the trail a canted rink. The last of the ships passed, plunging us into a well of night illuminated only by the feeble glow from the lampposts along the trail above.

"Ten thousand dollars. That's all I need to buy in."

"Get your hands—"

"Get away from him, you slut" a woman's voice roared.

Jake opened his hands. I slid backward, clutching Cheese Puff with my left arm, windmilling my right.

Feet pounded down the trail. Feet I'd heard pounding before. The redhead.

I screamed.

Jake shouted.

She hit me like that algebra-homework freight train that left Philadelphia doing 45 miles an hour.

Air exploded from my lungs.

I careened across the pebbly beach and into the river.

Quiz Answer:
I'm still working on a good response for this. Let me know if you have an idea.

The best way to motivate a sub to cover your class is to
a) remind her of her mortgage
b) promise that your students will respect her
c) leave chocolates in your desk drawer
d) praise her knowledge of the subject
e) tell her she can give a pop quiz

CHAPTER TWENTY THREE

Icy black water filled my nose and mouth and sucked me under. I swallowed, gagged, swallowed again, sank deeper into the river's brutal embrace. The twinkling lights from the ships grew dim and distant.

And then my survival instinct kicked in and I scissored my legs.

My right hand was stuck in something and jerked straight above my head. It was useless. I clawed for the surface with my left.

My lungs burned, my heart thudded in my throat. The lights seemed no closer, no brighter.

I clawed harder. The lights bloomed. I broke through into frigid air and hauled in a double lungful of air.

Cheese Puff yelped and I spotted him a few feet away, dog paddling like he was possessed. The pressure on my fingers increased and I realized they were jammed in the handle of his leash. When the redhead slammed into me, he had no choice but to come along.

"I'm here," I screamed, toeing off the one shoe still on and kicking to stay afloat. "Cheese Puff. I'm here!"

His yelps changed to yips and he did a 180. We collided and he scrabbled to the top of my head. "It's okay," I told him. "It's okay. We're alive."

But for how long?

The gap between me and the departing ships widened by the second. In the stern of the last one in line, a group of people raised a toast to those on shore.

"Come back," I screamed, knowing they'd never hear me over the rumble of the engines and their liquor-fueled laughter, never see me in the inky water as they drank to my demise.

No!

I flailed about and peered back at the shore, saw bobbing flashlights, heard faint shouts.

"Out here!" I shrieked, waving my arms. "I'm out here."

Cheese Puff barked, slipped, yelped, and clawed at my cheek as he regained his perch.

The flashlight beams crisscrossed, tiny as fireflies, sliding over something flailing in the water close to shore, something dark and broad and shiny.

A cluster of water droplets distorted the image but the fact that I saw it at all meant that somehow my glasses had stayed on. I felt a surge of joy, but that annoying little voice shut it down. "How will that help? Can you use them to send up a flare? Inflate them into a boat?"

"Shut up," I snarled. That stinking little voice probably had 20/20 vision. "If I can see clearly, I can think clearly."

"Oh, you're going to think," the voice sniped. "That makes me feel *much* better."

I slapped at the water. "I've had it with you! It's always negative. How about pitching in with a plan?"

197

Silence. The voice, like those politicians who oppose everything the other party sponsors, had nothing, nada, zip.

"Hang on, Cheese Puff," I wheezed. "I'm going to swim for shore."

That meant turning my back on the condo complex, facing downriver, and setting a diagonal course across the current—or trying to.

I reminded myself that I'd been a complete failure at volleyball, softball, and other team sports, but I could swim. Not fast, but I was buoyant, and I had stamina.

Telling myself my extra ten pounds would increase both floatability and insulation, I clamped the leash handle between my teeth, shed my jacket, and stroked for the bank.

After a few keening howls, Cheese Puff settled down to a soft whine, his front paws clamped at the corners of my eyes and his rear digging into my collar bones. I settled down to trying to breathe without swallowing more water, pulling leaden arms in half rough circles, and trusting that the feet I couldn't feel were still back there and doing something to propel me.

Relentlessly, the river swept us along, past a park and another condo complex. Yellow light streamed from the wide windows of a restaurant and I saw people, warm and well fed, just fifty feet away, their faces pressed against the glass watching the last of the ships disappear into the obsidian night.

I closed my eyes, fought tears that would do me no good, and thought of things to live for—Cheese Puff and chocolate and revenge.

If I got out of this river, that redhead would pay. No way would I wait for the wheels of justice to take their sweet time or for Mrs. B to see that she was "dealt with." I'd puncture the tires on her little sports car. I'd pour sugar in the gas tank. Then I'd come up behind her with a baseball bat and I'd—

Cheese Puff's whine escalated to a rising pattern of yips. The way he carried on when he heard a siren.

Deep in my numb chest, my heart gave a thump of joy. Someone had called for help.

But how would they ever find me out here in the dark?

I couldn't think about that. Better to concentrate on vengeance.

I thrust my arms forward for another stroke. Was I any closer to the shore? Should I abandon all hope of reaching land, let the current take me farther out, and hope to hit a bridge support somewhere downstream and hang on until help came.

But how long could I stay afloat? And what if I missed the support? I'd be out in the shipping channel, in the path of every barge on the river.

I focused again on revenge, imagined myself bashing the redhead's red head, and forced my arms out and back again. Everything below my neck was numb and above that I felt only a few distinct points of pain where Cheese Puff's claws pricked my skin.

"At least you'll go down together," the little voice chirped.

I plucked the leash handle from between my jaws. "Shut the hell up!"

"I was just saying," the little voice whined.

"Well, don't 'just say' another frickin' word!" I screamed. "I'm sick of you and your warnings and cautions. Thanks to you I have as much backbone as a jellyfish. If I get out of this river you'll be second in line after the redhead. I'll—"

"Keep yelling," a man's voice shouted. "I'm almost there."

My numbed heart thumped with joy.

Cheese Puff barked and anchored a paw in my mouth. I felt his weight shift and he barked again and again, at regular intervals, the way a telephone rings. A flashlight beam swept the river in front of me.

"I see you," the man shouted. "I'm coming."

I glanced over my shoulder and spotted a white gleam low in the water.

"Hang on," the man called. "I'm almost there." His voice was clear and confident, warm and reassuring. It was somehow familiar but my freezing brain couldn't place it.

A canoe filled my field of vision. "Hold up one arm," he advised.

I couldn't feel myself do it, but I guess I did and I guess he grabbed my hand, because I felt a distant pressure and my right shoulder rolled deeper into the water, pushing me close against that green forest painted on the side of the canoe. Cheese Puff barked again, used my arm for a bridge, and tumbled over the side into the canoe. Safe.

"Got him," the man said. "Let go of the leash."

By centimeters, I unfurled my fingers.

"Got it. Now raise your other hand."

With a grunt of concentration, I managed that, my glasses biting into my nose each time my head thudded against those painted trees. I wondered when shivering became full-body quaking, decided I couldn't remember, decided it didn't matter.

My rescuer clamped my fingers around the gunwale. "Now here's the hard part," he said. "I can't lift you into the canoe. We might capsize. I'll tie the leash around you to hold you up and paddle like hell for the shore."

Definitely not my idea of a good time, but drowners can't be choosers.

"You'll be out of the water in a few minutes." He threaded the leash under my arms. "The rescue boat is coming. I see its lights."

The rescue boat. I sighed and closed my eyes, thinking of hot chocolate and wool blankets. I felt warmer, relaxed.

How could that be? I was still in the river. But I was sleepy. So sleepy.

My frigid fingers straightened and my arms dropped. He grasped my wrists and forced me to grip the gunwale again.

"Look at me, Barbara. Nod your head so I know you understand." A flashlight beam swept across my eyelids. "You have to hang on. Don't give up. Not now."

With a supreme effort, I opened my eyes and tipped my head back. I saw Cheese Puff's face just inches from mine, watched him anchor his tiny teeth in my shirt cuff.

Beyond him, I spotted a familiar wet yellow shimmer. A slicker. Trash Guy II.

Saved by a man who grubbed through garbage. This had to be a dream. A really bad dream.

I closed my eyes.

The only way to deal with a bad dream was to sleep my way to the end of it.

So that's what I did.

Quiz Answer:
I've fallen for *c* and *d* many time, *a* provides motivation, *b* always makes me chuckle, and, depending on my history with the class, *e* could get me there.

Proposals for new educational programs often
a) contain language that's clear and easy to
   understand
b) are loaded with acronyms
c) require translation
d) use twenty words where five would do
e) will be dumped within a few years

CHAPTER TWENTY FOUR

I woke up to distant voices, the faint stinging scent of alcohol, and the distinct feeling that I was neither in my own bed nor my own room. The warm weight of a blanket lay across my legs and chest. My glasses were gone and my face felt naked and exposed.

By opening my eyes just a fraction of an inch and bearing down on the lids, I managed a squint that made up for about half my vision loss and allowed me to see a needle in my left arm feeding clear liquid from a sack above my head. Vases of flowers crowded a windowsill, and Iz and Mrs. B were posted on either side of the bed like the stone lions outside that spook-infested library at the beginning of *Ghostbusters*.

Mrs. B had bags under her eyes, but her hair and makeup were perfect. She wore white wool slacks, a pale green sweater, and a double string of pearls—twice as many as when she took on Atwell. I wondered if my sister was the target of the extra pearl power.

Iz wore a pale gray sweatshirt and skin to match. Her Mohawk lay flattened across the right side of her head like a bad comb-over.

They weren't talking and weren't looking at each other but, to my surprise, the atmosphere wasn't as cold as Nome in January. For a while I watched them through slitted eyes, suspecting their silence represented a lull in the sparring, but then Mrs. B closed the magazine she'd been flipping through, reached into an enormous black leather purse on the floor beside her chair, dug out a white paper sack, and offered it to Iz. "Chocolate truffles," she said. "You need to keep your strength up."

Iz shook her head. "Thanks, but I'm not hungry."

I struggled to hold back a gasp. Iz? Not hungry? Passing on chocolate?

Maybe I hadn't survived.

I shifted my right hand, pinched my side, felt the stab of pain, and wondered if that proved anything. If I could imagine that I was still alive, surely I could imagine pain as well.

Iz shifted in her chair. "I can't eat while she's . . ."

"I understand, dear. But she'll be fine." Mrs. B set the sack on the table beside my bed. "She's tougher than you think. And you can take credit; you helped bring her up."

Iz chewed at the nail on her ring finger. "I tried to swim to her."

Mrs. B nodded. "Yes, you did. You went into that river without a single thought for your own safety."

Iz snorted. "And without remembering I float like an anvil. A lot of help I was. How pathetic is it when they have to rescue the rescuer?"

"That river's cold and deep and dangerous. You tried, that's what counts."

Iz gnawed her nail in silence. I took shallow breaths, digesting this information. Iz had gone in after me. I remembered those flashlight beams crisscrossing something in the water and realized it must have been Iz in her long black coat. She hadn't paused to take it off. An act of foolhardy courage, of swaggering stupidity, of undiluted love.

Iz studied the ragged remains of the nail. "If you hadn't seen that redheaded harpy pushing through the crowd . . ."

"I knew she was up to no good." Mrs. B's hands curled into fists. "I wish they hadn't pulled me off of her so fast."

"And I wish we had a video of the fight. If we set it to music—maybe 'Hit Me With Your Best Shot'—we'd get a million views." Iz grinned and made a slashing motion with the edge of her hand. "She didn't have a chance against you and that cane."

The sword cane? I tensed and held my breath. Had Mrs. B skewered the redhead?

"I'll bet she's got more bruises than a week-old banana," Iz said.

Bruises. Not cuts. I relaxed a little.

Mrs. B flushed and fluffed her hair. "Well, the Committee helped."

Iz laughed. "Yeah, helped sit on her once you knocked her down and beat her like a rug. No, victory is all yours." Her lips crimped into a frown. "Do you think she'll charge you with assault?"

"Let her." Mrs. B flipped a beringed hand. "She's facing murder charges."

Murder charges? She only *tried* to kill me. She hadn't succeeded. Or had she?

I pinched myself again, still couldn't decide if that proved I was alive.

"I have an attorney on retainer who's done nothing for the past few years except give me tax advice. It's about time he earned his keep. Besides, I'm . . . well, let's just say

I'm a senior citizen." Mrs. B patted her silvery hair. "And after my doctor testifies to my height, weight, bone density, and physical limitations, no jury will believe I was physically able to take her down."

I wasn't sure I'd believe it either. Mrs. B worked out regularly in the condo exercise room, but she was whip-thin and, as she said herself, no spring chicken. Fear, anger, and a shot of adrenaline must have contributed to her triumph. And I didn't kid myself that she'd gone into battle solely on my behalf—I gave Cheese Puff most the credit.

Cheese Puff!

I opened my eyes. "Where's Cheese Puff?"

"You're awake," Iz crowed, squeezing my hand.

I squeezed back. "Is he okay?"

"He's right here." Mrs. B beamed. "Stand guard," she ordered Iz.

Iz shot from her chair, trundled to the doorway, and took up a sentry position, back to the room, arms folded, legs wide, feet anchored against the doorjambs. Mrs. B handed over my glasses, then lifted her capacious purse to her lap and made a kissing sound.

Like a prairie dog popping out of a burrow, Cheese Puff thrust his head and front feet from the sack and peered around.

"Cheese Puff!" I held out my hands and he leaped from the purse to the bed and licked every inch of my face. I stroked his back and scratched his ears. "You're not hurt."

Iz glanced over her shoulder and smiled. "Trust my loony sister to put her dog first. The vet says you probably saved his life by sticking him on your head."

Mrs. B laughed. "I wish I could have seen that."

"Trust me," I groaned, "we *will not* be reenacting that—ever." Cheese Puff wiggled in a circle and gave me a

205

high five. "How did you get him to stay so still in your purse?"

"Oh, that." She blushed. "We've been working on that little trick for weeks. I often go out to lunch or the movies and I see no reason why he should stay home alone, so I tuck him—"

"Nurse," Iz hissed.

"Back in your box, Jack," Mrs. B commanded.

Cheese Puff spun and dove into the purse. "Good boy." Mrs. B set her bag on the floor and brushed a stray orange hair from the sheet.

I eyed the purse and the white sack she'd removed from it earlier. "How did you get him to stay out of the chocolate?"

She slid the sack into her purse. "I keep the goodies in a separate compartment so temptation doesn't get too great, but the command is 'poison.'"

I blinked in amazement. "And he obeys?"

"Not at first." She smiled. "But he got with the program when he figured out he wouldn't get any filet later."

Filet. Naturally Cheese Puff got filet. He probably gorged on it almost every day. It's a wonder he had any use for the dog biscuits I could afford on my salary. "My job." I gripped Mrs. B's hand. "The high school."

"I called early this morning." She stroked my fingers. "Some woman named Frost said she'd get a sub for today and tomorrow. Sarcastic woman. Said she was *sure* that you'd made lesson plans."

I smiled, remembering that I'd done just that while I'd been putting off going home to Iz.

"She just woke up," Iz said, stepping back to make way for a slender nurse in pale green scrubs with brown hair swept back in a stubby pony tail. "I was about to come tell you."

206

The nurse brushed past, slid a thermometer under my tongue, and found the pulse point in my wrist with cool fingers. "How are you feeling?"

I ran an assessment. Body parts all accounted for and functioning, brain able to remember what happened and process new information, emotional dial set, as usual, to "find-reasons-to-feel-sorry-for-self." "Okay," I mumbled.

The thermometer chirped and she removed it with a twist of her hand, checked the read-out, and pointed a thumb at the ceiling. "Temp's almost back to normal. Doctor will be around later." She tweaked the sheet higher and departed with the subdued squeak of rubber-soled shoes, calling over her shoulder, "You can have a little water if you want."

I shivered, remembering that icy river, and shook my head. "No water."

"Don't blame you." Iz smiled and resumed her seat. She laid her hand on my forehead as if to confirm the thermometer reading. "Your temperature was around 90 when they got you in here last night. We were afraid you wouldn't—"

"But look at you now," Mrs. B said in a bright voice. "Almost as good as new. That will make Dave feel much better."

Dave? My brain synapses fired in vain. No mental image formed. "Dave?"

"He was afraid he'd capsize if he tried to get you into the canoe. Then you would have *all* been back in the river and who knows what . . ." Mrs. B glanced at her purse and I knew she was thinking that Cheese Puff might have been taken by the current and lost forever.

"It's okay," I consoled her. "It all worked out. But who's Dave?"

"Oh dear." Mrs. B's hands fluttered to the pocket of her slacks. "I told him we'd call when you woke up."

"Done," Iz said. "I texted him while I was on guard. He's downstairs."

"But who is he?" I demanded, struggling to sit.

"Don't get your undies in a bunch." Iz seized the control and the bed hummed and raised me to a sitting position. "That better?"

"Yes," I sulked, smoothing the sheet. "But who the heck is Dave?"

"That would be me," a smooth voice said. A sturdy man with a scruff of beard stood in the doorway.

His voice pinged through my mind. Familiar. But why?

"I've talked to you on the phone and seen you around the condo complex, but we were never introduced."

He strode forward and took my hand between both of his. I felt a tingle of electricity, tried again to place that voice.

"My daughter pulled you from the river two weeks ago," he said with a grin. "Last night was my turn."

I gazed up into eyes the color of coffee with just a dash of milk, conscious of that tingle, of my lack of makeup, my snarled and greasy hair, my missing undergarments, and the faded hospital gown with its stupid blue squiggles. "Your daughter? Allison? You're Allison's father?"

He smiled. "Guilty as charged."

"But we only talked on the phone. I never saw you."

"Yes you did." He chuckled. "You saw me almost every day." He released my hand and tented his fingers over his head. "Imagine a yellow rain hat."

I gasped. "You're Trash Guy II?"

"Two?"

"There were three of you hanging out back there." I shook my head. "But you have a job. Allison said you . . . you worked for the city."

"He does. He's a cop," Iz said. "He was on a stakeout."

"He was watching your ex-husband and that horrible woman who shoved you in the river," Mrs. B supplied.

Watching Jake and the redhead? "But why?"

Quiz Answer:
Read a few and let me know what you think.

When students leave a classroom, you're least likely to find
a) wads of gum
b) masses of used tissues
c) cartoon pictures of yourself
d) all the pens and pencils you loaned out
e) a note thanking you for filling in

CHAPTER TWENTY FIVE

"They were selling drugs," Mrs. B whispered.

"Steroids," Iz clarified. "And meth. Dave will tell you." She stood and offered her chair. "I'm going to the cafeteria. I could eat a dozen doughnuts."

Dave grinned. He had a great grin, warm and wide and boyish. Natural. Not like one from Jake's collection of self-serving smirks. "Organic doughnuts, of course," he teased.

I expected Iz to glower, but she grinned right back. "I may have to compromise my position on natural foods," she said over her shoulder. "Just this once."

"Compromise can be healing." Mrs. B smiled serenely. "If you find a doughnut with custard, the little prince and I would be grateful. Or a nice, fresh blueberry muffin with lots of butter. And a refill on my coffee, please."

"Consider it done," Iz said without a touch of her usual sarcasm.

I blinked. "Who was that masked woman?"

Mrs. B patted my hand. "You've heard of baptism by fire, dear. Well, your sister was baptized by cold water and the fear of losing you. She's changed."

Dave shrugged out of his windbreaker, took the chair she'd vacated, and scratched at his sprouting beard. I've always been a sucker for a man with stubble. "Not *completely* changed."

"No," Mrs. B agreed. "But she's not taking herself so seriously. And she's not expecting the rest of us to, either."

Wondering how long that would last, I pulled the sheet up to my armpits and finger combed my hair. Except for encounters with Jake and Atwell, this was as close as I'd been to a man in months and naturally I looked like something left rotting in the wake of a tornado. "Steroids and diet pills?" I prompted.

"In a minute." He focused on Mrs. B. "Where's that little dog? Rules or no rules, I'll bet you've got him in here."

She blushed, hoisted her purse to the edge of the bed, and kissed air. Cheese Puff popped out, licked my nose again, and then jumped onto Dave's lap and gave him a high five.

"Never had much use for critters this small, but this guy is a gamer." Dave scratched Cheese Puff's ears. "He hung over the edge of the canoe with your cuff between his teeth and when you started to slip out of the harness he yipped like a junior coyote until I got you roped up again."

Mrs. B reached for a tissue and blotted her eyes. "He was so brave and heroic. I'm going to write to the mayor and nominate him for a medal."

I smiled at the image of Cheese Puff weighed down under an enormous medallion. "A very small medal, okay?"

Cheese Puff stuck out his lower teeth in an expression of disgust and Mrs. B held out her arms. "Never mind her,

211

my little prince. You'll get the biggest medal they make."
He raised his chin, trotted across me as if I were a strip of
old carpet, and snuggled against her sweater.

I rolled my eyes, noted Dave also rolling his, and
smothered a laugh. "Back to Jake and the redhead."

"Right." Dave nodded. "They were dealing drugs out
of their condo. Well, we assume she—her name is Hillary
Dunne—was doing most of the dealing. His job was to
attract new clients by charming women and making men
envious of his physique and stamina."

A job custom-made for Jake with a desire to get rich
quick and laid often and with morality more flexible than
a rubber band.

"We got a tip from someone at another health club
about a month ago but the guy didn't have any specifics
and we didn't have the manpower right then to check it
out." Dave flipped a hand. He had great hands. Strong and
tanned, with fingers that weren't too long and spidery or
too short and sausage-like. "Sometimes tips turn out to be
all about professional jealousy. But then a couple of
mothers did a little checking on their kids and—"

"You can't have a dog in here!"

The ponytailed nurse stood just inside the door, a
deep frown creasing her forehead.

The heck we can't." Dave produced his badge. "I'm a
police detective working a murder case. That dog is a
witness."

The nurse's frown eased a little. "Well, I don't know.
He's still a dog and they're not allowed. Except for service
animals."

"That's what he is," Mrs. B said, her voice ringing with
honesty. "He's a psychiatric service dog. He's worked
wonders for my depression. Why, two months ago I was
so blue I could barely get out of bed."

The nurse narrowed her eyes. "Aren't service animals required to wear special vests or capes?"

"Yes, but the styles are so limited. And the colors are hideous. They clashed with his hair *and* my wardrobe." She brushed her sweater. "Being seen with him in that dreadful shade made me even more depressed."

The nurse shook her head in the slow way that said she wasn't buying that, but a smile twitched at her lips. "Well, you seem to be well-adjusted at the moment— except for an over-developed sense of fantasy—and I'm about to go off duty, so I'll let someone else handle this problem." She winked. "If they *notice* there's a problem."

"Back in your box, Jack," Mrs. B ordered. Cheese Puff dove into her purse and the nurse flashed a thumbs-up and strolled out.

"Service animal?" Dave rolled his eyes.

"He could be if he wanted to," Mrs. B protested. "But his schedule is far too busy."

I swallowed a laugh. For all I knew, that was an accurate statement. Just a few minutes ago I learned that Cheese Puff lunched and took in movies. Who knew what other activities he participated in while I was at school?

"I'll take your word for that." Dave shrugged. "Where were we?"

"A couple of mothers checked up on their kids," I prompted.

"Right. Well, it seems a guy named Jake told them that football scholarships would be practically guaranteed if they bulked up."

"He didn't use an alias?"

"I know you were married to him, dear," Mrs. B said as she patted my arm, "but he's not the sharpest pencil in the pack."

"And that was a break for us," Dave said. "The kids identified him and Hillary and provided us with plenty of evidence to hook them, but we decided to cast a wide net and see who else we could land. We collected photos and license numbers and we found their supplier. We'd intended to give it a few more days, but then—"

"That horrible redhead pushed you in the river," Mrs. B finished. "She'd been sampling her own drugs."

Dave nodded. "Probably had a short fuse to begin with, but steroids don't exactly mellow you out."

"And I hope you'll give your sister points for trying to save you, dear, even though Jim had to wade in and snag her with a boat hook." Mrs. B sighed and then plunged on. "She wants to have a good relationship with you, a real relationship, but you've both been stuck."

I winced. "Stuck back in the days after Bryce died."

She patted my arm again. "I think it will be much better, now."

"I think so, too," I said, only half convinced. Old habits are the hardest to break. "What happened to the redhead—to Hillary?" I asked, not wanting to give away the fact that I'd been awake and listening, eager to hear the story again, and anxious to turn attention away from the state of my life.

"Well, I saw her go by looking like a thundercloud and I felt quite a chill, a premonition." Mrs. B shivered. "So I went after her, hobbling just as fast as I could and calling for everyone to follow. I got to the top of the trail just as she plowed into you."

Shuddering, I remembered how she launched me into that icy water like a rock from a catapult. "What did Jake do?"

I cringed. That sounded pitiful—as if I wanted to believe he cared. "Let me guess—absolutely nothing. Right?"

Dave shrugged. "I was too far away to see. But he didn't go in after you."

214

"Well, who knows? He might have if that woman hadn't been punching him." Mrs. B gripped the cane I hadn't noticed leaning against the bed and thumped it on the floor. Cheese Puff peeked out of her purse, then dove for cover again. "She was so busy pounding him she never saw me coming."

Swinging the cane to illustrate, she whanged it against the metal nightstand, drawing a muffled yip from Cheese Puff. "I knocked her legs right out from under her."

I made wide eyes and feigned ignorance. "Did you use the rapier?"

"Rapier?" Dave sucked in a breath. His chest expanded, stretching his T-shirt, making him look even better.

"I never took it out of the sheath," Mrs. B told him. "The cane was all I needed. She'll be icing her knees for a long time."

"And sipping her meals at the jail through a straw," Dave added. "I'm glad I was busy commandeering that canoe and didn't see anything. Otherwise I'd be called to testify if she takes you to court."

"She won't," Mrs. B said as if issuing an imperial decree. "She's not that stupid."

Dave gave her a sharp look and I decided to let him worry about what that meant. I needed a nap. "Do you want to take my statement now?"

"No." He chuckled, a rich and full sound that made me feel melty inside. "Chuck will do that tomorrow."

"Chuck?"

"I think you know him as Charles. Atwell."

The melty feeling vanished. Despite the fact that I hadn't eaten for a day, I felt queasy. "Oh. That Charles."

Dave smiled. "Right now he's in a great mood. He's got the woman who killed Jessica Flint."

"She confessed," Mrs. B said. "To me and about a hundred others. She admitted that she saw Jake get out of Jessica's car. While Jessica was turning around, she jumped in and made her drive to that little park up the river. Then she whacked her with a tire iron and threw her in."

"But she took it all back when you stopped hitting her," Dave said with a frown. "The prosecutor is worried about that."

Mrs. B wiped his concern from the air with a flip of her fingers. "Oh, she did it all right. They'll find evidence." She twisted the pearl and diamond ring on her left hand. "You were smart to divorce Jake, dear. He has no moral compass."

This from a woman who'd been married to a mobster.

I sighed and nodded, thinking that if I hadn't divorced Jake he'd be bleeding me for his defense right now. Worse yet, I might be accused of aiding and abetting his drug trafficking. Talk about dodging a bullet. I'd dodged a missile with a nuclear warhead. "Did you arrest him?"

Dave nodded. "We've got plenty on the drug charges. As for the Flint case, Chuck's hoping that he'll turn on Hillary to save himself."

"He will," I said with a snort. "Jake's all about taking care of himself."

"That's what I gathered from watching him," Dave said. "Once he starts talking, it should be a cinch for Chuck to squeeze him for what he knows about the Stoddard killing."

Exhausted as I was, that got my mind churning. "Atwell thinks the redhead killed Henry Stoddard?"

Dave raised his eyebrows. "Just a wild guess here, but your expression tells me you don't agree?"

"No. They're from different ends of the universe." I held my hands a yard apart. "I'll bet Henry Stoddard never worked out a day in his life. And I'll bet he didn't do drugs, either—unless someone gave them away free."

"Now don't get too excited, dear." Mrs. B laid a hand on my shoulder and her fingers pressed into my skin. "There are a hundred ways their paths could have crossed. Maybe he cut her off on the freeway or jumped the line at the supermarket. You said he wasn't a very nice man, remember? And with her temper it wouldn't have taken much to set her off."

I suspected she was implying that if I went along with Atwell's theory, this would all be over. "That's true."

Her grip loosened. "Of course it is."

I closed my eyes and imagined Henry sliming his way into the express lane with two items over the limit and Hillary calling him on it. He'd tell her to buzz off and she'd punch him out. On the spot. That was the key. "Hillary seemed to be more about spontaneous action than planning revenge."

Mrs. B clutched my arm again, but I steamed ahead. "And how did she get into his classroom?"

Dave shrugged. "It's just one angle Chuck's looking at. The other—the one I like—is that Jessica Flint killed Stoddard."

Mrs. B's fingers pressed deeper. I kept my lips zipped, thinking that theory seemed more likely to fly—except for a little detail I knew was important but couldn't remember. I scratched my head. Memo to self: wash hair ASAP. My thoughts collided and fragmented like colors in a kaleidoscope and I yawned wide enough to make my jaw pop.

"You get some rest now, dear," Mrs. B said. "We'll talk about this later on." Meaning I shouldn't blurt out anything to put me back in Atwell's hot seat.

I nodded and Mrs. B released my arm, gathered up her purse, and set it on the bed. "Goodbye kisses," she ordered. "Then into your box." Cheese Puff popped out, licked my nose, then dove back into the purse. "We'll be downstairs, checking up on your sister and those doughnuts."

I nodded, betting Iz was so busy gorging she forgot her promise to supply Mrs. B. Could a leopard change its spots?

"How do you feel about talking to the media, dear?"

With greasy skin and tangled hair? I shook my head.

"They're camped out in the parking lot waiting for news." She nodded toward the windowsill. "And someone named Rick Rivers sent all those flowers. He said he'd try to pull some strings to get your job back at least part time if you'll give him an exclusive."

"When pigs fly," I said, meaning no to the exclusive *and* the idea of going back to work for Rick. That, I saw from this distance, had been the employment equivalent of marriage to Jake. "Why don't *you* talk to the cameras?"

Her eyes sparkled. "You don't mind?"

"I insist."

She was gone before I said another word.

Dave chuckled and shrugged into his windbreaker. "After they let you out, I'll take you downtown and we'll talk with Chuck."

That melty feeling returned. Maybe we could get a cup of coffee or even have dinner.

"And maybe he'll bring his girlfriend along," jibed that annoying little voice in my brain as the door closed behind him

"Shut up, shut up, shut up," I whispered.

I fell asleep trying to remember what I couldn't about Henry Stoddard's murder.

Quiz Answer:

e – but when you get one it makes your year

If a student's clothing isn't in compliance you should
a) remind the student of the dress code
b) ask the student to change into something more appropriate
c) ignore it
d) call for an administrator
e) strip down to your thong in protest

CHAPTER TWENTY SIX

They released me late that afternoon, we dodged the media by going out a back way, and Iz drove us home in Mrs. B's car—a huge older model with automatic everything, bright red and waxed to a glossy gleam. To my surprise, Iz insisted that I sleep in my own bed, that she'd be just fine on the futon. After a dinner of take-out Chinese with Mrs. B and a review of their sound bites— and a few sound barks—on the news, I crawled between the sheets and went down for the count.

Dave called the next morning while Iz and I were having coffee and French toast that she'd cooked without delivering a lecture on my lack of free-range eggs or organic whole-grain bread. In a voice that made me tingle all over, he said he'd be by to pick me up at 10:00.

"Will you let me buy you lunch afterward?" I asked before that nagging brain voice could remind me that he had a girlfriend.

"Lunch would be great," he said, "but I'm buying. Or maybe we'll bill Chuck. After all, your plunge broke the case for him."

I didn't argue. Payday was a long way off.

Ignoring the little voice reminding me that Dave had a girlfriend, I scooped up Cheese Puff and waltzed him over to Mrs. B's condo for a few hours of mutual admiration. Back home, I danced my way up the stairs, showered, washed my hair twice, styled it, applied eye shadow and mascara, and put on my most slimming outfit: black pumps and slacks, a black silk shirt, a jacket with vertical stripes of dark green and blue, and a pair of faux sapphire earrings.

When I danced downstairs again, Iz stood and straightened the back of my collar. "You look very nice," she said, sounding almost as if she meant it.

"Thank you." I strangled a little on the words, wondering how long it had been since I said that to her. Our relationship felt as fragile as those tiny figures crafted from molten glass.

Partly as a test and partly to relieve the pressure I assumed she was feeling, too, I gave Iz an opening. "You don't think this is too dressy?"

She wrinkled her nose. "It is for that Mexican place you like so much."

Two days ago I would have been annoyed by the implication that I needed to raise my standards, but now I just smiled. "He's buying, so he gets to pick the spot."

Iz frowned and I wondered if she was wrestling with the issue of etiquette or the concept of deferring to a man. In a moment she shrugged, warmed up another slice of French toast in the microwave and saturated it with butter and maple syrup. Just as she dug in, the doorbell rang.

"He's got a girlfriend," chanted that peevish little voice.

"Shut up, shut up, shut up," I sang as I grabbed my purse.

"I didn't say anything," Iz protested, staring at a dripping forkful of French toast. "I didn't even think anything."

"I know." I kissed her forehead, the Mohawk tickling my nose. "And keep it up. You're getting good at it."

She was still blinking when I opened the door for Dave Martin.

Damn he looked good. He'd caught up on his sleep and his eyes were bright and clear. He'd shaved off the stubble, but that had revealed a dimple in his chin. I sighed. The man was perfect.

"You look terrific. Much better than when I pulled you from the river."

"For the record," I said, closing the door behind me, "you tied me to the canoe and *towed* me from the river."

"Details, details." He chuckled. "I pulled your dog from the river, okay?"

"Technically, you didn't do that, either. Cheese Puff scrambled up my arm and jumped into the canoe."

"Ouch." He opened the passenger door on a rusted brown beater of a car that was as clean inside as Mrs. B's. "I can see that one lunch isn't going to be enough to resolve this. I'll have to book you for dinner, too."

As he walked around the car to the driver's side, I did a little seat dance, pumping my arms and tapping my feet. "Oh, yeah!"

"Need I mention," the bothersome little voice said, "that he has a—"

"La la la," I sang, sticking my fingers in my ears. "Not listening."

The driver's door opened. Dave swiveled into the seat and gripped my arm. "Are you okay?"

"River water," I improvised. "Can't seem to clear my ears."

"Alcohol might dry it up. I'll pick some up while you're talking with Chuck."

I nodded, thinking that alcohol—the kind you drink—could go a long way toward improving my rapport with Detective Atwell.

As it turned out, however, the interview was, if not cordial, then somewhere well on that side of antagonistic. Instead of the sweat box I'd been in before, Dave ushered me into a larger room with an oval table and chairs with actual padding. Atwell was waiting with his tape recorder and about forty percent of a smile.

Dave shot me a grin and closed the door with a soft click. Atwell motioned me to take a seat. "How are you feeling?"

Admitting to feeling better than I had in months wouldn't win me sympathy points I might need later. "Not too bad."

Atwell nodded, then tapped his pen against his notebook. "Dave said you have some concerns about the case we're building against Hillary Dunne for the Stoddard murder."

"He did?" I cast my mind back over a mesh of fuzzy memories, recalled my sense of doubt, found it still valid.

"Is there anything you'd like to fill me in on," Atwell coaxed in a sarcastic tone. "Little details you *forgot* to mention earlier or held back because I'm such a scary man and I intimidate innocent people?"

I winced, remembering how Mrs. B berated him. "It just doesn't feel right. I can't imagine how their lives intersected. And . . . well, his murder seemed too premeditated. Not her style."

"Ah, style." He raised his eyebrows and made a note. "And what about Miss Flint? Would premeditation have been her style?"

222

I thought about that for a moment. Jessica Flint had been supremely organized, and if she planned a murder, she would have worked out every detail in advance, set up alternate plans, made a checklist, and reviewed it later to assess and evaluate. My gut feeling was that she would have killed Henry Stoddard elsewhere in order to widen and deepen the suspect pool.

I recalled her face, inches from mine, her astonishment when I told her he'd been strangled, her raw, frantic need to get into his classroom, her search for what probably was that flash drive. If she decided to kill him, she would have gotten her hands on it before she eliminated him.

"Well?" Atwell prompted.

"She would have thought it through. Definitely. But I don't think she did it."

He leaned back and made a face like he'd tasted something sour. "And why is that?"

"She was desperate to get into his room right after I found his body."

Atwell smiled like a wolf spotting a spring lamb gamboling across a meadow far from the flock. "Did you know she minored in theater in college?" He leaned toward me, practically salivating. "She had the lead in *Hedda Gabler*. Reviewers said she was amazingly cold and calculating."

I felt a stabbing uncertainty in my gut and reran our argument outside Stoddard's room. Had her surprise and anxiety been a performance? Did she have the talent to be so convincing? Or had I convinced myself?

"He threatened her job. The proof is on the flash drive you found." Atwell leaned back and raised his arms, stretched, and laced his fingers behind his head. "And I believe we'll find more links." He rocked a little from side to side. "She was an ambitious woman. It all fits."

223

His tone implied that my lack of knowledge made the Dark Ages look downright luminescent. He was right—it fit. And it appeared that his intention was to make it fit even better. Jessica Flint, after all, wasn't around to argue.

"Think about it," Atwell commanded. "If she didn't kill him, who did?"

Out of ammunition, I drew a question mark on the table with my fingertip.

He stood, scraping his chair on the floor. "Well, let me know if you remember anything . . . concrete."

I got the hint. Don't bother him unless someone came to my door and confessed.

And that was fine. If I never saw Charles Atwell again I'd be a happier camper. "Sure." I set a leisurely pace for the door lest I give him the satisfaction of seeing just how much I wanted to be on the other side—with Dave.

But instead of Dave, there was a baby-faced uniformed officer thrusting a folded piece of paper at me. "Martin said you'd need a ride."

"Got called off on a case," the note read. "Sorry. I'll call you."

Sure you did, sure you will, I thought, as the freckled officer drove me home. Dave Martin was just like all the other guys. No way would I wait by the phone. And no way would I answer if he actually called.

"Told you so," the brain voice chanted. "He's probably with his girlfriend."

Quiz Answer:
a and *b*, and perhaps even *d*, but *e* would certainly spice things up

When leaving a note for a teacher you subbed for you should always
a) use correct grammar and punctuation
b) alphabetize student homework excuses
c) employ the word "allegedly"
d) suck up in the hope of being asked back
e) use recycled paper

CHAPTER TWENTY SEVEN

Deciding I couldn't face Iz—even the new and improved version—I went to Mrs. B's condo and found her at the dining room table, seated across from Cheese Puff. He had a linen napkin tied around his neck. His front paws were on the table and his rear on a puffy cushion. A bone china plate in front of him held three thin slices of rare steak, a tablespoon of mashed potatoes, and a few carrot rounds. A shallow crystal bowl beside the plate contained what I hoped was water. He glanced at me, didn't bother to wag his tail, and licked at the potatoes.

"I'm amazed he hasn't run away from home and moved in here where he's monarch of all he surveys." My tone was as bitter as dandelion greens. If my own dog didn't care about my feelings, why should I think a man would?

Mrs. B had the grace to blush. "You're back much sooner than I expected, dear. How was your session with Detective Atwell?"

"Preachy."

"He's got his mind made up?"

"Like an army barracks cot. He didn't listen to a word I said."

She nodded. "And how was lunch?"

"Lacking."

Her eyebrows arched. "In ambiance?"

"In everything. Dave got called off on a case." I pulled out a chair at the end of the table and slumped into it. "Or so he says."

"Well, if that's what he says, then I'm sure that's what happened."

"Want to make a bet?" I scowled at Cheese Puff who nibbled a carrot.

"You'd lose your money, dear." Mrs. B folded her napkin and set it aside. "I know men almost as well as I know diamonds. Dave Martin is high quality and he's *very* interested in you."

"According to Allison, he's also *very* involved with a girlfriend."

"He may be seeing someone, but I'd be surprised to find that he thinks of himself as involved." Mrs. B stood and bustled to the kitchen. In a moment she was back with a pink drink and the tin of giant cashews. "I put a frozen pasta dinner in the microwave for you. You'll feel better after you eat."

I didn't.

Knowing I was acting like a four-year-old, I sulked that evening and right through the weekend, refusing offers of meals and movies from Mrs. B. I took out my anger by attempting in vain to stir things up with Iz when she wasn't at her conference. She deflected my volleys with humor I'd never seen her display before, even laughing at herself. Seething, I took perverse pleasure in screening my calls through the answering machine and erasing Dave Martin's messages that he was still on a case and would get back to me soon to set a date for dinner.

Even dropping Iz at the airport Sunday morning didn't cheer me up like it used to. In fact, that afternoon, after the service for Jessica Flint, I felt lonelier than I had since the day Albert died or the day I kicked Jake out. But, on the plus side, I worked out lesson plans for a whole week and was rested and ready to face Monday.

Allison, wearing a pink sweater and blue jeans and holding hands with Josh, intercepted me outside the main office and waved a white envelope in my face. "This is for you. From Dad."

"Thanks." I snatched it from her fingers and stuffed it in my briefcase.

"It's a really cute card. I picked it out for him 'cause he was at work almost all weekend."

I bet the "almost all" part was where he took time to hook up with his girlfriend.

Allison frowned. "Aren't you going to open it?"

"Later." When I was alone. When I could tear it into little pieces and flush them. "I've got some prep to do before class."

"Oookkkkaaayyyy." She stretched the word out. "See you later." She turned with a flip of her hair and towed Josh off to the juice bar.

I felt a pang of loss, shook it off, and hustled up the stairs telling myself the important thing was that she was doing fine, and that I was, too. I didn't need Dave Martin.

Thanks to the news reports, my adventure was the hot topic in all my classes, with kids offering input on what they would have done with particular emphasis on how *they* would have gotten out of the river immediately and bashed the redhead with a rock or kicked her in the kidneys or taken her down with a few punches to the head.

I nodded, let them get it out of their systems, and forged on with the lesson.

It was much the same in the teachers' room during lunch. Susan seized my arm as I came through the door and clung to me. "I'm so sorry about what that dreadful woman did. You could have died. What a horrible experience."

"It's okay. I'm fine." I patted her back, feeling the knobs of her spine through the excess fabric of a corduroy jacket that had fit before Thanksgiving. The waistband of her slacks, I noted, had been taken in on both sides with safety pins. My trauma in the river had lasted only a few minutes, but her marital train wreck continued. I'd been rescued, but she would have to determine when she'd had enough pain and find the strength to save herself.

I was about to suggest that we get together for dinner when Aston slapped my back. "You're my kind of woman. As tough as an old boot. How about joining me New Year's Day for the polar bear swim?"

"Aston, you don't have enough common sense to fill a thimble. Jumping in the river again is the last thing she'd want to do." Brenda swirled a ladle through an enormous pot filled with viscous pink liquid. "I made some nice hot soup for you, Barbara. Cream of anchovy with dill, fennel, and diced beets."

"Thank you," I said, suppressing a gag and shifting my fabrication skills into overdrive. "Can I freeze some for later? I picked up a sinus infection and the doctor suggested I stay away from dairy products for a week."

Brenda frowned. "Freezing will blunt the flavor and the beets might get mushy."

"I told you to go with the braised ostrich, yam, and chard stew with sherry," Aston said.

"A little sherry is always good," Gertrude agreed.

"And a lot of sherry is even better," Aston grunted.

228

"I'll remember that." Brenda dished herself up a bowl and tapped the ladle against the pot. "How about the rest of you? Anybody want to try this?"

"Counting calories." Gertrude pointed to the carrot sticks and cottage cheese on her plate.

"Cutting back on salt," Doug yelped, shielding a heat-and-eat burrito from her view as he scuttled for the microwave.

"I'll have a bowl," Aston said. "Might go well with what I brought."

No one asked, but their sidelong glances at the foil packet in front of him told me that everyone wanted to know. Doug caved. "What is it?"

"A wild boar and turnip hash sandwich with horseradish."

I clutched my chilled PB&J with gratitude and bit off a huge chunk. Susan sat beside me and opened a plastic container half full of beige and brown flakes and chunks. "What is that?"

She stirred the mess with her finger. "Cracker and cookie crumbs and some cereal. From the bottoms of the boxes in the pantry."

Any bit of pity I had for my own situation evaporated. Was she too broke to buy something from the cafeteria? I tongued peanut butter stuck to the roof of my mouth and set my sandwich down. "Why don't I go get you a salad? Or a slice of pizza? Or you can have half of my sandwich. I only bit one end."

Her lips twitched into a faint smile, then she shook her head. "Thanks, but I'm not hungry. Everything tastes like dust."

Across the table Aston slurped bubble-gum-colored soup. My appetite withered. I wrapped up my sandwich, popped a generic cola, poured half into a plastic cup, and folded Susan's skeletal fingers around it.

229

The microwave dinged and Doug rescued his burrito. "You know, I watched every bit of the news coverage, and I don't doubt that Hillary Dunne killed Jessica because she was jealous, but when they started hinting that she knocked off Stoddard, too . . ." He slid into his chair and opened a jar of salsa. "I just don't buy it."

"Me neither," Gertrude agreed. "What's the motive?"

Brenda stirred her bowl of soup and frowned. "Well, to know Stoddard was to loathe him."

"True. But most of us try to avoid what we loathe." Gertrude aimed a meaningful glance at the soup and winked at me. "If we can."

"Right. She could have avoided Henry without breaking a sweat." Aston smacked his lips and helped himself to more of the viscous mess from Brenda's pot. "She didn't work with him or live close to him. You can bet Henry never went near a gym. And as for jealousy—" He snorted. "That dog won't hunt."

I nodded but said nothing, hoping for a fresh look at the problem, and wondering why I couldn't just let Atwell have it his way.

Susan sighed. "Well, we don't have the facts the police do. Maybe there's something in her background. Or his."

"Maybe they were distant relatives," Brenda said. "And she discovered a huge inheritance and didn't want to split it."

"You've been watching too many soap operas," Gertrude scoffed. "The woman was on steroids. Her temper was out of control. Who knows what could have set her off?" She crunched a carrot stick. "Maybe Henry saw her do something he could threaten her over—like shoplifting at the supermarket, or stealing money from the collection plate at church."

"I doubt Henry was ever inside a church," Aston muttered, "unless he was there to loot the poor box."

"Let's not squabble." Susan set her cup down hard enough to slosh cola onto the table. "I hate it when we argue, when we're not working as a team. It makes me sad."

Gertrude flushed, Aston bent his head to his soup, and Brenda smiled in triumph. Even though I hadn't said a word, I felt guilty. Susan thought of us as family—we should be better than Kevin and his brother.

"Besides," Susan continued, "if the police have enough evidence to take her to trial, it will all come out then."

"But if they don't," Aston said with malicious glee, "that detective will be back to grill us like sausages."

Brenda shuddered. "I don't want to go through that again. Every time he popped his knuckles, my heart jumped into my throat."

"It was the sound of his teeth gnawing on that pen that got to me," Doug said. "I was two minutes from confessing to sneaking a peek at Louanne Ryan's underpants back in second grade."

"That man made me feel like scum." Gertrude patted my hand. "Big Chill says he really raked you over the coals. Your job could have been in jeopardy."

Susan wrapped a claw-like hand around my wrist. "Why?"

"Bad publicity." Gertrude leaned across me to address Susan. "Because she found both bodies."

"You didn't tell me that," Susan gasped.

I shot Gertrude a barbed look. "I didn't tell *anyone* that."

Gertrude flushed. "Well, you know how gossip gets around."

Susan tightened her grip on my wrist. "I'm so sorry." Tears spilled from her eyes. "I'm so, so sorry. I had no idea. I'm so sorry."

231

Aston rolled his eyes. "Get a grip, Susan. You're always apologizing for stuff that isn't your fault."

"But this *is* my fault," Susan wailed. "I killed Henry Stoddard."

Quiz Answer:
c and *a* and *e* – in that order – *b* if you're that organized, *d* if you're that desperate.

A substitute teacher is like Santa Claus because
a) they both keep lists of who's naughty and who's nice
b) they both carry sacks
c) kids think they're both old
d) they both find joy in what they do
e) neither drives the latest model

CHAPTER TWENTY EIGHT

Time seemed to stop for ten long seconds, and then Aston erupted with a belly laugh. "And I fired a shot from the grassy knoll in Dallas. And Brenda has a little green man from Roswell living in her guest room."

Doug grinned. "That's a good one, Susan. You really had me going. I never heard you tell a joke before."

"I'm not joking." Susan squeezed my wrist so hard my fingers throbbed. "I killed him."

"And I helped," Gertrude giggled. "I knitted the tie she strangled him with."

"Stop making fun of me," Susan sobbed. "I did it."

I put my arm around her, pulled her against my shoulder, and stroked her lank hair. "I know you did."

I meant that. Because it had to be true. Like Big Chill said, I hadn't worked with Henry long enough to be on killing terms, but Susan had. Susan had a dream of building an award-winning department and Henry, as she told me on Thanksgiving, had been standing on the air hose. "Why don't you tell me all about it?"

"I never meant to do it," she whimpered. "I went to his room to ask him again to please help me build a better department. But he laughed and said teamwork created specialization and that bred idiocy." She drew in a shuddering breath. "He said I was a full-fledged idiot and only cared about the department because I didn't have anything worth going home to." The breath came out as a wailing sob. "I hated that he was right about my marriage. And he wouldn't shut up. So I grabbed his tie. I just wanted him to shut up."

Time seemed to stop for another wide-eyed, mouth-gaping ten-count.

"Holy shit." Aston broke the silence. "Holy shit on a shingle."

"What do we do now?" Gertrude whispered.

"Susan and I are going to take a walk down to the office." I nodded toward the phone on the wall by the door. "Maybe you could call ahead and make an appointment. And get someone to cover our classes."

"I expect we'll be a while." Susan pushed back her chair, stood, and smoothed her slacks. "Maybe all of fourth period."

"Probably." I took her arm and steered her to the door.

Aston rolled his eyes at me and twirled a finger beside his head and Doug whispered, "Shades of *Sunset Boulevard*."

"Do you think they'll let me teach in jail?" Susan asked in a wistful voice. "Will they let me have books?"

"I'm sure they will," I said in my most convincing tone.

"And I won't have to see Kevin, will I? Or clean the house? Or pay the bills?"

"You won't have to do any of that," I assured her. "Not for a long time."

Five days later I reclined on Mrs. B's fainting couch watching Josh steady Allison on a stepstool while she secured a silvery bone-shaped ornament to the top of the Christmas tree.

"Right there." Mrs. B clapped her hands. "That's perfect."

Decked out in a green velvet elf suit complete with bells and faux fur trim, Cheese Puff barked and danced on his hind legs, begging to be picked up. Mrs. B obliged, holding him up to view the tree trimming operation.

The entire Cheese Puff Care and Comfort Committee and many of their friends were involved in the project which, to my total lack of surprise, was all about the little prince. There were lights that looked like pizzas and ornaments shaped like sausages, steaks, chunks of cheese, and dog houses—not that he'd ever condescend to pass through the door of such a structure. Other ornaments paid homage to his status—glittery crowns, stars, and tiny glass dog ornaments with angel wings or reindeer antlers.

Selecting a crab puff from the plate on the table beside me, I wondered about Susan and what was on the Saturday-night menu at the jail. Word from Big Chill was that Susan declined her attorney's plan to try to get her released on bail. Aston and Doug were convinced that proved she was certifiably crazy, but I didn't blame her for wanting to avoid Kevin, Devin, and as much responsibility and publicity as she could. What she needed was a long rest.

Allison danced across the room, high heels tapping time to the beat of Vegas-style Christmas tunes, shiny blue dress swishing against her legs. It was hard to believe this was the same girl who'd huddled beneath a bush less than four weeks ago. "It's tinsel time," she said with a giggle. "Want to help?"

"I'll direct." I sipped my drink. "From here."

Allison giggled. "That's exactly how my dad does it." With a toss of sparkly earrings and curling hair, she danced back to Josh.

"It's such a shame Dave couldn't come this evening," Mrs. B burbled. "But it's wonderful that he's so dedicated to fighting crime."

I smiled, wondering if that remark would set her mobster husband rotating in his grave. "Isn't it, though?"

For the past few days, Mrs. B had worked overtime to put a positive spin on the elusive Dave Martin. He'd left just one message since Susan was arrested, and Allison had delivered no more cards. It seemed that he got the I'm-not-interested-if-this-is-just-business message. I came tonight only because Mrs. B admitted she'd invited him, but assured me he was working a case and couldn't make it. In retaliation for what I saw as her disloyalty, I refused to upgrade from jeans and a black sweater. Furthermore, I was prepared to stalk out in a huff if he appeared. Let it not be said I couldn't lug a grudge as far as the next person.

Mrs. B crossed to the couch and set Cheese Puff beside me. "I've got to check the ham. But the little prince needs to go out."

I drained my punch cup. "Delighted to be of service."

She disappeared into the kitchen and Cheese Puff nudged his head against my arm, working the belled elf cap loose and kicking it to the floor.

"Being adored has its price," I told him as I unsnapped the elf jacket and got him into his harness. "Consider that the next time you pig out on sirloin and noodles Romanoff."

236

I shrugged into my coat and we threaded our way across the room to the sliding door and out onto the deck. The security lights flashed on and I noticed that the privacy panel that marked the beginning of what had been Myra and Nelson's domain had been removed. Was a new owner about to take possession? Would he or she be an improvement?

Cheese Puff darted down the steps and wasted no time watering the base of a rose bush. The night was cold but clear, with a splinter of moon and undulating wisps of fog far out on the river. We strolled along the trail, neither of us in a hurry, Cheese Puff checking his pee-mail, and me considering how much less stressful a nighttime excursion was when I didn't have to worry about running into Jake, or having the redhead run into me.

But when we reached the end of the complex, a shadow loomed out of the night. "Finally," it whispered.

Too startled to scream, I staggered back, reeling in Cheese Puff. He fought me, whining but wagging his tail.

"What do I have to do to get you to go out with me?" the shadow asked in a normal voice. "Pull you out of the river again?"

Having planned on avoiding Dave Martin for the rest of my life, I didn't have a snappy comeback—or any comeback at all.

"Mrs. Ballantine says you're not returning my calls because you think I'm involved with someone."

"Mrs. Ballantine should mind her own business."

Windbreaker whiffling, Dave stepped onto the trail and bent to pet Cheese Puff who twirled in a circle and offered a paw. "I'm not involved."

"Allison told me you were," I said in a snippy tone. "Did she just *imagine* a woman? Did she just *imagine* you were dating?"

"Uh, no. But things aren't always the way they seem."
He shuffled feet clad in ratty tennis shoes with frayed
laces. "See, a few months ago she got interested in boys
and she started obsessing about how I had no one, that
she'd be going out on dates and I'd be home alone. I didn't
want her to pass up opportunities on my account, so I got
another detective to stop by a few times and pretend to be
my girlfriend."

My annoyance at Mrs. B withered like a Fresno raisin.

"I guess you know how that worked out," he said with
a bitter laugh.

"Allison didn't like her."

"Hated her. Hated me. Started acting out."

But Allison liked me! I shivered with joy. "Why didn't
you tell her the truth?"

"Teenagers are . . . well, you know. They're
unpredictable. I was afraid the truth might make things
worse." He pounded a fist against his palm. "And then she
got interested in Josh and I figured I'd give it a few weeks
and then pretend we broke up. But meanwhile she told
you and—"

"Things got complicated," I summed up, wanting to
avoid a potentially humiliating discussion of what I'd
thought and felt. Better to hold that until we knew each
other better—or until never. "So you've really been on a
case?"

"Yeah. You can read about it in the paper tomorrow. If
you're interested."

"I am," I said, not minding if I sounded eager.

"So, maybe we can take it from the top." He took my
free hand and wove his fingers with mine as if he'd been
doing that for years. "Would you like to have dinner with
me?"

"Yes."

"How about tonight?"

I glanced toward Mrs. B's condo. "Tonight?"

"Sure." He steered me up the trail, Cheese Puff racing ahead to the limit of the leash. "Mrs. Ballantine should be taking the ham out of the oven any minute and I hear there's rum punch, cornbread, yams, pecan pie, and—"

"No waiter bringing a huge check when we're done."

He chuckled. "Well, Muriel Ballantine has money to burn."

"Mob money," I pointed out. "Won't eating her food be a conflict of interest for a police officer?"

"It could, if that story had any truth to it."

I halted. "What?"

Cheese Puff yipped and I heard his toenails clawing at the asphalt.

"Marco wasn't connected?"

"Only to a huge inheritance. Marco had money and he knew how to make more, but there were dozens of men courting her—some who bent the law like a pretzel. They were dangerous and exciting. Marco wasn't. So he hired a few actors and wrote a new script for his life that included jetting around the globe allegedly avoiding crime kingpins and hit men until it was safe to settle down."

"How do you know this?"

"I walked up and asked him point blank." He chuckled. "I think he was almost relieved to tell me."

"Does Mrs. B know the truth?"

"Possibly." He squeezed my hand. "Probably. But let's not mess with her mythology."

"The secret is safe with me."

We climbed the steps to the deck and spotted her peering through the glass door, her face puckered into a worried frown. The security lights flashed on and a second later she smiled and turned to say something to the group inside, then spun back and beckoned us on. Cheese Puff barked and yanked on the leash.

I felt exposed, embarrassed, and manipulated. Dave's pace slowed. "There isn't a rock around here to hide under, is there?"

I laughed, delighted that we shared an emotional bond. "Not one big enough for both of us."

"Well, she's a force of nature. We can't change her, we can only reckon with her." He led me to the door. "So let's go reckon."

And reckon we did, dining, laughing, and holding hands until he had to leave, "to tie up a few loose ends at the cop shop."

"He's a good man," Mrs. B told me as I helped her put away the leftovers and stack dirty dishes for the cleaning service. "He reminds me of Marco."

I blinked. "Really"

"Well, not in the clothing department. We'll have to work on that."

"We?"

"Well, I have more experience shopping for men's clothing than you do, dear." She nodded to a photograph of Marco, wearing a cape, standing in front of the Sydney Opera House. "You'll let me know if I meddle too much, won't you?"

"And you'll stop?"

This time she blushed. "Probably not. But it might slow me down."

"That I'd like to see." I bent to scoop Cheese Puff from the fainting couch where he sprawled, bloated belly up. He groaned as I laid him over my shoulder, then emitted a belch worthy of a Great Dane, and went limp.

"Good night, my little prince." Mrs. B made kissy sounds and scratched his ears. "I'll see you soon. I have some steak in the freezer."

I felt a pang of jealousy. "Maybe Cheese Puff should move in with you," I suggested in a tone that took "catty" to new levels.

"Don't be silly, dear. I'll be traveling."

Traveling? Since I moved in, she hadn't left the city limits. "Where?"

"Oh, Easter Island, Antarctica, Borneo, the far reaches of the Amazon." She fluttered her fingers, diamonds flashing in the light from the tree. "Marco loved cities and nightlife, but I always had a yen to get off the beaten path." She patted my arm. "But don't you worry about the little prince; the Committee will see that he gets his walks and treats."

Of that I had no doubt. "But he'll miss you." I stroked Cheese Puff's back and he moaned and burped again. "I will, too. When are you leaving?"

"As soon as I get you all settled in."

"Settled in?"

"Tch. I'm spoiling the surprise." With another flash of diamonds, she tapped her fingers against her cheek. "Well, why wait for Christmas?" Digging through a drift of gifts beneath the tree, she pulled out a tiny gold box and pressed it into my hands. "You may want to start moving things tomorrow."

"Moving things?" I pulled the blue satin ribbon loose, lifted the lid, and spied two shiny brass keys. "What are these for? A storage locker?"

"No." She laughed and pointed toward Myra and Nelson's former abode. "The condo next door. I bought it. For you and Cheese Puff."

"What?" My voice rose to a near screech. "Why did you do that?"

"Don't get upset, dear." She took a step back. "It was in foreclosure. And it was the Committee's idea. We voted. It was unanimous."

241

Of course, a unanimous vote made it right. "I already have a condo."

"But it's tiny. There isn't enough space for you and Dave and Allison."

"Dave and Allison have their own place," I raged.

"For now," she said matter-of-factly. "But I expect that when I get back from Antarctica you'll be planning a wedding."

I sighed, set the box on the table, and headed for the door. "Thank you, but I can't take it." I wasn't sure if I meant the condo or her meddling. "And I'm never getting married again."

"Never say never, dear, you rule out too many possibilities."

"Well, then," I seethed, "if the day comes when I decide to get married, then I'll discuss housing *possibilities* with a real estate agent." I clicked back the bolt and grasped the knob.

"My heart will break if you and the little prince move away," she sniffed.

Her tears aren't real, I told myself, she's in manipulation overdrive. "I'm not going on this guilt trip." I opened the door, letting in a gust of damp wind. "I can't let you buy that condo for me. And I can't afford it on my own."

"But you can." Her voice was high and hopeful. Her heels clicked toward me. "It's a fact of the real estate market right now. Single units are selling better than doubles." She stopped just behind me. I felt a slight vibration and guessed she was scratching Cheese Puff's ears. "And I got it for a steal, so it will be almost a straight-across trade."

I thought about Dave saying that Mrs. B was a force of nature, that she could be reckoned with but not changed.

Still refusing to turn, I thought of the closet space, the river view, that expansive deck.

"If you turn this deal down, I'll never speak to you again," the little voice in my brain said.

I winced. Now there was a rock/hard spot choice. Pass on the condo and get rid of this mental pest. Agree and put up with its sniping.

"You're like a daughter to me," Mrs. B said. "You're the closest thing to family I have."

Family.

Chill wind swirled about me as I thought of my mother and father, uninvolved for so long, of Iz struggling to have a relationship with me and maybe finally getting the hang of it. I thought about Susan who traded a close and loving family for Kevin who didn't care enough to see she was going crazy. And then I thought about Dave and Allison. Finally, I thought about Mrs. B's last words and knew that they were true both ways—she was family to me, too.

Tears prickled my eyes and I sighed, aware of exactly what I was getting into, of the boundaries I'd have to set— mostly in vain—and the support, love, and laughter I'd get in return. No contest.

I cleared my throat. "Knowing you, I suppose there's already a fish on the line to buy my place."

"Um . . . yes," she admitted. "A nice young man who's moving here from Illinois. He says it's just perfect."

I let her sweat it out for another ten seconds, just so she knew I wasn't completely under her spell, that I still had the will to reckon. Then I closed the door. "Well, we wouldn't want to disappoint him."

She uttered a little cry of joy and I turned into her arms, both of us sniffling back tears, Cheese Puff waking up to lick our faces and burp once more.

"You'll be so happy, there, dear, I just know it." She plucked a tissue from a silver box on the table beside the door and blotted her eyes. "Tomorrow we'll go pick out paint colors and put new paper in the kitchen cabinets. The carpet cleaners are coming on Tuesday, and I have some ideas about window treatments."

I stroked Cheese Puff's back and let her words wash over me like tropical rain while she burbled on about deck furniture and mattress quality, thread counts and lighting.

"But all of that can wait until morning," she wound up. "You need to get your rest." She gave me a quick hug and opened the door. "Isn't it wonderful? You've got your life back on track."

"Back on track," I echoed with a shudder of apprehension.

As I said back at the beginning of this story, the problem with getting your life back on track is that there's usually another catastrophe rumbling down the rails to knock you off again.

Quiz Answer
For me, the choice is *d* – definitely and resoundingly *d*

BIO

Carolyn J. Rose grew up in New York's Catskill Mountains, graduated from the University of Arizona, logged two years in Arkansas with Volunteers in Service to America, and spent 25 years as a television news researcher, writer, producer, and assignment editor in Arkansas, New Mexico, Oregon, and Washington. She lives in Vancouver, Washington, and founded the Vancouver Writers' Mixers. Her hobbies are reading, gardening, and not cooking. For more information, surf to www.deadlyduomysteries.com

Also by Carolyn J. Rose

A Place of Forgetting
An Uncertain Refuge
Hemlock Lake
Consulted to Death
Driven to Death
Dated to Death

By Carolyn J. Rose and Mike Nettleton

The Big Grabowski
Sometimes a Great Commotion
The Hard Karma Shuffle
The Crushed Velvet Miasma
The Hermit of Humbug Mountain

13250666R00144

Made in the USA
Lexington, KY
22 January 2012